# The Border

## and other crossings

## RUSS DESAULNIER

LUMINARE PRESS
WWW.LUMINAREPRESS.COM

*This collection is a work of fiction. Although some stories were inspired by the author's recollections, all are finally and wholly products of his imagination. Resemblances to people, living or dead, apart from the few mentioned public figures, are purely coincidental and unintended.*

Published by:
The Literary Society of The Nagoya University
of Foreign Studies
Nagoya, Japan 470-0197
First Edition: 2001

3rd Edition Published by:
Luminare Press
442 Charnelton St.
Eugene, OR 97401
www.luminarepress.com

LCCN: 2022923778
ISBN: 979-8-88679-196-9

*For Bonnie*

*and*

*In memory of John Hermann*
*teacher and friend*

"I discovered that the short story is a
distillation of the personality of a whole world.
The way a particular writer chooses to
experience, edit and express that
is a matter of taste."

—AMY TAN

# CONTENTS

# The Border

----------------------------

L ife had seemed clear to James McClaren until he had been detoured to the Mexican border and been thrown into a whirl like that of a bull when it first blasts into the ring. There was still school to be finished, somehow. Could he ever make it to the big rings? Did he want to make the sacrifices required by that course? He had heard the stories about how long and hard that road could be, knew how it could be glory one day and tragedy the next, like Curro Ortega who that year had lost a leg after a grave horn wound in Mexico City. It seemed as though he was endlessly shifting around the imagined possibilities of his life like the sliding lettered squares in an alphabet puzzle, trying to get them in the right order.

All he could hear now was the quickening of his heart and Rafael's litany of instruction: *crúzate, crúzate, acércate, acércate.* With slow, sliding steps he crossed the sand toward the bull and profiled himself between the horns. Slowly sweeping the cloth around to the outside horn and giving it a little shake, he yelled, *ehey!* But the bull wouldn't charge and swung its head back toward him, ignoring the cloth. Sometimes bulls could be funny about where they were willing to take up the fight, so James motioned Rafael to lure the bull to another part of the ring, over in the shade by the stands where the bull might feel more secure, more willing. A half-hearted animal was more dangerous, often making choppy, unpredictable lunges, instead of the smooth, train-like, committed charges with which you could make the art happen. The first time, caping a calf in a club-organized festival had been easy, mimicking the 8 mm films he had carefully watched at the Los Angeles Aficionado Club, assuming the ballet-like postures from the photo books that had first piqued his imagination only a short year ago. *El toreo* wasn't just another high-wire act, or a contest. The *torero* created form and meaning out of brute chaos. The ritual, the silk, the gold, the trumpets, all entranced him like a Latin high mass at Easter, and all was acutely sharpened by the fear, relentless as the bull, whose horns made his thighs and balls feel naked in the tightly encasing silk pants. All his senses annealed into the core of the moment. Indeed, here was something that didn't circle life, but went to its center.

The bull seemed bigger than when it had been simply loitering in the pens, shaking off flies, when he and the two young Mexicans fighting with him on the program had held a *sorteo* to draw bull assignments. Rafael had assured him he'd drawn the best bull, which now stood in the shade near the barrier of the rodeo-cum-bullring, it's head and sharp horns held high, waiting, as did the hushed crowd, for James's finale, his *faena*, with the *muleta*. The hot, cottony afternoon seemed to soak up every sound as he approached, and the bull's flanks, spotted and caked with greenish dung, filled the still air with their rank smell. The big onyx eyes shifted with James's every move and the animal's heavy breathing collected thick saliva in strings at the bristled muzzle. It then drew a couple steps back like a long jumper about to dash, and the *banderillas,* like big candy canes, flopped about at its heavy shoulders wet with rivulets of blood. Again the bull hesitating, drawing back a line in the sand with a hoof as if marking off its territory.

Lining up his left hip with the bull's curly forehead, James crossed in again, this time closer, setting his feet in the sand. He was acting as if not really in his own mind and body, as if the little black ballet-like slippers were pulling his feet across the sand.

The bull lunged, going directly for him, hooking every which way, and he couldn't keep his feet still as the bull ripped into the cloth, almost tearing it from his hand. *Hold still, get lower, slow it down,* he thought. *There, a pass. Keep the cloth just beyond the horn tips. Now again slower.* He could hear the crowd's OOOOOLE stretch out in unison with his extending right hand as the black blur of the bull brushed by him. When he had finished the series, he culminated with a sweeping back-handed chest pass and strutted away from the stilled animal, flicking his head back with a cocky grin at the stands, challenging any scoffers.

There was an ovation from the crowd, accompanied by a burst of spirited *Dianas* from the tinny little band, and his beered-up fraternity brothers, whose block of prepaid seats had helped buy him a place on the program, wildly chanted and cheered as though at a football game. Catching his breath, he flashed a grin toward Isabel in front row center with her aunt and uncle, where his embroidered parade cape had been draped, signifying that she was his honored guest. He could sense her plea to be careful. Her eyes always spoke to him, could fix him in his tracks like a good *rebolera* did an eager bull. Today she was perfect in her embroidered peasant blouse, exposed shoulders, glossy raven hair taken up with a Spanish comb, exposing large golden hoop earrings. He reached inside his stiff brocaded jacket for the handkerchief she'd given him and wiped his brow. Her scent lingered in the lacy cloth, inflaming his already near reckless heat to engage the bull again.

*"Tranquilo, tranquilo, Jaime, despacio!"* Calm yourself, slow down, Rafael called with a patting motion of his hand toward the ground. Rafael moved ahead of him and with two expert flicks of his cape brought the bull around so it faced center ring. *"Andale,"* go, he said.

So this was what they meant by *mandar,* that point where you were no longer avoiding, sidestepping or deflecting, but engaging and guiding, even controlling the tempo of the bull's assault, like the lead in a tango. It was as though the muleta had become a rope attached to a ring in the bull's nose by which he could, at will, pull the lowered horns in semi-circles around his legs. Arching from the waist, legs together and straight, like a flamenco dancer, he presented his groin and thighs, inviting the horns. Having broken through some self-conscious wall, he became what he had only imagined before. No longer held back by focusing on the horns, he progressed toward the limits of his control over the beast.

The bull, perhaps dazed or catching its wind, stopped. Sensing that the bull wouldn't charge if he didn't make any sudden moves, James stood like stone and very slowly brought his left hand to rest on the flank of the left horn, while holding the muleta ready in his right. Then he slowly took his eyes off the bull and looked up and away, oblivious to the applause, intoxicated, as if he were only dreaming of the fluffy cloud that had floated in and etched the sky above the ring.

The time was right for the kill! The moment of truth. He had to get the bull's front hooves together so that the space

Russ Desaulnier

at the shoulders would open, and he would go in straight, locking his aim down the blade all the way. Holding the muleta out low in front in his left hand, he sighted down the curved blade in his right and drove in, pivoting out and away on his left foot as he met with the bull. Stunned and heedless of James's proximity, the bull trotted away with the sword to the hilt in its bleeding withers. But a sigh rose from the crowd, for when the bull turned, the tip of the blade, having been deflected, could be seen protruding from the lower flank. Flaco recovered the sword by snagging the pommel with his cape, and James lined up the bull again. This time he planted the sword three quarters of its length, straight and true. Stopped in its tracks, the animal shuddered and went to its knees and then rolled on it's side. One of the older bandilleros quickly delivered the *coup de grace* with a knife behind the horns, and it was over.

The band launched into a brisk pasodoble, and the crowd, an equal mix of locals and American tourists, including his now riotous fraternity brothers, stood waving handkerchiefs. He raised his hands in salute, and he began a slow tour along the barrier beneath the ten or so wooden rows of benches that formed the little amphitheater-shaped ring. Rafael followed closely behind, throwing back the hats and bota bags, even a brassiere, that were cast into the ring. Several of his drunken fraternity brothers climbed down into the ring, hoisted him up on their shoulders and began carrying him around the perimeter. Isabel threw him a bouquet of roses which he caught and held up to the handkerchief-waving crowd. Rigaberto Rodriguez, the head Charro cowboy, strode up to him, a wide grin propping up his handlebar mustache, and offered up a bloody ear severed from the dead bull. James took the ear and held it aloft to yet more cheers and more enlivened music from the band.

At dusk back at the La Sierra Hotel near the big downtown ring, where the bullfight crowd always gathered before the big Sunday fights, there were people to be talked to, congratulations to be received, a next fight to be arranged with the Charros. Maybe he could even get into a novillada in one of the smaller professional border rings of San Luis, Nogales or Agua Prieta. Also on James's mind was Isabel. Their moments together over the past semester since he had first met her on campus had been too few. Her dark Hispanic beauty was as striking as she was poised and clearheaded, unlike most of the chatty, blasé coeds he had met. An A student and fluent in Spanish, she enjoyed helping him master the language. On those few weekends when they could be alone, they often went dancing. Though he knew the moves for Sambas and Mambos, it was she who showed him how to dance, how the torso and legs danced separately, but in harmony. They were seeing each other exclusively, yet she continued to deflect and temper his passion with a grace as easy as that of the great Paco Camino's cape. Like the traditional religious icons of the La Macarena and La Virgen de Guadalupe, whose power he had unaccountably accepted without question and laid out on his hotel dresser before the fight, she had become a natural part of the course of events that led toward the ring.

As they stole a few moments in the quiet vestibule joining the Sierra lobby and the bar in the subdued light from small recessed spotlights in the ceiling, Isabel radiated like a burnished rose.

"I'm going to have to go back to San Diego tonight with my uncle after dinner," she said.

Russ Desaulnier

"I wish we could just jump on an Aeronaves flight for Mexico City, or how about a bus? It's only twenty bucks on the Tres Estrellas Line," he said

"Sure. What about school, our families? And what would we do when we got there, Jimmy?" She leaned back against the wall papered with vintage bullfight posters.

"Climb a Teotihuacán pyramid and watch the stars? Build sandcastles on Acapulco beach?"

"You're a dreamer, Jimmy boy," she said, pulling him closer.

They stood looking into each other's eyes, and for a moment even the din from the lobby disappeared as her nearness diffused the rush of his longing.

"Jaime! You were brilliant today," gushed Lance DeMarco, swooping in on them from the lobby. He was the secretary of the Los Angeles Aficionado Club, a fixture at the hotel during the season. He smelled of English Leather cologne and wore a deep-cut silky shirt exposing his hairy chest. He moved his hands a lot as he talked, his manicured nails gleaming through the air.

"Wherever did you get that lovely blue suit? It really fits you quite well, I must say. It's got to be a Manfredi." He flashed a toothy smile and then disappeared into the dark passageway of the bar.

"Come on, let's get out of here just for a while and have a drink in my room," James said.

"But Uncle Luis is waiting for us in the dining room."

"Having you there today, dedicating the bull to you, the whole fantastic afternoon. It's all slipping away so fast and I wish I could hold on to it."

"*Así es la vida,*" Isabel said and lightly ran her fingers through his hair. At his back he heard the strains of the mariachi trumpets striking up out on the patio, where the evening's party was getting into full swing.

"What are you lovebirds up to?" clucked May Hutton as she came out of the bar. May was a jolly dowager and a regular of the American bullfight coterie of Tijuana. "Guess who's in there? Torres and Garcia getting tighter than drums, having a *mano y mano* in butchered English. By the way, nice job today, Jimmy. Keep that up, you might get to Plaza Mexico," she said and started for the lobby.

Torres and Garcia, both *triunfadores* of the '63 season, were slated to fight a string of Piedras Negras bulls in the big ring the next day.

"A lot of odd people hang around the fights," Isabel said.

"Goes with the territory, I guess."

"My uncle says most bullfighters' lives are miserable."

"I don't know about that but being out there is something like loving you. I'm not me, but I am me... I mean, heck, I can't describe it."

"Geez, Jimmy, I hope you're yourself with me," she laughed. The familiar scent of her Emeraude perfume mixed with the alcohol fumes drifting from inside the nearby bar. He thought about Torres and Garcia. Maybe there could be a chance to meet them. He gave Isabel a kiss on the neck and caressed one of her bare shoulders and told her to go ahead to the dining room. He'd catch up with her in a few minutes.

As his eyes adjusted to the pitch-dark barroom, he saw Torres and Garcia and a burly man, probably a picador, sitting in a comer at one of the little cocktail tables lit by votive-like candles. At the mirrored bar were a couple of handsome young Mexicans in expensive summer suits, talking with several older American women in their forties, rich

West Los Angeles types, heavy with jewelry and dressed in colorful, revealing halters and skirts. Lance DeMarco, who was chatting with a young hotel waiter, acknowledged him with a nod. James took a seat at the other end of the bar within earshot of the matadors' table; he ordered a Tecate beer with half a lime and lit up a Delicado. He needed to think of a good way to approach the table.

"No, amigo, you are the best *torero,*" Torres was saying.

"But, amigo, you have the biggest *cojónes,*" Garcia replied.

"But you, amigo, have the most *arte.*"

"Perhaps, but you are still *numero uno.*"

"No, you are *numero uno.*"

"You are, amigo."

"No! you are the best."

"I said you are the best!"

Suddenly a sharp commotion from the lobby interrupted the matadors' heated banter. The mariachi band had stopped and there was a lot of shouting. People began leaving the bar to see what the ruckus was about and James followed.

Surging from the main patio through the big glass doors into the main lobby were several Mexican police in their usual pieced-together uniforms and sidearms from Colts to Lugers. In tow was Don "Moose" Moody, handcuffed and bleeding. Following close behind were four other fraternity brothers who, though not handcuffed, were also being hustled out of the hotel by the police. Mick Miller appeared from the wings. Miller probably had the best-looking flattop on fraternity row, like the ones in pictures of models barbers showed you before cutting, as if they could ever really get you to look that good.

"Fuck, man, where the hell you been? There was such a helluva brawl. Fucking Moody said the wrong thing to some Mexican asshole out by the pool and before you know it there was a rumble. I wasn't in it, thank God, I'd just come back from taking a leak."

The police were going to cool Moody in the proverbial Tijuana jail, and the others were being escorted to the border and sent home.

"Fuck, I got the hotel room to myself. I might as well stick around for the night. Hell, there's some nice pussy hanging out around the pool bar. Come on." Miller grinned, as always, with a hint of insolence.

"Sorry, got to see someone."

"The hot little tamale, eh?"

"It's too bad they didn't cart you off, too, Miller."

"Come on, Jimmy boy, be cool."

"See you later, if you're lucky."

"Come on, wanna hit the Blue Fox for a show later on?"

"How about you go alone and play with yourself."

"Fuck you, Jimmy," Miller called after him amiably. "Christ, you're getting a little too serious with the matador act, aren't you?"

In the dining room the waiters wore starched white waistcoats, and the tables were covered with thick white linen and laid with full dining settings. A trio of tenors in silver-buttoned black charro suits roamed around the tables, playing guitars and singing love ballads. James never ate there because it was too expensive for him on his taco stand budget.

Isabel, her Uncle Don Luis and Aunt Carmena were sipping wine and eating hors d'oeuvres. Isabel fidgeted with a long stern glass. Carmena asked James questions about the ring, while Don Luis kept readjusting his table settings and draining his wine too quickly.

"I guess you are a celebrity today," Don Luis said. He was a little paunchy with bushy eyebrows and gray wavy hair. He had the appearance of a young man who had been made up to look old.

"Not really. Mostly everyone's here for the *corrida* in the big ring."

"Of course," he said dryly. The aunt frowned with disapproval at her husband. James knew Don Luis didn't approve of his niece hanging out with a gringo and a not-so-very Catholic boy who played with bulls.

"What does your family say about your bullfighting?" Don Luis asked.

James said his mother was afraid that he might get hurt, but his parents had not forbidden him, so long as he kept up his grades. The truth was they didn't know about his double life between the fraternity house in Westwood and his numerous trips to Tijuana to practice with Rafael, mostly financed with smuggled liquor he retailed for a profit at the fraternity house. He had even branched out and developed a clientele at other houses on the fraternity row, taking orders each time before going south. Less and less he had come to think about his school responsibilities. Spanish 2b, which he took to fulfill the general education language requirement, was the only class in which he was likely to pull a good grade. He had become interested in his English 2b lecture, ever since the class had been assigned Hemingway's *The Sun also Rises,* but there was no appeal in the carbon chains of Chemistry 102, or in the theories of Economics 200. The fraternity gave him a place to live near campus and the brothers still considered him one of theirs, even if some did jag him about his longish hair (which he had grown in order to attach the matador's fake pigtail). But he had become increasingly less connected to the rituals of beer, poker and talk about which sorority girls put out and what the Bruins' chances were for the Rose Bowl. That vague, distant promise of the future signified by his being at UCLA couldn't be sustained during these days along the border that glittered like the gold filigree of his bullfighter's suit.

Then Uncle Luis, as if having perceived something telling in James's eyes, gave his wife a smug, I-told-you-so look. Carmena just sighed and looked away.

"Jimmy wants to go to Mexico City, maybe even to Spain," Isabel said, as if to impress her uncle that he was serious and not just a crazy college boy.

"I'm sure your family will appreciate that," her uncle said.

"I thought the boy was really quite good today. It's been so many years since we went to a *corrida.*" Carmena spoke with a hint of recrimination. Time had not yet hidden how she'd once been a beauty.

Luis responded with a grunt into his glass of wine. The combination enchilada dinners came, and Uncle Luis seemed to warm as dinner progressed and as another bottle of wine was served. He offered to give James a ride back to San Diego and invited him to stay at their home. But James declined. He said he had to stay the night to take care of business and would only have to come back to see the Olivar-Tirado *corrida.* Although he wanted more time with Isabel, he knew he wouldn't get much time alone with her with the old man around. Besides, he had his own car, and it had to be loaded up with contraband liquor before the trip back to Westwood.

"Business, hmmph! Don't you have schoolwork? Education is the only glory a man needs, hombre. This is... *una ilusión de pobres y tontos,*" he said with a wave of his hand, as if to include the hotel and everything in it.

"Luis, we are Americans. We can speak English," his wife chided.

"The boy knows what I have said. He has at least learned some Spanish. Haven't you, boy?" the old man said, turning to his wife.

Shortly after finishing dinner, they moved to the lobby where they waited for the old man's Plymouth to be brought around by a parking lot attendant. Carmena purposely hustled the old man away to a lounge couch, leaving James and Isabel to talk alone. The floor-to-ceiling plate glass of the lobby made the outside patio with its milling, drinking and dancing crowd seem like a giant aquarium.

"You're always a step ahead of me, you know, Bel?"

"There'll be other weekends, Jimmy."

"Sure," he said absently, a nearby cluster of incomprehensible Spanish conversations reminding him of monotonous school lectures and the long weeks of school relieved only by weekends that sped by all too soon. Could he even continue school? This thought cued the image of his father's admonishing face which bolted through him like a sudden chill.

"Jimmy boy, are you okay? Look at me," Isabel said.

She moved closer to him, her eyes inviting, cool and fathomless. She glanced at her uncle who wasn't watching them for the moment, and then she suddenly leaned into James so that he had to put his hands on her waist to keep her from falling into him. She kissed him fully on the lips. He kissed her back, and she brought a hand to his neck and pulled him into her mouth, her tongue meeting his for an instant before she let him go. The old man perused a newspaper, appearing uninterested in them, and Carmena turned away, suppressing a smile.

They gathered at the driveway entrance of the Sierra where the car had been brought around. James had felt a bit sheepish and avoided the old man's eyes, but Isabel held her head high as if to defy her uncle. Carmena surprised James with a parting peck on the cheek, while the impatient old man already at the wheel threw him a perfunctory *adios*. Before getting into the backseat, Isabel hugged James tightly, as if to leave a lasting impression of the topography of her body. As soon as she got in and her door had clicked shut, the uncle drove away. James watched the car gradually disappear down the dusty road, until he noticed the parking attendant studying him and smiling.

A scruffy little boy about ten, like the ones you saw everywhere selling gum, perhaps to help put food on the family table, came up to him with his box of cellophane packages of Chiclets. He gave the boy a crumpled dollar from his pocket, took the gum and refused the change. A shoeshine about the same age as the gum seller tugged at his pants cuffs and pointed at James's dusty shoes. *Why not?*

When he returned to the lobby, the Saturday-night party was hitting full swing. He went out to the patio and bought a Cuba Libre at the pool bar. A mild musty smell of something like old cooking oil permeated the night, and a canopy of stars blanketed the sparsely lit townscape surrounding the hotel.

"Take a load off, kid, and have a smoke." It was Jolene Rayburn grabbing him from his blind side and pushing a thin wood-tipped cigar in his face. She was a habitue of the fights and the club meetings in LA, and even though she looked like the Marlboro man, she had always been kind to him, had even taught him a few graceful pointers with the cape, which she had studied and perfected *en salon*.

Russ Desaulnier

Her girlfriend Maria, always very lacy, almost never said anything and would dutifully sit by in a cloud of strong perfume. Across the table, littered with empty cocktail glasses and paper beer cups, Santa Monica Rico was trying to give a hickey to some giggly, drunken American woman; and from the Capote aficionado club Burt Jessel's nebbish daughter was smiling too sweetly at James from across the table. Lance DeMarco was engaged with the same young waiter as before, but now he had an arm loosely draped about the waiter and was excitedly carrying on in fractured Spanish. Jan, from the Orange County club, cigarette and Margarita in either hand, was chatting with an erstwhile Mexican bullfighter turned bull breeder, while her husband Harry, already drunk, was slumped at the table muttering to himself.

One drink led to another and, despite a promise to himself not to do so, James got very drunk. Around noon the next day, when he stirred from sleep, the fingers of his right hand ached with several raw bums from cigarettes allowed to bum too far down, and his head felt as though his brain stem had been twisted like a wet towel. Miller, who had managed to get into his room with help from the cleaning woman, leaned over the bed and talked doggy breath down into his face, inquiring if he could have the next dance. James mustered a swing at Miller but missed, his stomach rebelling at the sudden movement. Miller brought him a glass of water with an Alka Seltzer which settled his urge to retch, and when he was able to sit up in bed, Miller told him about his evening, how James had danced with every person wearing a skirt and with a few who didn't, including, Miller gleefully reported, "the bleach haired dike." His final act of the night had been a quasi-flamenco dance on a table from which he had stumbled and staggered, flopping into the nearby swimming pool. James's act, Santa Monica Rico later said, had been as flamboyant as anything seen at La Sierra in recent seasons, as crazy as the out-of-ring exploits of Matador Jaime Bravo who, according to legend, had chased a woman around the parking lot late one night, like a satyr after a nymph, both near naked. James decided he couldn't hang around to see the Garcia-Torres *corrida;* he was just too weak and sick to try to sit through a hot afternoon in the bullring stands and then have to crawl home with the heavy Sunday night traffic. So he bid farewell to Rafael, Escuinapa, Flaco and a few others from the inner ring. Miller, down for James's fight and what partying he could find, was glad to get back on the road to Westwood.

After leaving the Sierra, they stopped downtown near Caesar's Hotel on Revolucíon Street to have some hangover-stabilizing *menudo* soup, and while they had the car parked on a quiet back street, Miller helped him get every crevice of his old, beat-up Ford stuffed with bottles of inexpensive, tax-free contraband liquor.

With a San Diego pop station playing like a clarion call to home, they made their way out through the dusty roads between downtown and the border, past the many quickie car upholstery shops and roadside hawkers pushing plaster of Paris statuary, souvenir banderillas, tooled leather purses and acrylic paintings on velvet. The traffic lines at the crossing stations were not so long, nor did the border checks seem particularly intensive. But there was no way of knowing whom they would choose to search. Most cars were just waved through. Sometimes they took a cursory look in the trunk or in your luggage, if you had any, before letting you through. Sometimes a car would be waved over to a side area where a special team of customs officers did a thorough search. In any event, crossing was easier if you left early on Sunday and missed the surge of returning traffic that climaxed the tourist weekend orgy of cheap drinking, shopping, raunchy floor shows such as those at the Blue Fox, gambling at the Jai Alai Palace and the Caliente Racetrack, and, of course, the thrills of the bullfights.

While they were waiting in line to cross the border, a hawker came up to the car window with an assortment of paintings of buxom nude women on black velvet. Miller purchased one of the more voluptuous pieces for a couple of dollars.

"Nice set of jugs on this one, eh?" Miller said, turning up the radio that was playing the new British quartet with the strange haircuts who harmonized like the Everly Brothers.

"You're such a connoisseur of art, Miller. I wonder what you'll be when you grow up."

"Ah, let me see... a gynecologist? What are you gonna be, Jim? No, don't tell me, lemme guess, a matador."

"Maybe. I dunno."

Geez, not a matador? That's a relief. I was beginning to worry. Now tell me about the cute tamale. Did you get any?"

"How would you like me to barf on you?"

"Hey, now that sounds more like my old brother frat rat."

"Don't count on it," James said, driving forward into the crossing dock with the waiting border guard.

"The moment of truth, eh? Isn't that what you call it in the ring, Jim?" Miller grinned and sank into a slouch, preparing a nonchalant attitude for the guard.

The officer looked in the car at Miller first, asking him to turn the radio down and then questioned him about citizenship, place of birth, and reason for going to Tijuana.

Miller was quick to point out his velvet cheesecake with a conspiratorial chuckle. The officer responded with a tired sigh. He'd seen far too many college boys come across from weekends of strip shows and cheap prostitutes. Then he turned to James. He felt naked and heavy under the officer's gaze, counting off to himself the assorted bottles of illegal scotch, bourbon and rum, as if calculating the degree of their offense, concealed in the door panels, in the air conditioning vents, under the dash and inside the seats among the springs. He and Miller even had a few half pints of scotch lining the inside of their belts. If they were going to get busted, they figured they might as well go for broke.

"Well, you got anything to declare, young man?"

"No sir, nothing."

Feeling his bullfight poster that lay rolled in a plastic tube on the seat next to him, he knew he possessed something he could always declare, and as the guard waved them across, James could see the ramshackle hills of Tijuana in the rear view mirror, now golden in the late afternoon sun.

# The Whole Nine Yards

T he fog had rolled back out to the bay and left the city clear and bright. From the 10th floor offices of Marketing Consultants in the Alcoa building, Jim McClaren studied the new towering Bank of America building with his first cigarette drag of the day rinsed with sweet coffee. It was nine, the best time of the morning when hope was fresh and focused on scoring a deal or two. His SOD sheet (spins of the phone dial) was laid out on his desk and prepared with some thirty bird-dog calls to be made to district managers in the Bay area—Hunt & Wesson, Kraft, Black & Decker, Kimberly Clark, etc. And there was the usual flow of applicants to interview, classify and arrange for interviews. He'd been one of those job seekers when J.B. Bradley recommended that he start out at Marketing Consultants and passed his resume along to Bob Hansen, the office manager, who hired him.

Last week had been good with three job placements, putting him only two behind Bradley on the office score board. Things had slowed a bit, but he still had one hot job order in the works with Clark Equipment. The job paid 25K which meant a commission of about $500, but he was having trouble finding the right man for Wayne Williams, the regional manager. The candidate had to be experienced, have Madison Avenue image and be tough minded. For sure, to get the job a candidate would have to sell himself to the scrutinizing and picky Williams.

"How you doin' this morning, guy?"

It was Bob Hansen as he came down the aisle, pinching a perpetual cigar between his teeth. He was the Vince Lombardi of the personnel industry, a chunk of a man about fifty or so, well known to his competitors, Tom McCall Agency and Management Recruiters. In his day, it was said, he filled the sales staff positions of almost every major industry with offices in the Bay Area.

"Are we going to go out there and get 'em today, kid?"

"Sure, Bob, gangbusters," he replied.

"That's what I like to hear." He readjusted the bite on his cigar and moved on down the aisle between the other agents—Tupper, Enright, Jones, Bradley—all with phones propped between ear and shoulder.

McClaren had been with MC almost six months. It was the first full time straight job he'd had since he got out of grad school and LA. Too old at 28 for the draft and the divisive war in Vietnam, he'd floated about for two years with part-time jobs and a brief marriage. So, when he landed at Marketing Consultants in San Francisco, he didn't have a solid track record, the very thing he had to look for in job applicants who came into the office.

But J.B. and Hansen had liked him, for whatever reason, and Hansen had said they'd put him to work, give him a shot, that he was obviously smart, but they'd have to toughen him up a bit. He got through the probationary period and made his first job placement within the first month. Hansen was pleased and averred that he knew a good man when he saw one. With Hansen's confidence, McClaren followed his dictum, always go for the first down, never punt. Press and persist. Only Regional Manager Williams of Clark Equipment had become an especially tough defense, stopping the advance of three applicants. Williams, it seemed, wanted nothing less than a triple-threat All-American applicant.

The afternoon dragged on, but he scheduled several new applicants who'd read the ongoing want ad in the Chronicle for salesmen, self-starters, looking for great potential, degree and some experience preferred. When he had first interviewed, Hansen had been in his Lombardi mode, wanting to bring up a rookie from the bench. *Okay, kid, this is your chance, show me what you got,* or something like that. He remembered how Hansen ceremoniously brought his new name plate to his assigned desk—James McClaren, Consultant. As he set the plate on the front of his desk, Hansen put an assuring hand on his shoulder as if he were being sent from the sidelines to join the team huddle on the field, all in the spirit of winning one for the Gipper.

In between fielding calls and making appointments for job seekers, he went back to his SODs to get some listings, but he was running into more than the usual number of obstinate secretaries screening their sales managers' incoming calls. The district manager offices were not as tightly screened as the regional manager offices. The regional offices had secretaries who were masters of stonewalling—Mr. X is in a conference, not back from lunch, leave your number, leave him a message, and so on. All excuses meant to delay you, put you off. Some days he felt like he was in the fourth quarter of a game too far behind in points to mount enough enthusiasm. Come Monday mornings, Hansen gave a pep talk, always reiterating you've got to want to win, you got to have the desire to close deals, get those managers in here to the interview rooms. We'll run the ads and get you the talent.

The interview rooms were large cubicles with Danish mid-century modern conference tables and chairs. The walls were decorated with large photo prints of turn-of-the-century San Francisco, as if the company shared such a long tradition and provenance. The interview cubicles were at the back of the office separated by ceiling to floor tinted plate glass. One of the office secretaries had the job of keeping the managerial clients and the interviewees plied with fresh cups of coffee and soft drinks. If you got as far as the interview rooms, you had to be sure you put people in the room with your client-employer who fit the bill or else you were wasting the employer's time. Preferably, you lined up three or four winners. Men with business degrees and good grooming were high on the list. No long hairs. Better yet, if you can poach a district manager from somewhere, we'll get him a regional job, Hansen had said.

During late afternoon, there was a trickle of applicants, even a few pros looking to trade up. But mostly the consumer product corporations were looking for young trainable guys to service product territories that offered a good starting salary, full use of a company car, commissions and opportunities for advancement.

Then there were the Willy Loman types, middle-aged and unemployed, and not able to get another comparable position in middle management. Burt Powers was a classic example, forty-eight with a big mortgage in Half Moon Bay, a wife who worked and two kids going to college. He came around the office now and then, just checking to see if on the outside chance there might be something. There were others in his age bracket, victims of mergers and downsizing who rarely were able to make a lateral move to a job paying the same money as they'd had. And nobody wanted them for lesser positions. McClaren made a few cursory checks for Powers without much hope. Any lateral move Powers might have made was usually taken by someone from within company ranks or by someone a bit younger with a cracker jack resume. Powers reminded McClaren of lost-at-sea movies where the lost people afloat in rubber rafts waved frantically and futilely to passing aircraft. Every time he stopped by the office, he hated having to tell Powers that there was nothing new for him in consumer products or that a middle management position advertised in the Chronicle had been filled. He didn't want to lay any more disappointment on the man than the business world already had. It was hard enough to watch walking humiliation, never mind add to it.

McClaren had a second story studio in an old building at the top of Ashbury Street, a few blocks up from the Haight, at the corner of Clayton where he could look from above at Kezar Stadium out his kitchen window. It was roomy enough with a small bathroom and galley kitchen, but the problem was that his life hadn't enough breadth for him to not feel listless. He would often just sit on his fire escape balcony with a Scotch and soda (or two) after work. Or he would take aimless walks around the neighborhood simply so he wouldn't feel constricted. Occasionally he'd smoke some pot but that usually left him feeling solipsistic and sorry for himself. He had taken to heating cans of Campbell's soup for his dinners, eaten with chunks of San Francisco sourdough bread which filled the hunger but left him unsatisfied. So occasionally he would go out for Chinese. Sometimes his walks took him down the hill to the

Haight, where he was always awed by the waves of young people who dressed and acted in ways that seemed silly and bizarre, meant perhaps to advertise that they didn't care a jot for the real world of making a living and having society's respect. Their antics didn't seem like nonconformity, but just a lot of lost young people conforming to pop fashions for being looped out on drugs and dressing as odd looking as they could. Perhaps a girlfriend would be a good change, but his divorce was still fresh, and the schedule of his life didn't seem to present any opportunities to strike up any friendships with women. He was becoming like all those serious faced people on the morning bus to work, enduring routine, the grind.

He would clean the kitchen, dishes, sink, pots and pans and vacuum the apartment about once every five or six days which was the intermittent frequency of his periods of ennui. The cleaning was sort of an absolution for the sin of boredom. In addition to house cleaning, he'd attempt to balance his check book. A soft Bay breeze drifted through his open French doors to the fire escape, and so he took his second Scotch and soda and sat out on the small landing. Upper Ashbury was quiet except for occasional strollers, and there was surprisingly little traffic. It was that time of day when people often walked their dogs. A man, still in his workaday suit but with a loosened tie, strolled by with two German Shepherds and patiently watched them as they fouled the sidewalk, which he left behind as he strolled on. Another man, tallish and thin, dressed in skin-tight white clothing, walked by like a female model on the fashion cat-walk. Although the sun had almost gone down, he wore large wraparound sunglasses. Then two choppers roared into the intersection, each biker with a young woman behind on the narrow high-backed seat. Suddenly they came to a halt at the corner of Clayton and at once started yelling obscenities at each other. One of them yanked a piece of heavy chain from his handlebars and proceeded to menacingly whip the pavement while shouting, *fuck off* which the other biker promptly did, giving the finger as he rode off.

McClaren continued sitting on the landing through another Scotch and soda. Across the street at the Clayton Arms, a young couple embraced in the stone arched portal. Lovers, they tarried at the iron gates to the building, perhaps trying to part for the evening but not making progress. The young man kept pulling the girl closer with his hands locked around her waifish waist. She laughed and tossed her straight blonde hair away from her face and kissed him. Then they reconnoitered the street and finally disappeared into the portal of the building. The young man appeared again not long after, his long hair disheveled. A moment later he was picked up by a vintage Oldsmobile whose windows were partially curtained with Indian tapestry. Windows in the buildings around him were suddenly lighting up. McClaren hadn't noticed that the night had crept up on him like a cat and that the Scotch had insulated him from the cold air now coming in off the Bay.

Although he had gone to bed early, the Scotch still hung with him in the morning. He must learn to eat a real meal in the evenings and drink less. Hoping to allay the effects of his hangover, he bought a large ham and egg sandwich at the concession in the lobby of the Alcoa building. In the office, he was eating his sandwich and trying to get down some coffee at his desk when Hansen came by. It was only ten minutes to nine and he already had a fresh unlit cigar in his mouth. He tilted his head down to look over his rimless specs, studying McClaren's face.

"You look a bit rough this morning, kid," he said, rolling the cigar in his teeth and coming around the desk to peer down at McClaren's SOD sheet.

'That's good, uhuh, uhuh, uhuh, uhuh." he affirmed for himself as he scanned the SOD list. "What's going on with the Clark account? Let's get that job on the score board."

He raised himself up and with his head turned upward, he struck a match and ignited the tip of his fresh cigar. In that moment he was an amalgam of FDR and Woody Hayes, the legendary Ohio State football coach, wily, confident and triumphant. Washing down a mouthful of sandwich with coffee, McClaren then excused himself, a time out to the restroom.

"Sure, kid, sure, you're doing fine. Remember just don't...."

"Punt, I know!"

"You got it. Carry on."

Everyone in the office was busy spinning the dial or was buried in the mouthpiece of his telephone. J.B. was, as usual, leaned back in his swivel chair, a picture of composed relaxation, speaking into the phone as if making vacation plans with his wife, his eyes roaming the office. McClaren had begun with follow up calls, obviating the necessity of going through the Marketing Consultants' sales pitch to new clients. Then he got a call from Ned Cooper at Levi-Strauss.

"Hey, Jim, maybe you can help me out." This was good. He assured Manager Cooper he would help, and he felt some loosening of the tautness in his head. Cooper continued.

"There's some pressure on us to hire minority staff, and, well, to be frank, we have to hire at least two black guys for the region. The company is going for a big Fed contract and so, well, since the Civil Rights Act, there's been a diversity requirement for doing business with them. It might be hard to find some black applicants, but that's why I'm calling you, right? I'm sure there's some applicants with degrees out there who look good and present well, you know, can talk straight."

"Straight?"

"Come on, Jim, you know. Not like some Fillmore jive talking pimp."

"I get it," he replied, feeling himself stumbling for words. His head felt taut again. He hadn't seen a black applicant in over three months. "How pressing is the company's need?"

"Pressing."

"Fine. Send me details—starting salary, benefits, commissions, the usual. I'll see what I can do." Cooper thanked him and hung up.

He would have to go through his files to find the black applicant who had come in months ago. There had been nothing for him at the time and it was likely nothing was going to develop, so McClaren had filed him away. But his filing was as about as orderly as his check book which never seemed to balance, catching him with several overdraft fees in recent months. After a trip to the restroom and more coffee, he remembered the name of the black applicant. It was Madison! Yes, that was it, Madison. Presidents' names were ever popular. But what was the last name? He started taking out thick stacks of old applications, going through them one by one until he found Madison, Madison Aubert in Berkeley, a French name. Perhaps his ancestors were from Haiti? He called the phone number on the application but got no answer. There was no answer after several more calls, so he decided to call from home that evening. When he finally got Madison on the phone, he was interested but couldn't come into the office because he was working a 9-to-5 in a haberdashery shop on Polk. That was a good sign.

He recalled Madison was a natty dresser and well groomed. It made sense he would be working in a classy men's clothing shop, but probably for minimum wage with commissions. Yes, he could fill Cooper's need at Levi-Strauss. So, he made an appointment to see Madison at the office at 5:30 pm the following day. He would have to stay a bit longer in the office while the janitor made his evening once over, emptying wastepaper baskets and vacuuming.

Madison arrived on time. He was well-groomed and handsome, medium height, square jawed with a soft roast coffee complexion, and short trimmed hair. He wore a British style dark blue blazer and a red regimental tie. His Cordovan shoes were polished to a mirror finish. He was warm and quickly initiated a handshake which was firm and sincere. The application had him at 26 and he told McClaren he was an only son, for the moment living at home in Berkeley with the family, who were of course all anxious for him to establish something more than selling shirts, slacks and ties. He saw the men's clothing store as temporary and said he was glad to receive McClaren's call. Because they were alone in the office and not under any scrutiny, which surely wouldn't have been the case during business hours, they relaxed, and the meeting became more personal. Madison had graduated from UC Berkeley in history, had traveled a bit and was still single. The companies liked married better but Madison possessed the overriding requirement. As expected, Madison liked the idea of a certain degree of autonomy a rep job would offer. Having a company car was a great perk for a young man who didn't have a car and had always gotten around by public transport. They found they had both traveled a bit in Europe, the thing to do as an undergrad, if you could get some help which they both had as only sons. Madison didn't smoke, which reminded McClaren how much his desk job had caused him to sink deeper into the nicotine trap. His respect for Madison, even admiration, welled up. At this point, they had almost forgotten about the business at hand when McClaren went through the position in detail without mentioning anything about Levi's business with the Feds. A half hour sped by before they brought their meeting to a close with fixing a timetable for an interview with Levi-Strauss. He was happy that Madison might find his niche in corporate America, a good steady salary and happy parents. McClaren knew about that brass ring.

Because he just missed his usual bus into town, he got to the office a bit late the next morning. There was bad news waiting. His two placements with Crown Zellerbach had fallen through, one placement failing a deeper credit check and the other quitting after one day on the job. Hansen had left a note on his desk. That said not to sweat it, it was only the first half.

He slumped into his swivel chair, gazing over the city scape toward Chinatown. Then he saw Enright chalk up another sale on the graph. Hansen stood to the side, rolling his cigar in his teeth. What was the watchword from Hansen? Look after the interest of the employer. *We find people for jobs, not jobs for people.* McClaren spent several hours interviewing drop-ins looking for work. The MC ads pulled them in with regularity. It made one aware that jobs were scarce or there were a lot more people looking for work than labor statistics tended to show. Cooper called and had promised him a bonus on the affirmative action hiring and said there was no point in going through all the prelims. Just send Madison over to his office and they would get him suited up. He asked for confirmation that the candidate looked good and was articulate. McClaren assured him. He felt guilty, even sorry for Madison, who'll think he's finally got the brass ring, but then perhaps he was smarter than that. Nevertheless, he still felt sorry that Madison's worth to Cooper wasn't based on his character or abilities. He called Madison and gave him the time and address for the interview.

"Just take the time off from the store. Ned Cooper's expecting you. Make sure you bring all your references and commendations, a copy of your degree, etc. I doubt you'll be needing the clothing store job anymore."

"How can you be so sure?" Madison asked.

"I know the business. Trust me. Just keep the appointment and dress well, like the Ivy League you wore when you came here last time. Got it?"

"Right on, brother."

"And, Madison, drop the brother talk. It doesn't go down well with these corporate guys who are apple pie, flag waving and sorry to say—hyper white. Got me?"

"Thank you, Jim. I understand a hundred percent."

"Good luck, Madison."

After the call ended, he felt exhausted and needed a break. He swung by Hansen's office and put his head in past the glass door. *Ironic how doors and walls in the office were all glass.*

"I think I'll have one on the board by the end of the day. Got a live one for Cooper at Levi. I need to take a time out, okay."

"That's the hustle, kid. Go water down", Hansen said and winked and went back to his phone.

There was a light breeze blowing across Alcoa Plaza. He put his head into the breeze and breathed deeply as if his breathing would cleanse him somehow. He went into the

Plaza bar and ordered a Scotch and soda, but his stomach began to heave as a swallow went down, and he couldn't finish. He asked the bartender for water, drank it down and left his unfinished Scotch on a five-dollar bill which included a tip. He swore to himself he wasn't drinking any more. When he stepped out of the dark lounge, the brightness of the afternoon blinded him. When his eyes adjusted, he saw a dozen or so flower children banging tambourines, chanting and snaking their way around the plaza's grass islands and sculptures. They coursed across the plaza and down the stairs to Front St. and the lower level until the fading sound of their tambourines became lost in the traffic.

Back in the office, he stopped at Hansen's office again. He was invited in and he sat down, trying unsuccessfully to ignore the strong stench of cigars.

"I want to leave, Bob." *Leave* sounded better than *quit*.

"Where you goin', kid?" he asked, absent mindedly shuffling papers.

"I'm leaving Marketing Consultants," McClaren added firmly.

"Did you get a better offer somewhere else?"

"I thought about that, but no."

"Whatcha you gonna do?"

"I don't know yet."

"So, what's this about?

"I just can't do this anymore. Sorry."

"You need to get your signals straight, kid."

"Are your receivers down field, Bob?"

"What!?"

"I'm punting."

# Memory

One had a lovely face,
And two or three had charm,
But charm and face were in vain
Because the mountain grass
Cannot but keep the form
Where the mountain hare has lain.

—W.B. YEATS

# The Hotel Cadillac

····················

Back in LA with San Francisco behind me, I discovered photography. Needing more income in addition to my part-time teaching at the local college, I took an idea and made a business out of creating old time portraits, dressing my subjects up with a collection of antique clothing and accessories to look like they came out of the era of Mathew Brady and daguerreotypes. I air brushed the 8 X 10 prints around the edges, sepia toned them, cut them in perfect oval shape and then mounted them on brown art board. People loved them, and it didn't take long for a steady stream of customers to develop, which helped pay for the rent and photography supplies. On the side, I made serious portraits and other subjects in black and white, available light candid shots of people. I was trying to emulate Henri Bresson. My large, very old apartment had spacious rooms and vintage high ceilings, and so it made a perfect photo studio and a walk-in size closet made for a workable darkroom. The bathroom, two steps across the hall from the closet, was convenient for rinsing prints in the tub. I even made 16 X 20 prints that I stapled on frames and let dry like drum skins. I got the big prints by projecting images from the worktable to the floor where I got down on my hands and knees to wash the large prints down with sponges dipped in developer and then with sponges of fixing solution, finally carrying the prints across the hall to the bathroom for washing. With drying prints hung on lines everywhere, the apartment suggested a laundry service.

After nearly a year of this venture, I decided that with my part time classes wrapped up at the college, I needed a bit of travel, a summer holiday. I paid the rent in advance and I left my place in the hands of Rosie, a past girlfriend, who needed a place to live for a couple months. She would field my phone calls while I was gone and take care of my place. I was still at an age when rather than thinking of consequences, I thought more about missed excitement.

Almost a decade before I had spent a lot of time at the border but never got to Mexico City. The time and circumstances were right to finally go there.

I packed up my Canon camera and lenses in a sturdy attache case with a foam padded interior and a small valise of personal items and clothing, and I headed for San Diego and the Mexican border. Now I had the skills to take great shots of bullfighting and some candid shots of life in Mexico City. I had a couple contacts from my bullfighting days on the border who still might be around. Mexico was old world compared to California; people stayed put. With my fair command of Spanish and Mexico's bargain basement prices, I'd be okay.

Tres Estrellas bus line from Tijuana to Mexico City cost twenty dollars and took a grueling 48 hours non-stop with changes of drivers at pit stops along the way. Sleeping much of the way, I still felt exhausted by the time we arrived at dusk. I had the address of a hotel not far from the bus station and took a cab for a few pesos. The Hotel Cadillac on Jose Maria Izazaga was designed for lower tier Mexican businessmen visiting from the provinces. More of an old

Chevy rather than a Cadillac, it was reasonable and clean at 20 pesos a night or about four dollars. My room on the second floor had a large tiled shower stall where I luxuriated in a long hot shower, then slept until the next morning in the clean, comfy double bed. Waking up ravenously hungry, I could smell food down the hall where I discovered the hotel *comedor* and ate a huge breakfast of *juevos rancheros,* fried eggs and tortillas, smothered in green chili salsa. I was ready to start my adventure.

The assistant manager of the hotel, Antonio, was young, solicitous and spoke fair English. If I needed anything, Antonio said he'd take care of it. If I needed to call anyone, he told me to dial the desk from my room and I would be connected. By the end of my first day I had made my contact calls, first to Alejandro and then to Manuel, both from a decade before, hoping the numbers were still viable. Matador Alejandro was happy to hear from me and would call and come by the hotel in a day or two and we would go out for an evening meal. I tried to call my old acquaintance Manuel Sanchez, the bull breeder, but the number was defunct. I felt lucky I was able to get hold of Alejandro who warmly remembered me. A lot of changes happen in almost 10 years.

On Saturdays, in Plaza Mexico, the biggest ring in the world, young aspirants trained *en salon,* one playing the bull and the other the bullfighter. I thought this would be a good place to start taking some photos and maybe get to socialize. I parked myself at the surrounding sturdy barrier with my Canon resting on the edge, a good place from which to observe and take photos. Before long, one of the practicing boys was curious enough to come over to the barrier and address me. He wondered if I worked for the American press. I guessed that my expensive camera, uncommon in Mexico, except among a few pros, made him think so. Young unknowns were always angling for some good photos for their resumes. It was my goal to get entry to as many bullrings as I could for ground level shots. My rusty Spanish was smoothing out with each encounter since I'd arrived. Chamaco was his ring name. Indeed, he was small, dark and delicate like the famous Spanish bullfighter back in the 50s nicknamed Chamaco, a flamboyant gypsy from Huelva. I asked my new acquaintance how the *temporada* was going for him.

"I'll soon have a contract to fight, *si quieres venir*," if I wished to come. Of course, he wanted me to take photos. This is exactly what I had planned for. The next problem was getting to these villages outside Mexico City.

"*No preocupes, vayas conmigo por coche*" Don't worry, you can go with me by car. This was perfect.

Ignacio Vazquez was his real name and at 24 he'd been aspiring for five years, *en pos de la gloria*, in pursuit of glory, as they say, fighting in the provincial villages where they made very little after expenses but accumulated a track record, while hoping for contracts in bigger rings. A wad of black and white photos from me couldn't hurt his publicity collection of calling cards. Chamaco was congenial and I could understand his Spanish, which was not the case with everyone I met. Many working-class Mexicans lacked clarity for me. I told him about my past along the border, and after exchanging a little *toreo en salon*, we established a rapport. Chamaco bid his buddies goodbye, and then we dropped off his equipment in his ancient beat-up Ford in the parking lot and we went to lunch nearby at a taco stand where I treated.

Days passed quickly at the Cadillac. In Mexico City during summer it rained lightly almost every day in the late

Russ Desaulnier

afternoon, which is sometimes not good for the novice bull-fights that are held in the summer, beginning at 5 pm. Long lunches with Tecate beers began to often lead to long naps and lost afternoons. I had done the obligatory tours around the environs of Mexico City—Teotihuacan, the museums, Plaza Garibaldi and walked the length of the verdant Paseo Reforma to the Palacio de Bellas Artes. There were beautiful Mexican girls everywhere and I was feeling lonely.

Seeing Alejandro Ortega, billed nearly a decade ago as *El Rey de la Elegancia* on the big posters, brought back a rush of memories. I had originally befriended him at a meeting of the Los Angeles bullfight aficionado club when I was still at UCLA and had become dazzled with bullfighting. Thereafter I met with him every time he was in LA or fought in Tijuana. He came to one of my ragtag economical fights in Tijuana's Lienzo del Charro, a small ring near the Caliente racetrack, and I dedicated my bull to him. The last time I saw him, he had been in route to a Juarez *corrida* and we got happy with a bottle of Manzanilla at the Matador restaurant on Pico Blvd in Santa Monica. He later did the obligatory tour of Spain with modest success, returned to Mexico and had a string of mostly unnoteworthy afternoons and a couple gorings, one very grave. To complicate matters, he took the losing side in a union dispute with the bullring empresarios. His career then became a trickle. He spoke good English with a charming accent, even better than Antonio, the assistant manager at the Cadillac. During those few years of successful border fights and his appearances in LA, Alejandro had quietly married a knockout American airline stewardess with Western Air who flew the connection between LA and Mexico City.

It was a late afternoon when Alejandro finally arrived at the hotel Cadillac and a slight drizzle had started. We went to a cozy place near the hotel, and we ordered some steaks. I ordered a bottle of wine.

"Sorry, amigo, not for me. I quit drinking a few years ago," he said.

"Really?"

"After Spain, I had some bad afternoons and I began drinking."

"I have to be careful. I get sick easily"

"I lost Karen because of too much drinking."

"Wow, I'm sorry. *Qué pena!*" What a pity seemed more appropriate in Spanish. "Does she still work for Western Airlines?"

"Yes, out of Los Angeles where she lives with our kids."

"I'm sorry, hombre."

"It's not so bad. She comes to Mexico occasionally and brings the kids"

Almost ten years hadn't physically changed us that much. Alejandro was just as lean and ramrod straight as ever, his hair just as thick, oiled and swept back over his head, his cheek bones just as sharp, his eyes just as penetrating. He was dressed as impeccably as ever in a light grey suit and a simple thin black tie.

"I was very surprised when you called. It's been a long time."

"Yes, my life has been busy too—finishing college, two degrees, a brief marriage, a year in San Francisco, some teaching." I was a bit embarrassed that it had taken me so long to get to Mexico City. "How about you and the bulls?"

"Very little, my friend. Mostly I've been working fulltime in customer relations with Western Air. Karen helped me get hired when we were still together. So, I've been with them about six years."

"So, how is it?"

"It's fine. I mainly take care of upset passengers."

"You said very little *toreo?*"

"Si, I don't get many calls to fight anymore, amigo, and when I do, it's for provincial festivals. But I never travel far from the city."

"Anything booked while I'm here?"

"Well, yes, at Tlaxcala, August 24th with Eloy Cavazos and Emilio Rodriguez. That's a Sunday. About an hour and half drive."

"Great! That's a good ring, and good company."

"It was Cavazos who got me on the program as a favor."

"I remember he was a good friend of yours."

"*Si, un buen amigo.*'"

"I'd love to see you fight again!"

"I'm driving, come with me and take photos from the *callejon*"

"I would be honored, my friend. Gracias. I'd love to take photos."

I was happy to have reconstituted my old friendship with Alejandro There was still hope for him to round out a fine career. After all, he was only 35. I would make sure I could give him a great collection of photos of his *corrida* in Tlaxcala.

The following day after I got back from my local camera shop, I picked up messages from Antonio at the desk. A young man named Vazquez had been to the hotel to see me. Chamaco, yes, of course, but he had become secondary in my mind now. I wouldn't mention that I was connected to matador Alejandro Ortega. That might make him feel slighted by my friendship to a senior matador. My past experiences taught me Mexicans can be possessive and jealous in friendships, old world.

"And you received this letter, Mr. McClaren" announced Antonio, handing me a letter which was from Linda Ganz in LA. In the enclosed note she wrote she'd called my studio and got the address of the hotel from Rosie. *Why didn't you let me know you were going to Mexico? We could have planned a little side trip to Acapulco together. Maybe we still can?* That was Linda, persistent. She was coming to Mexico City for a few days to see me. She wasn't asking— she was just coming, and I could expect her in a couple of days. I'd never made a clear statement about my feelings for her, mostly because I didn't understand how I felt and I figured it might be hurtful if I told her I liked her well enough only to see her now and then. Perhaps that's what she wanted too. The 60s weren't far behind us and relationships between the sexes were evolving. Linda was smart, kind, and attractive, and so how could I not enjoy her company? But I had no choice *again*. Anyway I decided I could do with a few days of distraction, and I'd do my best to show her a good time since she was coming so far. I had only been in Mexico three weeks and it was already getting complicated. But I was drinking less.

I had been to a *novillada* at Plaza Mexico with Chamaco and then one by myself to the Aurora ring, a sort of neighborhood bullring just outside the city where they held economical bullfights with unknown local aspirants. I had no problem walking through the cuadrilla gate, the main entry to the ring, and establishing myself inside the *callejon,* the passageway behind the barrier abutting the sand. I was simply presumed to be *La Prensa,* the press, and nobody asked for credentials. I didn't see anyone with camera equipment at the level of my Canon and telephoto lens. At the end of the afternoon, the boy who'd fought the best, dressed in

Russ Desaulnier

a very worn, fading green suit of lights, asked for copies of photos, so I gave him the Cadillac hotel address and told him to come by in several days and I'd give him some prints.

Back at the Cadillac, Chamaco and I were having lunch and he was all excited about being contracted to fight in Cuautitlan, a village forty miles north of the city, a *novillada* with four bulls and three other *novilleros,* none of whose names I recognized. He was topping the bill as a *triumphador* making a return appearance.

"I had a fight there last year and cut an ear from *a pandulci,* a sweet little *novillo* that did everything I asked. They should have pardoned him. But I put him away very quickly. One thrust. *Patas arriba.*" He raised his arms to represent the bull on its back with hooves in the air. I would have liked to offer to buy him a decent pair of shoes, but I didn't want to insult him. I had no idea how he supported himself and I didn't ask, not wanting to encroach on his privacy. I would go to Cuautitlan with him in his Ford jalopy and pay for the gas, the least I could do. He was taking along his main assistant, an old-timer named Luis, maybe 50, who acted as his *banderillero* and subaltern, advising with the complexities in the ring, a bit like a caddy advises a golf pro on the course, or the corner man who directs the prize fighter. Luis knew the personalities and the quirks of the bulls.

The Cuautitlan bullring was at least a permanent structure and not a temporary kit assembled for the event. It had a rough stone base from where the balance of the wooden ring structure rose about twenty feet with more seating and some decorative canopy shading over the top rows. Maximum capacity might have been seven or eight hundred people. I saw the bulls in the corral, all maybe 300 kilos and well-armed, decent looking cattle for such a backwater bullfight. Chamaco acquitted himself well with a lot of low right-handed passes displaying command and tempo, fighting valiantly close to the horns, and then killing well with his second attempt. They gave him a well-earned ear, and he did a triumphant circle around the ring to applause, collecting bouquets of flowers and tossing back hats thrown into the ring. We got back to the city late that evening and Chamaco dropped me off at the Cadillac. I was glad to get back to a long hot shower. It had been a good day with lots of good shots from the *callejon*.

A few days later, I was having breakfast in the *comedor* when Mgr. Antonio appeared at my table. He told me there was a young torero in the lobby who wanted to see me about some photos I took for him at his *novillada* in La Aurora. I instructed Antonio to tell the kid to wait a bit and I'd be down to the lobby with the photos. I washed down the last of my eggs and tortillas with the *cafe con leche,* strong coffee with hot milk, which I had largely substituted for beer over the last few weeks and went to my room to retrieve the prints I'd had made at a local camera shop. I had put together a set of two each of matte finish 5X7 selected passes he'd executed that day at the Aurora ring: *un natural, un derachazo, un pase de pecho, una veronica, una chicuelina,* and so on. They were a complete pictorial revue of his style and bravery. He was grateful for my gift and asked me which picture I liked the most and I told him his veronica cape pass, which he then inscribed with best wishes and signed with his name, Alberto Valle. I thanked him and wished him much luck in the difficult path he'd chosen and sent him on his way.

Two days later, Linda arrived. I was happy for the company but a bit afraid what else her arrival was going to involve and hoped I'd be up to it. As usual, she was dressed well, now in an expensive scarlet ensemble, with extra eye liner heightening the large dark eyes of her Levantine face. If I were making a movie about the Queen of Sheba or Cleopatra, I would have cast her. Her ample raven hair was pulled back tight in the Spanish style, a decorative comb set in the rear bun. She had a valise too large for just a couple days stay. I had already decided before she even brought it up, I wasn't going to Acapulco. Mgr. Antonio and I exchanged a knowing look as I took hold of Linda's valise and started for the elevator, with Linda trailing. There was no need to check her in, she was my temporary guest. Once in the room, we simply went about getting her settled.

"Better than I'd expected," she said, surveying the room and then the bathroom. "The bathroom is nicely tiled. I'm going to clean up a bit and change," she continued, taking some clothing items and a small bag from her valise.

She was no doubt happy to get away for a bit from her high-pressure job and had probably calculated she was getting a little vacation with an already booked hotel, a tourist guide and most likely, a lover. Money wasn't in her calculations; in the elevator, she'd already slipped a C note into my breast pocket, saying, *that's to help out with the party.* I would show her a good time. I had cleared my schedule for her and had an itinerary already in mind from the Zocolo to the Plaza Garibaldi with its mariachis and then to La Plaza Angel for dinner and dancing. But for the moment, Linda was tired and didn't want to do anything until she'd had a good night's rest, so we had dinner in the *comedor,* which she found clean and quaint and the menu inviting. The waiter made a fuss over her, stumbling around with his meager English to explain what she might like best.

The dinner menu could be splendid at times. We started out with some Mexican wine, then an infant Mexican industry, but it was passable and we both ordered the *solomillo,* filet of sirloin. Beef in Mexico had always been free range and always tasted better than store-bought meat in the States. The side of *papas fritas* were browned just perfectly and the *guisantes* were a large sweet variety of pea I had always enjoyed. All was accompanied with small bowls of rich red and green salsas. The waiters, familiar with me from my frequency in the *comedor,* were especially attentive because of Linda. They couldn't do enough for her, refilling her wine glass when half empty, and bringing her a small plate of complimentary *camarones a la plancha,* a plate of grilled shrimp. She gave lots of grateful smiles to the waiters and I a generous tip. We were both stuffed by the end of the meal, and it was clear there was nothing to do but retire for the evening. The wine had also made us both sleepy. At the room, she unpacked a few things and placed them in an empty drawer I had made available in the dresser and then she excused herself to the bathroom. A few minutes later she came out in a silvery colored, clingy nightie with her black hair down past her shoulders. She could be alluring. In bed I stroked her hair softly and she fell asleep almost immediately, a slight smile on her face.

Two more days passed with museums, a Reforma stroll, the Zocolo, and dinner and dancing in Plaza Angel. I had maintained the delicate balance at bedtime, neither reaching for her nor resisting cuddles. She, for her part, was not taking the lead or forcing anything. We hadn't been together in three months. We both needed to slowly feel our way back. Midweek before her return, we laid out my collected prints on the bed. She was quite interested in what I'd been doing.

"Oh, now that one! ...and this one, too! The photos of passes are nice but it's the little moments in between the fight that I like," Linda said, as she picked up several more photos she claimed had artistic merit aside from what we usually expect of bullfight photos with stop-action moments of matadors making passes or being calamitously tossed. She'd chosen a close-up I'd taken of Chamaco at Cuautitlan with his head bowed and kissing his crossed thumb and finger just before making the paseo into the ring. You could see the depth of prayerful hope for an unscathed day etched in his face during his last quiet moment before stepping out into the arena. Another photo she chose was of the kid at Plaza Aurora, scowling into the ring at the bull while an assistant wrapped his sword hand with supportive bandages. Yet another was a shot I caught of Chamaco behind the barrier, frowning up at the stands, annoyed by hecklers.

"Jimmy, you should have a show in LA when you get back. Photos of the small moments, or, say, the bullfighter as a man, or how about what you don't notice at the bullfights, I don't know, I think you know what I mean," she said.

"I think I've always had an inkling of what you're saying, which is why you see a few moments here, but I hadn't really thought about this kind of candid stuff for the focus of a photographic essay. But you're right. Those shots do tell a larger, personal story."

Of course, she would have a fine-tuned aesthetic vision. It wasn't just business savvy that landed her as a buyer for I. Magnin, one of LA's hottest purveyors of young women's fashions. She gave him the seed of an idea which he would take to Tlaxcala where he would focus more on Alejandro the man, rather than just on his dance with the beast.

The last evening with Linda was at Plaza Garibaldi, Mexico City's fabled entertainment hotspot for roaming mariachi bands and open-air food stalls from *carne asada* to *ceviche* bars. Linda took a special liking to the traditional Grenadina cocktail served at the bars, a concoction of tequila, pomegranate syrup, soda and a twist of lemon. That evening, even I was a bit tipsy by the time we caught a cab back to the Cadillac. Linda was looking especially good, her hair in a French twist with stray strands hanging from the temples, and her Faberge Babe perfume was intoxicating. On the way back to the hotel, we kissed reservedly and sweetly in the back seat of the cab, a ritual then commonly practiced in Mexico between *novios,* unmarried lovers. The American sexual revolution hadn't yet reached south to Mexico and dating mostly only went as far as kisses. Back at the room, it was pretty much a clothes-off-and-strewn-on-the-floor finale to her visit with us making abandoned love until exhausted, passing out, and sleeping peacefully until late the next morning.

The next day we had a simple brunch in the *comedor* of *caldo de polio,* Mexico's version of chicken soup, a clear broth with a few large pieces of chicken, a couple slices of onion and carrot, accompanied by a stack of warm tortillas. Linda said the soup reminded her of her mother's cooking. The likely conversation might have been, *where do we go from here?* But I was consciously moving the conversation in other directions, her work as a buyer for I. Magnin fashions, my plans for the photo studio in LA., my fall semester classes at the college, perhaps a photo show about the unseen moments in the life of the matador. She apparently was content with her visit, and I was happy she was patient and not pushing for avowals and commitments.

"Jimmy, do you know why I care for you so much?" Here it comes, I thought. I suddenly felt dumbfounded. How does one respond to such a question?

"Yes, you are interesting and full of surprises...and, of course, sweet."

"Oh, thank you!"

"But the icing on the cake is you don't put demands on me and you let us be in the moment." I couldn't disagree. Our times together were mostly occasional gems, memorable vignettes all, cured with time in between.

"I never thought of it that way." I really hadn't. My detachment, tempered by some occasional passion, apparently fit her agenda.

"I have a life, and you have a life," she said. "You let me be me."

"Now you're sounding like Sammy Davis Jr."

That got a laugh out of her, and I got her surprising import. I began to see that we had a certain, working balance. Gratefully, we didn't drag out the discussion.

We both agreed that in our times people, especially Californians, spent too much energy analyzing everything, especially relationships. Know what you want, be what you are and live in the moment was Linda's motto.

The day of her departure, we were standing in front of the Cadillac, waiting for the cab Antonio had called. She'd dressed in a navy-blue business suit with a turquoise blouse, nylons and black heels, her hair pulled back tightly from her face. I began thinking how really special she was. We were on the same plane. That was it. Then I had a thought of her seated in her spacious fancy office behind a large glossy wooden desk, sorting through paperwork that had piled up while she had taken her short vacation to Mexico. Reflexively, I pulled her to me and gave her the most passionate, long tender kiss I think I had ever given to a woman in public. I was momentarily in a movie with Ava Gardner, and it had caught the attention of not a few ogling pedestrians.

"Do call me sometime, won't you, Jimmy, when you get back, and let me know how you're doing?" she said as she got in the cab for the airport. She watched me from the rear window as the cab pulled away. I felt something strange between sadness and joy and relief. I went to my room to study my proof sheets to choose what prints I'd make from my shots from around the neighborhood, and Chamaco's *novillada*.

It was already the middle of August and I was wondering about Alejandro's date with the bulls in Tlaxcala. I hadn't heard from him, so I called. He said he'd been especially distracted lately with many things happening, but he would come by the Cadillac the following evening. When he arrived, he was dressed in his usual attire, a firmly fitted dark suit, pressed shirt, thin tie, business-like. He said he'd come straight from his job at the airport. He took me to a Spanish restaurant on San Juan de Letran where we had a paella. After the meal, when we were having coffee, his face grew very serious and he made an announcement:

"Tlaxcala has been canceled, Jim."

"What?... Why?"

"The corrida will go ahead as scheduled with Cavazos and Rodriquez *toreando* three bulls each *mano y mano* because I pulled out. As the Tlaxcala corrida approached, I realized I had lost something." Then Alejandro's words became strained with emotion.

"I couldn't feel the old *aficion* which drove me for so many years. I wrestled with my decision ever since I last saw you. That desire that kept me coming back to the rings, even after the horn wounds. I just couldn't feel the fire anymore." With this announcement he took a deep breath and shrugged. I was lost for words.

"Surely you recall the heat in your blood when you fought, Jim."

"Of course! I can never forget!"

"It's an overpowering aficion that moves us beyond the fear. I don't feel that anymore." Now Alejandro spoke without emotion.

"So, what will you do now?" I asked.

"I'll just keep working for Western Air. I've come to enjoy the work and the money is very good, more than it was with the *toros*—except for in my early days when I was near the top and got big money. Things change. *Así es la vida, verdad?* I'm a *matador de toros.* I still have some pride and a reputation. It's best that I stop now. There comes a time, my friend, when we must retire. So, I called the Tlaxcala empresario to take me off the program. I also decided to get rid of my *trajes,* capes and swords and so I gave them to a poor young *novillero* I like who has promise, but I saved this for you."

I had seen him come in with the package under his arm, but I didn't expect it was for me any more than I expected his Tlaxcala cancellation. I opened the brown paper wrapping immediately and found a lovely, hardly used Spanish magenta and gold fighting cape. It still had Alejandro's name stenciled on the inside.

"The cape will always remind you of my *veronicas, verdad?*"

"*Verdad, Alejandro, El Rey de la Elegancia! Muchisimas gracias!*"

We spent another hour in the restaurant, talking about the bullfighting world, about his career with Western Air, his young growing kids, a boy and a girl. If he felt sadness for retirement from the ring, it didn't show. For myself, I talked about making a book of taurine photos, of doing some writing perhaps, and finally, about finding a woman I could love unconditionally. When we left the restaurant, we both promised to keep in touch, and he would call me when he came up to LA to visit his kids.

I was disappointed I wasn't going to take photos from the *callejon* at the Tlaxcala *corrida* with the big bulls. I was surprised I was even feeling a little lonely for Linda. I was beginning to feel my time in Mexico City was indeed nearing an end. I felt restless and had to change the view, take a walk in some cleaner air, a day to devote to clearing my mind.

Chapultepec Park is Mexico City's equivalence of Griffith Park in LA, only smaller. It was the one landmark I'd not been to. I had visited the Teotihuacan pyramids on the outskirts of the city but not Chapultapec which featured a forest preserve, a lake, a zoo and a hilltop castle, which once housed Mexico's only monarch, Maximilian. Sundays were especially busy at Chapultapec with recreating families in every corner, tourists, and roaming food and trinket vendors. I stopped to see what was going on with a small crowd of people encircling some demo or show. It turned out to be a shell game with the elusive pea under the walnut shell. I watched for a while and I seemed to be able to follow the whereabouts of the pea. I watched several participants walk away with some winnings. I don't remember exactly what possessed me but it no doubt was what possessed those people whom P.T. Barnum described as suckers who were born every minute. And I was born in that minute in Chapultapec park. I had been up the equivalent of $200, over and above what I had started with, but then I got over-confident *(which is the goal for the scammers)* made some big bets and lost. I left the game near broke, losing the equivalence of about $300 and feeling blood rushing to my head in disbelief and my stomach sinking with shock. By the time I got back to the Cadillac, I was numb. Because of my foolishness, I wasn't going to have the means to make it through to my return. I had hotel bills to make good, a load of prints to pick up at the camera shop and I still had to live through the next two weeks. There was only one thing to do. I had to sell my camera kit, which I had noticed several Mexican taurine photographers coveting at some of the bullfights I attended. So, I put out the word. It didn't take long for a string of professional photographers to show up at the Cadillac to check out the gringo camera kit for sale. Even Mgr. Antonio dug up a potential customer. For the Canon SLR body and two lenses, a 35mm and a 70mm-250 telephoto, including the case, I was asking $500, which the third photographer to come along gladly paid, peeling off the equivalent in fresh Mexican notes from his wallet. I paid up my hotel bill, which included a running tab at the *comedor* and made an advance payment for my room until my departure date and booked flight to LA. I picked up my prints, including those for Chamaco, and put aside the rest of the cash to carry me through the remaining week.

Chamaco came by and I gave him his prints, bought him lunch again and recounted with him the many good times we'd had over the summer, including his triumph in Cuautitlan. He told me he might try to get up to LA in the off season in order to earn enough money to get him through the coming year. I knew he'd need some help if he came up to LA, so I told him to look me up and I gave him my address and phone number. There would always be a restaurant that would employ a young undocumented Mexican kid to bus and wash dishes. I loved the fire in him I had once known, the narcotic effect of the bulls, the rush, the out-of-body moments. I wondered if I could burn again like that for something.

Back in LA, my apartment/studio sorted, my temporary caretaker Rosie relieved of duty, I began feeling an unusual fatigue. I was getting weaker every day and I had no appetite. I decided to see a doctor who no sooner arrived in the exam room and saw me that he shook his head. He knew something.

"Feeling weak and have a loss of appetite, huh?" I nodded affirmation.

He got up close to me and looked in my eyes with a small flashlight and proclaimed that I had contracted hepatitis, but not to worry, I could be cured. He explained how the virus is usually passed through unsanitary food preparation. I flashed Garibaldi Plaza and all those other open-air food stalls where I had eaten so many raw *ceviche* cocktails over the summer. When I told the doctor I'd been in Mexico, he said in that case the diagnosis was no surprise. He gave me some shots and sent me home with instructions to get lots of rest and liquids. After two weeks of convalescence, my pallor dissipated, my stools normalized, and my appetite returned. I remember looking in the mirror to check the fading yellow in my eyes and saying to my reflection, *one day you'll have to write all this down.*

Feeling myself again, I returned calls from the list Rosie had kept over the summer, including people wanting old time photos. In ten days, I would begin classes at the college. Meanwhile I worked furiously in the dark room for several days, developing and printing 8x10s of my store of shots from Mexico, now strung around the apartment. I needed someone with a good eye to see them and help me pick out the best prints. I thought I was too close to my work to be sure. I needed another opinion from someone with a discerning eye. So first I got a clean bill of health at the clinic, got my hair cut and styled and set aside some new clothes for the evening, a pair of hound's tooth bell bottoms and a sky blue Van Heusen shirt. I bought a good bottle of Cabernet for a toast and I was ready to call Linda.

# In the Year of
# Becoming John Garfield

J ust a few blocks up from the beach on State St. in Santa
Barbara, on the SW corner of Ortega St. is the old two-
story Park building, or at least it used to be there. The
building had been built in the early 1920s and already was
worn and tired by the 1970s. It even smelled old. The second
floor was hardwood throughout, a few business offices, a
small press publishing firm, private rooms and a center
piece little theater with a dozen or so raked rows of seats that
encircled the stage like an amphitheater accommodating
around 100 or so patrons. Flat black paint on the interior
covered a lot of wear and tear, and rows of velveted seats
made for a sweet little theater venue. On the street level
of the building, there were several retail shops, a modest
little marquee and a busy liquor store on the Ortega St.
corner. It's probably all changed now. A lot of changes take
place anywhere in forty years, but especially in Southern
Californian coastal towns like Santa Barbara which is a
short drive from LA and a popular weekend destination
for tourists. But in the 1970s Santa Barbara was still quaint
and mostly under exploited. I had inherited tenancy at
the Park building in one of the second story rooms from
an acquaintance who had moved to LA, from where I had

escaped not long before. The room was 250 square feet of bohemian living with tall windows and a high ceiling that allowed a sleeping loft. There was only a cold water tap and small sink. Toilets were provided by communal restrooms on the second floor. I supplied myself with hot water by rigging up a used electric cafeteria size hot water maker that I poured into a plastic concrete mixing tub, making an adequate bathing stall for sponging off, standing or sitting. When done, I carefully picked up the tub and poured the used water down my cold-water sink. I had a hot plate for making coffee and the occasional home cooking and a hotel size refrigerator. At fifty dollars a month, the garret had all the comforts of home while I lived off my unemployment insurance and pursued my life as a theater bum. Meanwhile I had put together a pretty good actor's portfolio with flattering photos which I naively mailed off to agents everywhere. My head was in a wonderful cloud, hardly considering that Southern California had the highest number of wannabe actors per capita in America. But I had to give it a shot.

Living within steps of the Park community theater put me on the inside in many ways. I got to know a wide range of people connected with theater—actors, directors, designers, and techies. I was easily available for auditions that had something I liked and otherwise I got to work properties or build sets, set lights, or sell tickets in the box office. I did just about everything except clean the toilets in the year I was there. I got cast in several plays, working myself up the ladder from a few lines per play to supporting roles. But I really hadn't been tested yet, for I hadn't yet played a difficult major dramatic role. But I wanted a chance to prove myself.

I was nearing nine months in residence at the Park building and the theater, when Mary Grace Canfield entered the scene. All I knew was that Chuck Wilson, the general manager of the Park Building and the theater, had opened the back door for her, so to speak, and was happy to have her. When you saw her, you knew you had seen her somewhere before because she'd been on a popular TV sitcom for years, playing a character named Monroe on *Green Acres,* a sitcom starring Eddie Albert and Eva Gabor. She was a small middle-aged woman with an impish look, carrying a fixed hint of a sardonic smile. Now she was retired and living in Montecito, a tony enclave just down the coast from Santa Barbara proper.

"What else was I going to do here in retirement? One gets tired of just walking the beach," she'd commented when we first met. A lot of serious actors harbor the desire to direct once they are through acting, and Mary Grace was no exception. Because I was around the theater all the time, I got to meet her early on, before she was big news, and as luck would have it, she took a liking to me, having seen me in a few Park shows. Now she was going to direct something for the Park. Her first suggestion was the stage version of Hermann Melville's sea story *Billy Budd.* I have no idea what it was about me she saw, but she told me I would make a good Claggart, the sinister master-at-arms in that sea story, played in the film version by Robert Ryan with whom I had no resemblance. I was relieved when she told me she'd discussed the *Billy Budd* proposal with Chuck Wilson who advised her he didn't think the theater could technically handle such a big show, and so she opted for her second choice, the stage version of *Mice and Men* by John Steinbeck, and she wanted me to play George. But she told me to keep her decision under wraps until auditions had been completed.

Thrilled but scared, I got a couple of Samuel French playbooks immediately, cutting them into loose pages and gluing them into a standard size notebook, giving me large margins in which I could write notes. I read the play completely through every day and then continued to memorize a page at a time, until I could recite it without the book. But Mary Grace, MG, still wanted me to read at the auditions. The play called for a gang of itinerant farm workers during the Depression and only one woman, the ranch owner's son's wife. Being MG's first casting and a main character of the play and being at the theater all the time, I was gradually becoming her de facto producer because she turned to me to answer who could do this or that; did I know someone who might best play this or that character; what did I know about this guy or that; who could build us a great set? These questions were always asked outside of auditions when she came around the theater. Of course, I had some of the answers. But she still had to find a Lennie. I was a good height for George at 5 feet 7 inches, (not your leading man type) so any actor over 6 feet could physically make a good match with me, the short smart one next to the big tall simple one, partners in the Depression era, roaming Californian farms, looking for work. I couldn't think of anyone I'd met at the theater who could fit the bill.

At the first Park audition for *Mice and Men,* about thirty people showed up, some from the shows I had been in or worked on. MG sat in a front seat in the middle to get a close up look at her potential actors. There weren't too many women since there was only one female part in the play for someone in her 20s. MG had me read with some of the secondary characters, but mostly scenes with potential Lennies. Many of the would-be Lennies overdid Lennie's slowness. Finally, a guy about 6 feet 4 inches, big but not bulky, broad-faced and a bit loose-jointed, read with some others so I got to watch. As he read the character of Lennie, he had a vacant stare into space, as though he were in his own world. It was a beatific, peaceful look that contrasted with his considerable size. Reading Lennie, he became a man trying to excuse and diminish his size and power, and he projected gentleness. I knew MG liked him as did I.

Joe Brennen turned out to be a postgraduate in theater arts and a veteran of a dozen or so productions up and down the coast from LA to San Francisco, Sacramento and now Santa Barbara. He couldn't have been more qualified in my comparatively inexperienced view. I had come to theater on a lark and I had learned a little about blocking, the difference between a Fresnel and an Ellipsoid light and could interpret direction. I was naturally a mimic but untrained. I knew nothing about acting except what I felt when I interpreted a character. I figured that either you could act, or you couldn't. No number of classes could teach acting in my view, just like classes alone couldn't make a novelist or a painter. Even Marlon Brando had taken a dim view of all the ado about acting. Easy for him to say, I had thought, but then he had a point. I had learned that the most common pitfall was overacting. When I took on a role in a GB Shaw play and was out of my depth, trying to play a British *toff*, I was duly panned in the local critic's opening night review. That taught me something about acting and what roles I was best suited for.

Mary Grace being a television star helped her easily make friends across the theater community. She made acquaintance with Bob Tyson, at that time Santa Barbara's undisputed maven of all things theatrical. I had been in a couple of his shows and had been on stage with him in a production. He was an all-around artist who worshiped the legendary Orson Welles, and Bob wanted to emulate him. Bob could design playbills, posters, sketch out stage sets, design costumes, direct and act. He'd recently played *Beckett* at the big Lobero Theater and had directed *Long Day's Journey into Night*. He was 40ish, handsome and discreetly gay. In my time at the Park Theater I became accustomed to the high incidence of gay people. Perhaps the theater had always been a refuge where gay people could express themselves without the need for closets. In the theater there is the tacit acceptance that we all harbor many personae. Outside the theater, it was the 1970s and general societal acceptance still wasn't on the horizon. Celebrated playwright of the time, Edward Albee, author of *Who's Afraid of Virginia Woolf* made concerted efforts to keep his sexual preference a secret.

Bob Tyson came up with the idea of making the bunkhouse the anchor of the set, an upstage wall of aged wood with windows, a few strategically placed bunks, a simple table and chairs and a door for exits and entrances. What Bob needed was a great quantity of aged wood, to which I just happened to have access. A real estate friend had a rental property that had a lot of weathered wood fencing and a decrepit shed he wanted removed. The wood was totally gray and deeply etched with decades of wear. Again, I fulfilled my role as a budding producer. Producing community theater on shoestring budgets demanded resourceful people. My real estate friend gave us a day we could remove the wood, and I had Tom O'Malley go with a crew and a truck to break down the wood fencing and shed and bring the wood to the Park. Tom, a theater regular, had worked on a lot of sets before. Tom loved theater and exercised that love in between his itinerant construction jobs. People who gave their time to community theater rarely got any renumeration; they did it for the excitement of being part of a group creation. The house manager Chuck Wilson was on salary from the absentee building owner for managing the building and collecting rents. But whenever there was a play, which was mostly regular and consecutive, he'd take a percentage of the box office receipts, a percentage which I was never privy to. But I heard these receipts were taken as guarantee against a set monthly rent. In this age of the bottom line, I doubt that few little theaters like the Park exist. For most of the hip residents of the Park building at that time, a few painters, a sculptor and a musician called Pinche Pete, art was the goal, and money secondary. If everyone paid their modest rents on time, the absentee landlord and the manager Chuck Wilson seemed to have no complaints.

After two more evenings of auditions, the roles for *Mice and Men* were cast. As expected, Joe Brennen was cast as Lennie, local old timer Frank Underwood, a SAG member, as Carlson and Slim by a new guy named Grayson, a brooding sort of a Henry Fonda type. Candy, written as a sagacious older man, was cast with a Robert Brandt who was new. The one female part went to Laurie Woodland, an attractive petite brunette, a locally seasoned actress. Crooks, the one black cast member was filled by a fellow named Jim Harmon. Lucky for us because Santa Barbara had few blacks and likely fewer experienced black actors. The balance of the cast were all new faces to me, but we'd get to know each other over the weeks to come.

The rehearsal schedule was posted and construction on the set was begun. Rehearsals were mostly evenings from

Russ Desaulnier

7-10 pm every weeknight for five weeks. Not everyone was scheduled until we did run-throughs of the whole play which came in the ten days before opening. Other production people had not been assigned other than some people not cast who were happy to be put to work by MG and O'Malley, or Bob Tyson. The final touches with costumes, makeup, the setting of lights and soundtracks would happen when we got close to dress rehearsals. Meanwhile Bob Tyson was working on a poster to put up around town.

Funny how I liked my Lennie but not so much when he was out of character. Maybe that was just my inexperience. For me the emotions generated on stage tended to carry over into real life. I think I became George in my everyday life for some time after the play ended. At rehearsals I just couldn't drop my character like a pen and then pick it up again. Maybe I lacked the professionalism of Joe who'd logged so many productions. When he wasn't in character, he was almost unapproachable. During the five weeks of rehearsal, we never sat down and had a beer together, never got cozy, personal. But in character on stage, he was a great Lennie, soft and vulnerable, yet irritating with his absolute mindlessness. In a word, we were great together. On stage. I had to hand it to Joe. At that time when I was just getting my stage legs, he was already professional. Indeed, he went on to make a successful career on the stage. I had melded with the character of George and my relationship with Lennie so much that in our third performance when I dropped a couple lines and we went off script, I just kept going in character with improvisation and so did Joe until we brought the gap back onto script. No one caught our flub except MG and a couple of the cast members.

Properties and costumes were run by Dee Reynolds. She'd lost out in the auditions for Curley's wife. Dee loved theater in general and was happy to take on the responsibilities of production detail, while working for a local graphic design company. She was good at costumes and she herself dazzled with her ever changing getups constructed from second-hand clothing. She was lovely in an odd way, not a stunning beauty, but she had expressive eyebrows that filled gaps in conversation. When she spoke, she was usually brief but precise, and she never relied on *you know* for lack of words. Once she engaged you, her outsized cerulean eyes could be hypnotic. She was sure of herself but stepped lightly, not your usual actress type. At twenty-eight, she was experienced enough to be careful. In the theater where adrenaline and intensity ruled, she wasn't going to be a fool. She had gathered a huge supply of old clothing, mostly Salvation Army stuff which she bought with the small budget allotted her by MG. Being that the play was about men wandering in search of work during the Depression era, her bag of costumes was perfect. I secured an old forties gray fedora from her that I took to wearing on and off stage. As I said, I tended to be in character all the time, not just at rehearsal. Dee also got her hands on the needed properties, including a track starter pistol for the play's sad ending, and all the other assorted but meager possessions of the men that inhabited the ranch bunkhouse. When Lennie and I were off book with our lines and cues memorized, Dee stepped up as script girl and cued us when needed as rehearsals wound down. Familiarity grew between us and gradually a clear attraction. And so, one evening after rehearsal I invited her to my theater adjunct residence for coffee. When we got in the room, Dee took in all the details and exclaimed that it felt so Parisian. I think this was when I really began to appreciate the place. There is no doubt that my living arrangement steps from the theater enhanced that year of living in fantasies of the stage.

Lennie and I were at the center of the company's efforts, the story that all the company gathered around with expectation, a centripetal force pulling everyone closer together as we neared opening night. Dee was no less in that gravitational pull. It wasn't easy to decelerate after rehearsals and so it wasn't unusual to keep each other company, have a drink and smoke a little pot into the wee hours. Theater people keeping late after hours is a custom that made Sardi's restaurant of New York such a success. But not having that luxury, I made some instant coffee and put out some oatmeal cookies, and Dee and I settled into my inherited lumpy old upholstered chairs and fired up a couple of mild joints. We were almost too tired to talk much and so we mostly studied each other through sips and tokes, slowly escalating a shared mood comparable to the lusty eating scene in Albert Finney's *Tom Jones,* Then Dee's expressive eyebrows began doing their work as she undid the top button of her blouse, and complained it was getting warm in the room. Minutes later we were scaling the ladder to the loft.

"Cool, this really is climbing into bed, isn't it," Dee said.

"It took me a while to get used to."

"Makes me think of that old romantic song, *stairway to the stars.* Is it?"

"It'll be whatever you want it to be."

"Okay, Georgie!"

I loved her playful style—and her extraordinary nubile breasts, small waist and womanly hips. But most of all, I was swept away by her soft breathy whisper in my ear, *please be gentle and sweet.* We contentedly spent the night together, and early the next morning, tired but happy, we went to breakfast at Little Audrey's cafe across the street.

The turning point for the production came when a city fire department contingent showed up one afternoon, barging into the theater by surprise, like police making a bust. They announced they were making a long-delayed inspection for code violations. They found several, including the absence of push bars on the exit doors and an absence of code conforming exit lights. There were also backstage violations, all of which would be too expensive and too involved to be remedied before opening night. This was when a producer had to be keenly resourceful.

That same day I went post-haste to see Father Challinor at the Episcopal church further up State Street, a large stately Gothic gray stone building in the tradition of the old English church. I'd met him before, a big kindly vicar with a solicitous manner. I got him alone in his office and laid out what we had been doing with our play and that we had a celebrity directing, that we were already a couple weeks into our show but had been shut down at the theater by the fire department. Could we do the play in his assembly hall, a large hardwood floored wing of the church proper that had an ample supply of folding chairs?

He agreed. The play would be presented by the church and the Park Theater and we would split the proceeds with the church. Chuck Wilson would have nothing to say about this because all deals were off the table with the fire department cancellation. We had neither time nor $3000 to make the corrections needed at the Park. The good vicar happily agreed to our use of the church assembly hall while emphasizing that the no smoking rule was to be strictly observed. The set could be left in place, but the hall was to be left clean after rehearsals and performances. Fortunately, our aged wood upstage facade had not been built at the Park yet, and so we hauled the planks to the church where O'Malley and crew got to work on the set in the broad space of the hall. Lighting and strategic arrangement of folding chairs would make it all come together. Mary Duval, our lighting technician, surveyed the new venue and thought the spacious hall would bring a fitting openness to the production with her envisioned lighting and be ideal for the outdoor exterior scenes. The upstage facade of the bunkhouse wall would recede into darkness when the lighting came up on the downstage outdoor scenes.

In the last week before opening night, we had our full complement of theater help—a makeup team, sound board operator, lighting operator, dressers, ticket takers and ushers. Dress rehearsals went well with Mary Grace, her usual calm self, smoothing out the wrinkles. She had few comments for me and Lennie, except to keep the pace we had established. I loved working with Joe. He gave me a reality to play off, and he never faltered. I'm not sure he always felt the same about me. On opening night, I felt as tense as I had in my high school days when I was called for the final heat of the 100-yard dash league title. But once Lennie and I launched out there in the opening scene along the imaginary Salinas River, I was *there*. Our soundtrack even piped in the murmur of crickets and a moving creek to lull our audience into the opening evening scene. I could almost smell the river, and I easily called up that crazy mix of irritation and affection for my simple sidekick Lennie as we were trying to bed down for the night.

We received a standing ovation at the end of the play with prolonged applause for each character joining me and Joe on stage until all were assembled, finally joined by Mary Grace who raised yet another long round of applause. When we were back in the dressing room, removing our makeup and changing, patrons stopped in to offer congratulations. Among them was Kenneth Rexroth, the eminent American poet and his wife.

"You guys were great," he opined. "Your performance was as good, if not better, than what I saw on Broadway. Thanks for a great evening!"

We all joined in thanking Rexroth for coming and we savored the satisfaction of that moment which no doubt would be remembered by us all. After cleaning off makeup, changing back to street clothes and breaking down the folding chairs, we all retired to the Park for a cast party on the abandoned stage where we ate take-out food and drank wine. MG was cutting loose for the first time in five weeks. All the bunkhouse gang were elated and getting tipsy. O'Malley was near drunk when the party began. Bob Tyson tippled some champagne and talked theater with everyone. Joe was not there. After the crowd had dispersed at the church, he had quietly disappeared with his wife who'd been in the audience. Dee and I maintained a distance but exchanged knowing tender looks. Some discretion was good so as not to feed company gossip. By midnight, everyone was exhausted and ready to call it a day well worth the celebration. We had to be ready for the following night's performance and three more weekends yet to follow. Dee and I slipped away and down the hall to my garret where there was little left to do but sleep.

We had breakfast late the next morning at Little Audrey's and read the review in the News-Press:

*STRONG PERFORMANCES GIVEN IN POWER-FUL STEINBECK PLAY.*

*The fire department shut down the Park Theater, but it certainly didn't dampen the ambition—or the talents—of the Park Playhouse. After a brief delay, while relocating to the Trinity Episcopal Church, John Steinbeck's Mice and Men opened last night and produced an evening that would have been a credit to any theater.*

*Steinbeck's play is a difficult one and Mary Grace Canfield directed it with sensitivity. Because it is so emotionally sensitive, it is easy to overact the parts of the tragically retarded Lennie and the lonely protective George, But Joe Brennen as Lennie turned in a touching performance. And James McClaren as George was a natural. While the suspicion might have been at the beginning that the actors were chosen for their size ratio, it was soon apparent that there was a great deal more to the casting than met the eye.*

*The character of Lennie is a real enigma for an actor— and for the director. The fine line between tragic fool and a dangerous lunatic was never breached by Steinbeck, but it is very easy one to cross for an actor. At the beginning of the play, Joe Brennen approached the danger of overacting. His facial expressions were a little twitchy and he was a bit too dramatic, but as the evening wore on, he settled into the characterization and by the end of the play he had it mastered. McClaren's George is hard to criticize. He did what every actor tries to do. He acted the part so well that it didn't seem like acting...*

The review continued with praise for all the other actors, for the lighting and sound, the marvelous set and Mary Grace's superb direction.

After the heady experience of *Mice and Men,* I didn't feel inspired to try rising to that level again, and my enthusiasm had begun to wane. It was like having conquered a peak, survived and triumphed and then not wishing to attempt such a perilous height again. I felt that all the stars had lined up for a once in a lifetime event. Bob Tyson, Mr. Theater, liked my George so much he complimented me at the cast party by dubbing me Santa Barbara's own small-town John Garfield and told me he was seriously thinking of directing *The Big Knife* by Clifford Odets and that he would like to cast me in the lead which Garfield had played when the play debuted in 1949 on Broadway. Although greatly flattered and tempted, I had become bone tired of living in the garret and struggling on a shoestring budget. And my unemployment insurance was winding down. Had I the wherewithal, I might have been able to afford a continued relationship with Dee. In any case, she moved on to New York where she had some connections and got a paid internship with a fashion magazine. I was happy for her. Like her and so many others, I was called to the theater, but I was already 35 and couldn't see any light at the end of the tunnel, no future. And I wasn't moving back to LA to look for it, which some people advised. I decided instead that I would throw the dice and take the course for a real estate sales license. I knew people in the business who were making good money, and I saw it as more theater anyway, putting on a suit and tie costume and charming clients. Surely John Garfield could do that!

# The Million Dollar Club

- - - - - - - - - - - - - - - - - - -

With the smoothness of a Mohammed Ali combination, Ralph slid the contract under the buyer's nose and fumbled his gold Cross pen onto the floor. The client went for it. Ralph settled back in his chair, folded his hands and prepared a passive face. The client, again upright in his chair, found himself facing the contract, pen in hand. Ralph began shuffling through some property files.

"I'm going to have to run this by my wife," the client said, clearing his throat and placing the pen down.

"Mr. Alsop, if you came across a fifty-dollar bill lying on the sidewalk would you go home and discuss it with the wife before picking it up?

"I think the property will be there tomorrow after the wife and I have had a chance to sleep on it."

Of course it would. And it was also likely the buyer would get cold feet by tomorrow. Ralph smiled benignly and led client Alsop to the lobby. He wondered about his closing technique. He'd done it just like he'd been taught by Valmore, but it just wasn't going to work with everyone.

There had been leads, inquiries, property showings, even a few lowball offers that he had timorously presented to irritated sellers, but after three months at Brownstone Realty he had managed to close only one small condominium deal. That commission had been eaten up by his initiation dues and multiple listing subscription fees to the Board of Realtors. He had reached the limit on his Visa card and soon he would be out of the startup money that was supposed to get him launched in his real estate career. He needed to close a deal soon or get something solid into escrow he could borrow against.

But J.J. Valmore, his boss and mentor, would help him through. At thirty-eight, Valmore had already become a real estate legend around town. Many of his people were consistent members of the Million Dollar Club, selling millions worth of property each year. Valmore had personally groomed many of them, as he had promised to do with Ralph. Brownstone was not a big brokerage, but under Valmore it accounted for one of the biggest volumes of business in the county.

The excitement touched Ralph every day when Annette, the office secretary, chalked in the latest sales and listings up on the big blackboard. There would be a round of applause from the associates in their glass-partitioned cubicles when she'd write out a big sale or listing. As she added on the last zeros, calculations would buzz around Ralph's mind like mosquitoes—three percent of sales price, split fifty-fifty with Brownstone, minus expenses, came to a night out at his favorite bar and grill, Visa Card paid off, his Nikon and lens collection out of hock and a wad in the pocket, like the one Valmore carried and conspicuously whipped out over business luncheons or at the Pelican's Perch during Friday night happy hours. It was at the Pelican where Ralph had got to know a little about the man behind the three-piece suit and constant telephone. Valmore collected art and liked cruising small galleries up the coast for bargains.

Sometimes he would have to take Ralph with him, he said. But it would be "predicated" on listing a vineyard he'd been trying to nail down. He'd show Ralph the way it was done.

Having bid goodbye to Alsop in the lobby, Ralph started back to his cubicle, passing the tinted glass walls of what Valmore lovingly referred to as the "war room," the conference room where he liked to close his big deals. At its center was a huge antique oval table surrounded by ferns and miniature palms. Valmore was in conference with two Mexican-looking men, dressed as though they were planning a round of golf at Pacific Meadows with Gerry Ford, except they wore a little too much gold jewelry. An easel was set up with an architect's drawing of a large ultramodern building. Valmore was leaned back in his leather swivel chair, his thumbs hooked in the pockets of his vest. He winked at Ralph as he walked by.

The main cubicle area was busy, phones ringing, agents hunched over phones, some with clients. In the cubicle behind Ralph's, Al Ingram, semiretired stockbroker and self-described Texan, had his boots up on his desk and was reading The Wall Street Journal. He had his stock dividends to depend on. He could take it easy, and he did. Across the aisle, Rossi, an ex-cop working part-time on an MBA, was writing in files, intent as usual, like a monk hand copying scriptures. He wore an Ivy League tie each day and his shirts never seemed to lose their starched crispness. But he hadn't been up on the board recently, either. Directly in front of Ralph was "Charging" Marge Robideux. She was the only one at Brownstone who called Valmore Jimmy Jay. She usually had clients and she was always up on the big board. She was like a big happy truck stop waitress whom one somehow didn't want to displease. Big Al, who took no nonsense from anyone, was the only one she didn't get along with. He didn't like people calling him *buddy,* he said. Ralph didn't mind this occasional appellation and was happy to have Marge provide a quick and experienced answer on some real estate detail or other. *Why sure, buddy,* she'd say.

Ralph sat in his cubicle and thumbed through the new multiple listing book. A lot of the same properties just sat on the market, usually because they were either dogs or overpriced. Overall, the market had spiraled upward so fast, it now seemed to be leveling off and slowing down. He wondered if he had come into the business too late. But there just weren't too many immediate careers around for thirtyish guys like him. Ten years of part-time odd jobs since graduating college didn't recommend him for much of anything. But he had to do something worthwhile, had to make something of his life, as his folks had said when he visited home for his thirty-fifth birthday. It was time for him to do something instead of just being "into" things. After all, he wasn't a kid anymore. Real estate offered an immediate place, a flexible schedule and the promise of something more than an hourly wage.

He had bought a dark three-piece suit *(a closing suit, Valmore called it)* at Guy Gamble's in the mall, had his hair tapered up the neck and around the ears and leased a new, but modest Ford. He still hadn't gotten around to going to Valmore's manicurist, whom he recommended. One of Valmore's maxims of success held that when the client wasn't looking in your eyes, he looked at your hands. *So keep your nails manicured.*

Valmore's recently built home, as manicured and spar-kling as his nails, was modern California Spanish, red-tiled, turreted, rising from a bluff up in the Hillcrest district that commanded a view of the city and the ocean. Ralph had been there once, just after he had been hired, for a Sunday afternoon that culminated the company caravan of new property listings. It had been one of those typical iridescent coastal days, the city far below seeming little more than a sparkling village.

The spacious, vaulted living room with its pastel couches, signed Tamayo prints and gleaming hardwood floors was something right out of Better Homes & Gardens. Valmore's wife appeared only briefly, excusing herself to see to the children. She tended to the matronly, but it was her large brown eyes, like those of some nocturnal animal, that dominated her presence and seemed to take in everything in that majestic living room. It was said that she was from a wealthy Mexican family, still in Mexico, whose money had seeded Valmore's establishment of Brownstone Realty.

Trays of Margaritas in chilled crystal and plates of colorful canapes were served by a stony-faced Mestizo housekeeper the shape and color of a copper pot, while classical guitar floated through the air from a quadraphonic sound system. About mid-afternoon, just before breaking up the party, Valmore announced the opening of a new company to operate out of Brownstone. It was to be the answer to the company's problems in the present climate of rising interest rates, Valmore Trust Deed & Mortgage Company. He said the industry was entering an era in which survival would depend on *creative financing*. Ralph was wondering how he was going to create enough financing for his rent.

On Monday morning he entered Valmore's private office. Valmore motioned him to sit down while he continued talking on the phone, alternately smiling and frowning into the phone. A Valmore maxim held that when you talked on the phone you should always think you were face to face. A smile could be heard, he said. The row of square buttons corresponding to separate lines were all flashing. Valmore pushed another and shifted in his chair.

"Well, sure," he was saying, "why not just take back a third after we get the new loan approval? Makes sense, right? No need for any end runs on this one, Ed."

Valmore spoke with an ease only afforded by someone dead sure of himself. Although he often knitted his brows in public, projecting a serious and determined nature, once engaged, he could be irrepressibly friendly, and even his mustache and professorial glasses couldn't hide his essential boyishness.

"Yes, Annette... okay, put him on," he said, pushing another button and motioning Ralph to wait. "Alex, everything has moguls. But I tell you this one's like virgin powder at Vale. We refinance the second T. D. and trade the ground lease for the down payment on the second property. Easy."

More flashing buttons, but Valmore told Annette to take messages on his calls. Then he asked Ralph why the worried expression, which Ralph then explained.

Valmore leaned back in his high back leather chair. Staring down from the wall above was a Picasso scribble of a janus form head. Valmore held his hand in a prayer position just under his nose. He looked intently at Ralph.

"Okay," he said with a flourish, picking up his phone and pushed one of the buttons.

"Annette, I want you to make out a ninety-day promissory note payable to Brownstone," he said, pausing and looking over the tops of his glasses, "by Mr. Thompson for the amount of one thousand dollars at ten percent straight interest. Issue him a check from the Valmore & Associates Mortgage account.

"Normally I don't lend unsecured money, but this loan is predicated on my faith in you. I hired you, didn't I? You're coming along, but you've got to go for the full court press. I know you'll make the Million Dollar Club. Don't let me down." Ralph had barely said a few words of thanks when Valmore reached for his phone and started reeling off orders to Annette.

"Well, what are you waiting for? Go out and get me some listings," he shot at Ralph, who was still trailing the action.

"And, Thompson, God bless."

A week later there was a sudden credit crunch, announcements by the Fed sending a shudder through business in general and real estate in particular. There was more activity around Brownstone than usual. Valmore was rarely to be seen except going somewhere in his 300 SL, usually talking on his car phone en route. He had even been skipping his ritual T.G.I.F. stop at the Pelican.

Ralph still had no listings, but he was showing properties. Client Alsop finally made an offer on a property which was accepted, but now there was a financing problem. Alsop just wouldn't have any part of new conventional financing which had climbed to 11 percent plus. The seller, on the other hand, couldn't be convinced to carry back a second mortgage if Alsop assumed the low interest existing first. This was a time when in-house financing could grease the wheels of a difficult transaction. He had to see Valmore. His mind full of real estate contingencies, Ralph was relieved to have a late afternoon patio lunch with Blair at Tolkien's, a small low-budget veggie cafe on the west side of town that she had introduced him to. Blair was not his girl. That is, he wasn't sleeping with her. He did that now and then with Patti, the Safeco Escrow receptionist, who was too young for there to be much else going on. If they spent more than an hour together out of bed, they fought. And so their meetings had become less than occasional, while his meetings with Blair became more frequent.

"Earth to Ralph, earth to Ralph," she was saying.

Her face was small and serious with a high intelligent forehead. Ralph thought she looked European. Perhaps it was her style of dress that never included jeans or off-the-rack Californian sportswear. Or perhaps it was because she didn't have that fixed, practiced smile that characterized so many West Coast women.

"Sorry, just thinking. I was thinking about Europe."

"What about it?" she asked.

"I've never had time or money to go, mainly not the money."

"I almost went once, with this older guy, to Greece. Some island or other, I don't remember the name. But I can get all the *moussaka* I want right here in town at Johnnie's Deli."

"It's not the same."

"It's not? Look at this weather."

"Still not the same."

"You know, when I finally made it out here from the East, just a kid crashing around Venice in bell bottoms and belly chains, I thought something was supposed to happen. Nothing did, I mean nothing that wasn't going on before. Only there was lots of sunshine."

She chomped down on her avocado and alfalfa sprout sandwich as if to emphasize the finality of her words on the topic. She smiled in between chewing. It was refreshing to be with her in these days when everyone was taking

Russ Desaulnier

showers together soon after introductions. It wasn't that he didn't feel attracted to her. But too often relationships that began as performances played short runs. And so he was agreeable, even relieved, when Blair had suggested that there should be "nothing pressing" in their friendship. The designated space between them became an ease rather than a tension, and yet one might have guessed they were lovers by the way they chatted away in a cafe or theater lobby or strolled Shoreline Drive. As they waited at the cash register to pay the bill, Ralph's eyes wandered across the street to the mock-adobe Mexican restaurant painted with Saguaro cacti. At that moment the restaurant door swung open and out stepped Valmore followed by an attractive woman in business dress Ralph didn't recognize. He didn't give it much thought until the woman suddenly swung in front of Valmore and caressed his neck. It lasted just an instant, as Valmore abruptly deflected her hand, looked around, as if for someone or something, and hustled the woman and himself out of sight toward the rear parking lot.

Valmore liked to joke around a bit about women, but that's all it ever seemed to be, just joking. "Annette gives good phone," he would aside to the boys, or about some passing woman "I wish I had that swing in my back yard." But he always showed restraint and timing, as if he only wanted to sustain the impression that he was easy going, good ole boy who could hold his own in the locker room. He just as easily fell into talking about the NFL and the Dallas Cowboys with Big Al Ingram, although Valmore wasn't a big sports fan. What Ralph had seen across the street had to be nothing. Valmore wasn't screwing around. Not in the light of day. He was too smart for that.

Ralph had been married once, had lived with a few women, but it was always one at a time. It wasn't a question of morals, or even being true blue. He just got in too deep, except in a few cases like Patti where depth wasn't possible, to ever think about roaming. He always chose with the hope of staying.

"You know, my parents have been married for forty years," he said.

"I wonder how many people will be able to say that in the year two thousand," Blair replied.

"God, I'll be almost sixty then," he said, catching the blurred reflection of his face in the window next to their table.

When they left the restaurant, Ralph took a less direct route back to Magnin's where Blair worked, thinking he might catch sight of Valmore's candy-apple colored 300 SL. But no sign.

"Hey, Mr. Businessman," Blair said when they parted at the Magnin's entrance, "when you slow down this week, give me a call and come on by. I got some good smoke, if you're interested."

He went back to Brownstone. Rossi was buried in paperwork, and Big Al was doing a crossword puzzle. Charging Marge wasn't around but she had been busy because she had two new listings on the big board. There was no Valmore.

Annette would give Valmore his message. Outside in the parking lot, the afternoon was bright, another boring day in paradise, as the local expression went. Only the haze had set in, the constant reminder that LA wasn't far away. There wasn't much to do but go back to his apartment or he could cruise the beach, stroll on the pier, feed the gulls.

Hadn't Big Al said one day when Ralph had been slamming desk drawers, "Hoss, you gotta slow down and get out on the range and smell the flowers."

Parked next to his Ford was a black Lincoln. At the wheel was one of the Mexican country clubbers Ralph had seen in Valmore's office. He was smoking and reading a newspaper, as though killing time. Seen up closer, the man's face was heavily furrowed like tooled leather. Ralph faintly acknowledged the man when he looked up from his paper, but the man's expression was unmoved, as though Ralph were invisible, and he returned to his paper, a gold-braceleted, meaty hand turning the page.

That afternoon Valmore called Ralph from somewhere on the coast highway en route to a development site. "Thompson, what are you doing at home, fucking off? 'Scuse my English, but that ain't gonna list or sell properties."

Ralph lied and said he didn't feel well and he told Valmore about needing some stopgap financing to swing the Alsop deal. Valmore said he'd have Annette prepare the mortgage papers for escrow when Ralph gave her a copy of the title report and property appraisal.

"Remember, Thompson, success isn't an accident. It's a commitment. Don't let me down."

There were only three days left to clear the financing contingency on the Alsop transaction. Alsop was already sounding apathetic about the deal, and Ralph suspected if the deal didn't move along like dominoes, Alsop would take the first chance to step away. It was hard for these aerospace-engineer types to invest. Although their business was higher math, they couldn't seem to read the simple numbers on a good investment. There was a lot like Alsop all over the Towering Oaks suburb where Randall Corporation, subsidized by the Defense Department, kept them in oversized homes with pools. Maybe engineers like Alsop couldn't help becoming cynical, knowing their good life depended on refining ways of human destruction.

Two days ticked by and the mortgage papers had not been signed and were still lying on Valmore's desk. He had called for his messages, Annette said, but that was all. Ralph could wait no longer. He marched into Valmore's office where the wife and two plump children smiled at him from a desk photo as he snatched up the Alsop file.

"If he's around town, I'm going to find him."

"Good luck," Annette said.

Cruising a half a dozen places where Valmore was likely to be and not seeing his car, Ralph decided to cross town to Valmore's house. Hillcrest Drive, a heavily wooded, snaking road with hairpin curves, still had a few bald patches on either side of the road, scars left over from the big fire a few years before. The fire had destroyed millions in pricey homes, most of them since rebuilt. The driveway to Valmore's house was like the approach to a medieval castle, the turreted section of the house looming above like a stucco keep. The red 300 SL was parked in the drive-in front of the expansive four car garage, along with a Black Porsche Carrera. Valmore had to be there.

The heavy oak door creaked open, revealing the stolid housekeeper from the party. She spoke before he could introduce himself.

"De Señor ees not heer," she said and began closing the door.

"Wait, how about the Señora Valmore? Is she here?" Valmore's wife then appeared at the door and Ralph explained his urgency. She said she didn't know where he was and had no idea why his car was in the drive.

Russ Desaulnier

"Mr. Valmore is so busy, you know. I never know when he comes or goes. You know how busy he is, Mr... ?"

"Thompson."

She smiled for the first time. She said she remembered his face and she was sorry he'd had to drive all the way up to the house. She wasn't as matronly as Ralph had remembered her. She wore heels and black stockings and appeared shapely in her fitted dress. She said she would tell her husband he had been to the house.

If Valmore was out in the Rolls, he must be closing a big one, Ralph was thinking, as he wound his way down Hillcrest Drive with the radio thumping out a new Blondie song. Suddenly a silver BMW cornered wide, careening right at him, barely missing a head-on collision. Jarred from his preoccupation, he cursed. Why were people who drove expensive cars so damn careless? He slowed down and changed the radio. News. No break in the Iran hostage negotiations. Wasn't everybody a hostage in one way or another?

The next morning after taking a jog, Ralph called Alsop before driving to the office. Alsop was getting skittish. If the financial contingency of the contract to buy was not met within twenty-four hours, Alsop would no longer be obliged to comply. Where was Valmore with the financing? After all, the Alsop deal also meant a few thousand to Brownstone.

At the office three police squad cars were parked in the reserved spaces, including Valmore's. A uniformed policeman guarding the entrance asked Ralph if he was an employee or a client. The policeman wouldn't say what was going on and just told Ralph to go inside. As Ralph entered, another uniformed policeman hustled him into Valmore's office. A big, but pleasant-faced man in a baggy suit was looking through Valmore's desk, while a uniformed policeman was packing Valmore's files into cardboard boxes. The big man introduced himself as a lieutenant and began asking questions about how long Ralph had worked for Brownstone, how well he knew Valmore, had he been to Mr. Valmore's house, did he know any of Valmore's acquaintances or friends other than those who worked for the company? All the while, Ralph's attempts to ask what was going on were pushed aside by questions. He mentioned the Mexican he'd seen around the office.

"Middle-aged, heavily-lined face, drives a black Lincoln?"

"That's the one," Ralph said.

"Family. One of Mr. Valmore's brothers-in-laws," the lieutenant said.

Ralph was told he may be contacted later and he was to collect his personal effects from his desk in the main work area.

Across the street from the office at Larry's Bar & Grill, Rossi and Big Al were having a beer. Rossi had a few details that he had managed to get from an old friend on the force. The company was being indefinitely closed by court order, pending police investigations and lien procedures against Valmore & Associates Inc. Existing escrows would be expedited through McCarty & Slavin Realty, who it was revealed had an option on Brownstone.

"Where the hell is Valmore?" Ralph asked.

Over at the long bar, charging Marge stood laughing and drinking with a cluster of people.

"He's probably already down in the Bahamas having a rum cooler with Robert Vesco," Big Al said.

"Come on, Al, Valmore's no crook," Ralph said.

"I guess we'll all know soon enough," Al said.

"Anyway, I'm moving to McCarty and Slavin's," Rossi said. "How about you, Hoss? What're you going to do?"

It was too soon to make any decisions. Ralph gulped down the beer before him, even though it was only eleven a.m. Lunch soon flowed into the mid-afternoon.

That evening and the following day Ralph walked circles around his apartment wondering what to do. He hoped for a phone call to set him in motion. He couldn't call Alsop. A Valmore maxim: never call the client unless you have good news. He couldn't keep his mind on reading a novel and his apartment didn't need any cleaning. Blair wouldn't be home until later in the afternoon. With nothing to do but wait, he heated up some canned raviolis for lunch and settled into watching afternoon TV. After a predictable rerun with Starsky & Hutch laying rubber around LA and pummeling hapless bad guys, the local news came on. No movement in the Iran hostage crisis, Idi Amin on the run, Three-Mile Island lawsuits. Locally, The Water Board upholds no-growth ruling, coastal oil exploration questioned, a well-known local realtor found dead. Ralph sat up.

*...member of the Rotary Club and noted for his activities on behalf of the Pueblos Charities Association, he had been an outstanding member of the business community for the last seven years. His body was reportedly found on a deserted road outside Tijuana, Mexico. Investigating detectives say Valmore may have been in Tijuana in connection with his charity activities. They say probable cause of death appears to have been a single gunshot wound to the head, sustained in a suspected armed abduction and robbery...*

Murdered?! Shot in the head for a lousy handful of money?

Ralph reeled with visions of Valmore on his knees, his manicured nails digging the dust, begging for his life, then crying, shouting, pleading perhaps, finally whimpering, everything else suddenly and absolutely worthless—the house on the hill, the money, the power, the Rolex watches, the expensive cars. The raviolis danced in Ralph's stomach. He thought about Valmore's Mexican wife with the big eyes already mourning in the huge emptiness of that house. Valmore had been only three years older than Ralph. Just a kid, really, playing Monopoly.

Alsop called. The office number was disconnected, he said. He was sorry but he had to drop the deal. Interest rates had climbed too fast and were still edging up; cash would be better invested with an equity fund. Ralph couldn't disagree that it was hard to turn down a secure double-digit cash on cash return. Alsop promised he would be in touch if he had any real estate needs. Sure.

Blair called. She'd be off work soon. Did he want to come over? Nothing pressing, of course. Did he want to do a little smoke, take a walk on Shoreline Park, grab a baklava at Johnny's Deli, in between making millions? He did. He would tell her later about his boss.

He started to get dressed, throwing on some slacks. He was just cracking the cleaner's plastic wrap on a dress shirt when the phone rang again. It was Rossi.

"Did you hear the news?" he said.

"Yea, just a minute ago. I can hardly believe it. They're not telling the whole story."

"What?"

"The wallet was empty and the Rolex was gone, but Valmore still had a wad of bills tucked in his trouser pocket. You go figure."

"So what? The bastard who wasted him was in a hurry?"

"On a deserted road?"

"Whoever did it got careless then. Overlooked it."

"Thompson, don't be so naive. If it was robbery, you can bet your sweet ass whoever did it would have picked the body clean, especially one in a three-hundred-dollar suit."

"Okay, Columbo, is that why you called? To tell me all this shit?"

"Not exactly. You coming down to M & S? McCarty's recruiting."

"I got to think about it."

"Don't think long. They're not holding slots indefinitely."

"I'll keep that in mind, Rossi."

Outside Ralph's apartment it was another day in paradise. Everything his vision panned—the aloe plants, the loquat tree, the jacaranda, the rusted barbecue grill, the trash cans and his Ford in the drive—seemed extraordinarily focused and vivid. But it could have been raining and it still would have been paradise. It was a good day to see Blair, a day to take her arm and stroll along Shoreline. Disregarding the dress shirt he had started to open, he surveyed the line of casual shirts hanging in his closet and pulled out the brightest one he owned, an Erte design. Nothing was pressing, after all. The rent was paid for another month. Something had always turned up, as sure as the winter tides kept the beachcombers busy.

# It's Always Hot in
# the Beginning

- - - - - - - - - - - - - - - - - -

He had raced up the coast to Santa Barbara on many weekends like this, the convertible top down in windblown abandon, pushing the little blue Triumph past towering, menacing trucks, and when the last leg of the 101 merged with the beach, the sweet sea air inspired images of Nadia's auburn hair and slim body as insistently as the pulse of the surf.

From the coast highway toward the Sierra overlooking the city, it was only a few minutes to her door. Upon pulling up in front of her house, he honked his car's distinctive tenor horn, which had become his customary signal of arrival. It was a small stucco cottage with a red tiled roof, reminiscent of an earlier Mexican California, nestled among a riot of bougainvillea and jasmine. She'd always wanted to get out of Los Angeles, like almost everyone they knew, and so one get-away-from-LA weekend around the time they were talking about a trial separation she had bought the place and then moved up several weeks after.

Now framed in the Spanish doorway, Nadia stood between light and shadow. There was deliberation in her makeup, in the blue knit dress, slightly padded in the shoulders, an unmistakable promise of love in her controlled

Russ Desaulnier

smile. Her style always minimal, she said nothing until he reached the step. Then simply *hello,* as though she knew anything more might blunt the eloquence of her greeting. He was sure she could break if he were to embrace her in any but the gentlest manner. Once in her arms, he was almost dizzied by her familiar perfume. He could have easily fallen to the couch with her right there and then in the living room, but he sensed her resistance. He absorbed such little tensions, storing them away like unstable chemical compounds, until eventually they distilled and condensed into emotional tugs and shoves.

"I don't care if we go out," he said, kissing her neck.

"Not now, George."

"You know, that's the only time you use my name."

"What are you talking about?"

"When it's *no* to something."

"That's not true," she said, kissing him on the cheek.

"It seems that way sometimes," he said and instantly felt he'd betrayed himself by quibbling.

They had agreed the 125 miles separating them might be good, and it had exerted a force, pulling them back together intermittently by accumulated stores of passion, until something could be settled, or until that unspoken possibility occurred of someone new entering the picture. He reflected on their tenuous arrangement as typically Californian and an example of their generation's phobia for commitment. But he didn't worship *freedom* and was actually tired of being on his own, tired of the empty evenings that capped his frantic days as a salesman in Los Angeles. Nadia had never been alone, had always had a man around. She was capable but not in the habit of being on her own.

"I was thinking of buying more real estate. The market just keeps going up. It's a great place to live."

"If you don't have to work for a living."

"I'm working."

"Really?"

"I just took a part-time job at a flower shop."

Despite her practical side, she loved delicate and beautiful things. She could actually sit and ponder paintings at exhibits and museums, while he would be racing ahead merely scanning the walls. Her living room was testimony to this spirit—the throw cushions she'd covered with scraps of tapestry and velvet, her own primitive weavings on the wall, the staghorn ferns she'd cultivated, a Mozart piano concerto tape filling the room. A print of Klimt's lovers was new, it's size and brilliant contrasts somehow invasive. Was this addition to the room an extension of her longing for him in his absence? Did she, like him, sometimes ache?

"Just have to put on my earrings and lipstick."

"Where did you make reservations?"

"A place down by the beach," she called from the bathroom.

He always felt an odd mixture of familiarity and strangeness whenever he came into her house after a few weeks of absence. Were there actually slight changes each time or were there blanks in his memory? The place was neat with no signs of Tracy, her seven-year-old daughter, away for the weekend with grandparents. Though Nadia's ex-husband had been long gone, rarely even in contact with his daughter, his parents were gracious, never interfering in Nadia's life and giving Tracy some genuine family. Nadia hadn't had any family of her own for years. Her mother had left when she was a child and her busy, indifferent father hadn't been able to keep her, and so she had grown up at boarding schools.

He scanned the room for a new magazine, a new book, any detail he didn't remember from his last visit. He went into the tiny kitchen and opened the fridge, looking for any shifts in her tastes. The pale green of a near empty bottle of prime Chardonnay dominated a shelf. He poured off the balance into a water glass and took a couple large swallows. He was still holding the bottle when she came back in the room, her lips full and mauve, large gold hoops in her ears.

"Nice wine," he said, looking for a response, perhaps a clue.

"Help me close up the windows, we're running late."

He looked at the empty bottle, chiding himself for his suspicion, and polished off the rest of the wine.

Santa Barbara is the Riviera of California with endless sunshine cooled by sea breezes. But there were no jobs. It had been said Santa Barbara is a town fit only for the "newlywed and nearly dead." But Nadia had no need to work since her grandfather passed on, leaving her with the means to get out of LA. The windfall had been timely, coming when their relationship—that's how they talked about themselves, *their relationship*—had become like some fruit they had chewed over until the juice was gone and only an indigestible fibrous pulp remained.

The convertible top up, Nadia's perfume filled the Triumph, and he remembered how she had once described herself, her reserved nature, as a *flower without a scent*. Ironically, the comment had lingered with him. She was, indeed, a dark rose with her flawless, tawny skin and thick tresses, but rarely, he thought, was she equal to the passion he felt for her. Yet he remained patient, believing devotion would bring her around, pay off. She was patient and persistent in her quiet way, even while their lovemaking was becoming strained and anxious. Long distance phone calls between Los Angeles and Santa Barbara in the months that followed her move, sustained the thread, his trips up the coast their habit of each other.

"Turn left at De La Guerra," she said.

He could tell she was anticipating this evening out as she hummed a few bars, a rare thing for her, from the Vivaldi on FM. Dining out had almost become a ritual with them since the separation, the dressing up, the slow dining, a sort of foreplay. She ate slowly, almost sensually, and his feelings would intensify by the necessity of restraint.

The Top Hat restaurant was full when they arrived. The hostess, a woman in her sixties, wearing false eyelashes and jangling wrist bangles, told them there would be a short wait and seated them in an anteroom with a Swedish fireplace where they would be served drinks. He ordered a bottle of Pinot Blanc, pricey but the cheapest on the wine list. The wine steward attending them, deftly opened the bottle and offered him the cork, but too conscious of this pretension, he ignored it and insisted on pouring himself.

The Top Hat was not as stiff as something you might find in Brentwood, but it still had the obligatory oversized menus bound with soft leather and selections described with liberal sprinklings of French. The general lighting was subdued, lending intimacy, but hiding the fading and the blemishes caused by years of smoke, food spills and vaporous grease. The patrons were nearly evenly divided between affluent retirees who shouldn't have been eating such rich food and younger couples playing out their own dating rituals. He enjoyed good food like anyone else, but a more relaxed place would have been better. It would have been lovely, he thought, if without his suggesting, she had prepared a simple light dinner at home with a little California Chablis, some Jobim bossa nova in the background—and then invited him to an early bed. After all, he'd put in a long week on the road in his West LA sales territory and had fought the Friday night coastal traffic for hours.

"Why do they give you the cork?" Nadia asked.

"It's to prove the wine has been well stored, no leaks. A pointless little tradition that I suppose most people don't really know and maybe think you are supposed to save it as a souvenir. Some fools even smell the cork."

"Funny, I never thought about it much before. I just thought it was a symbolic courtesy, you know, your wine, your cork."

The glow from the fire highlighted the perfect delicate bones of her face. In the reverie inspiring flames he imagined himself in her yard, finishing up an afternoon of much needed yard work and being beckoned in for a well-deserved home-cooked meal.

"I'm hungry," he said.

"Too bad you won't see Tracy on this trip."

"Yea, how's she doing anyway at her new school?"

"Better now. She's got some little friends. You know how she's sensitive."

*Sensitive?* Where was the sensitivity he and Nadia had once congratulated themselves on, that gentle spirit of tea, poetry, long walks and afternoon lovemaking that had marked their first year? *It's always hot in the beginning,* she had once explained, as if love were a cup of coffee. The comment had stayed with him like a picked-at scab.

"We were good once," he said, the phrase caught somewhere between statement and question.

"George, please."

"Well, we were. Where did you go?"

"I'm here."

They both looked into the fire, as if to find an answer. They were still staring when the hostess came to announce a table was ready for them.

His appetite was now dulled by the wine, the stuffy air and the tension. Flushed, he slipped off his sports jacket and hung it on the back of his chair.

"Think I'll order something light, maybe a seafood cocktail and a salad," he said. His mood had changed and he looked about the restaurant trying to distract himself.

"We could have done Chinese take-out at home," he said.

"Maybe we need a longer break."

"Would that suit you?" he shot back.

Before she could answer, the waitress intervened, informing him that gentlemen were required to wear coats. He hadn't noted any sign when he came in. George curtly replied that he was uncomfortable and perhaps they should have some air conditioning. The waitress said the air conditioning was operating just fine and that he would have to comply with the house rule.

"Come on, I'm not bothering anyone," he said. The waitress insisted, and he insisted on talking with the manager.

"Maybe you ought just put your coat on, George," Nadia said, tugging at his wrist.

Her plea, rather than softening him, hardened his determination to challenge the absurdity of the rule. A sturdy, middle-aged Mediterranean type in a dark, natty suit approached the table.

"I'm sorry, sir, but it's a house rule... as you can see, all the gentlemen are wearing their coats."

"All pretending to enjoy themselves."

"Sir? You seem to be the only one who minds. It's either the coat or you'll have to leave." The smile and the sir had been dropped.

"Right. We've lost our appetites anyway," George said in a flurry of rising clumsily from the table, while fumbling through his wallet and flinging a dismissive twenty-dollar bill on the table, more than enough to cover the wine.

"Come on, let's get out of this dump." He wasn't loud, but a few patrons had stopped in the middle of talking, chewing, and smoking to look his way. He caught hold of Nadia and marched for the exit, hardly aware of his muttered expletives.

"Pardon me," the hardened voice of the manager trailed after him. Nadia's luminous eyes had the beginnings of tears. But George pressed on.

"Pardon me?!" The manager was more insistent.

He must have caught some of George's muttering. In any case, the manager's solicitation rang of resolute challenge.

"You should at least apologize to the young lady," the manager snarled from a few paces behind.

"This is my wife, if you don't mind," he threw over his shoulder at the advancing manager, as if that explanation excused him from any apologies, while Nadia was looking away dreamily, mournfully, as though she were somewhere else. The manager overtook him at the door, swinging it open defiantly.

"I don't want to see your face around here ever again, Mister!" Away from the dining area, the manager was apparently less compelled to restrain himself.

"Why should I want to see yours?" The words escaped George, a sudden inspiration of bravado, but ill-advised under the circumstances, and so he hurried through the door, dragging Nadia with him toward the parking lot. The manager followed in pursuit but, fortunately, discreetly stopped outside the canopied door, shaking a fist and shouting what sounded like Italian profanities.

They didn't try to go to another restaurant. Time had flown and the mood was gone, and he was feeling the effects of too much wine without food. They drove back to the house in silence. Once in the house, he made a bowl of raisin bran.

"Bad choice of restaurants." he said.

"A friend said it was good."

"What kind of friends you making up here?"

"You could have put your coat on."

"You could've said something."

"What do you mean?"

"Something to that Al Capone manager?"

"Like what? Excuse my boyfriend for being an asshole?"

"Never mind."

He wasn't sure where to begin explaining and he was tired. They finished their snacks and Nadia said she was going to go to bed and read. He knew it wasn't his style to make a scene, but this had been an exception. It was as though something had been caged in him, pressing for a way out.

He fixed another bowl of raisin bran and turned on the television. He stopped at a rerun of *Kung Fu* with David Carradine. Nadia came through the living room in her nightgown. She paused for a moment near the end table lamp where her hips and legs were silhouetted by the light through her gown. *Flower without a scent.*

"You coming to bed?" she said. There was no come-hither in the question, just the behest of habit.

"Is that an invitation?"

"I'm brushing my teeth," she said flatly and left the room. The old, blind Shao Lin master was saying to David Carradine, the fledgling monk, "but, Grasshopper, a journey of a thousand miles is begun by one step." Carradine's puffy eyes seemed to widen with recognition, and the old sage chuckled.

About a half hour later, the light went out in Nadia's bedroom. He turned off the television, undressed and made himself comfortable on the couch with the Afghan cover. There was a breeze rustling the overgrown bushes in the front yard, and the scent of the night-blooming jasmine wafted in with the cool air from the open window. Soon he was drifting into sleep, floated away, off to the coast, at first driving his car south on the 101, and then, without logical transition, sprinting effortlessly on the hard sand at the water's edge.

# The Man Who Loved Fat Women

------------------------

H e quit the lulling medley of pop songs midstream, hunkered down on his guitar as though for maximum intimacy and then slowly picked his way into a classical piece like the patter of rain before a storm. When he burst into the theme, heads turned and conversations evaporated.

He was new at the Bistro and he went by the name of Gabriel de España, pronounced Gawbriel. He didn't look Spanish to me, nor did I detect anything in his speech that might suggest he was a genuine Latino. He was a paunchy sort of fellow of indeterminate age with a pasty complexion, thinning hair and thick glasses, as if he had spent too much time indoors reading large volumes of small print. I thought inviting him to our table between sets would liven up the evening. Gloria and I weren't getting along too well again, and there was still a strain in our communication, even though we had stepped out for the evening for a little distraction and a few glasses of wine.

Gabriel, as it turned out, hadn't near the eloquence of his guitar. I almost regretted the invitation to our table. When we ordered him a drink, he insisted on something non-alcoholic. He didn't approve of smoking either, eyeing

Russ Desaulnier

the cigarettes dangling in our hands. He had recently come from Chicago and was working in some high-tech job in the R & D complex on the outskirts of town, until he got his artistic career going. The few evenings a week at Le Bistro were a warm-up. He was serious and unsmiling, as though life had dealt with him poorly, but there was no denying his music. Even Gloria was brightened. At any rate, a little third-party stimulus had us talking again. She was moody and sometimes she found things disagreeable, including me. Most of the time I couldn't figure out what I'd done or not done. Young women were like that, I figured. She'd be okay once I taught her a few things. I had exposed her to good California Cabernets, Bergman and Fellini, her first real orgasm, so she said, and now, by chance, to some really good local music.

"What did you call that song you just did?" she asked our new acquaintance.

"*The Concerto de Aranjuez,* by Rodrigo."

"It's sad and beautiful," Gloria said, genuinely moved. I always knew she was sensitive. She was just young.

"There can be no beauty without pain," Gabriel pronounced. Gloria looked at me as if to ask for a translation. I wasn't quite sure what to say. But then Gabriel excused himself for the next set and resumed with more classical pieces, and for the moment I forgot about connecting pain with beauty. I invited him to the party I was throwing the following evening at my cottage. Gloria agreed that a little live entertainment would add class to the party. Anyway, Gabriel indicated that he'd like to meet some new people, which I knew meant women. It wasn't hard to see he probably didn't do very well in that department. But I couldn't think of who might be a match. Anyway he'd get a night out, some company, hors d'oeuvres, and maybe, I hoped, a few laughs. The party turned out well. There was a generous selection of bring-your-own booze and smoke. Before the party got really rolling, when people were just warming up to each other and were into the first round of drinks, Gabriel's music got lots of attention. He was the only one wearing a tie. I kept his glass full of ginger ale and had him play more Rodrigo pieces and movements from De Falla. The arabesque turns of Gabriel's strings had me imagining I was galloping across plains at night to a Bedouin tent where Gloria lay restlessly waiting in something cool and diaphanous. I sat close to her while we listened.

After a while, most people got too loaded to sit still, preferring the Stones and Elton John to Gabriel, who got left in the background. One of Gloria's friends from her typing pool, a girl named Barb, seemed to take a liking to Gabriel, but I could tell he wasn't impressed. Barb was cute but was built like the old stuffed chair in the corner of my living room. Around midnight Gabriel packed it in. He thanked me for inviting him, shaking my hand almost too firmly, that same serious expression on his face, as though we'd all just been called up for a tour of some war zone.

Gloria stayed after the party broke up. But she never liked to stay the whole night at my place because of her kid with the babysitter and because she said my place gave her the creeps. Sure, it was rickety and sometimes you'd hear a rat or two scratching around in the walls, but you never saw them. The cottage was old, but it was charming, especially with all the work I'd put into it. Besides, the rent was cheap, considering it was only two blocks from West Beach. But she would never stay the night and would get up after a while, get dressed and drive home.

"It was a good party," she said, reaching behind her back to hook her bra.

"How'd you like Gabriel's guitar?"

"The music was fine, but he's weird. Does he like women?" I told her I thought so, while thinking how much I enjoyed watching her drag her bikini panties up her long thighs.

"When are you going to stay the night?" I asked.

"Here? Not a chance."

"Some people think it's romantic."

"Some people? You seeing someone else?"

"Did I say that?"

"I gotta get back, the babysitter."

"Right."

I guess she thought I was sulking because she came to me and kissed me on the forehead. I tried to slip my hand under the bikinis.

"Look, I'm not ready to start playing house, particularly in this dump."

"Who's talking about house. I'd just like all night now and then."

Then the clothes started going on quickly as though I wasn't supposed to see her naked.

"Why don't you get a decent apartment with a decent bathroom," she said. I hated that word *decent*.

Suddenly feeling tired, I yawned. I didn't want to argue and ruin the mood any more than it already was. There was still the whole weekend ahead. I saw her off, cleared away the dirty glasses and debris from the party and climbed back into bed that still smelled of Gloria.

Then the rats started, as if they had a network of stairways within the walls. I had estimated there were three or four, like a human family, that had taken up residence, but now it seemed they had invited a few cousins. Maybe I ought to do something about them. I had done almost everything else for the old place—plastered walls, replaced chunks of dry rot, repaired a few leaks in the roof, refinished the hardwood floors, put linoleum down in the kitchen. The cottage wasn't grand, but the rent didn't strain my income that mainly depended on unemployment checks.

I started stopping in at the Bistro more often to hear Gabriel play. There was no cover and the house wine was cheap and tolerable. Gabriel looked tired and his face was getting more puffy every time I saw him, which was always evenings.

"You should stop smoking," he was saying, looking at the Pall Mall cocked in my fingers.

"You ought to get some sunshine. This is California," I said.

He didn't respond to my comment and sipped his ginger ale. I wondered why I bothered. But I knew he wanted some company, and I was curious.

"Is *España* really your name?"

"No."

I waited for the real name, but nothing.

"How's your lady friend?" he asked.

"Gloria? She's okay."

"Does she really care about you?"

"What?"

"Nothing, forget it. Look, I want to show you something."

He took out a large wallet and extracted a laminated black and white photo. A man in tails on a cane chair was playing guitar on what looked like a big stage. The guitarist was slim and had a full head of wavy hair.

"This you?"

"Turn it over," he said, nodding.

It read: *The Andres Segovia Awards Recital 1968, Carnegie Hall.* He took the photo back and carefully slipped it into his wallet. Though no expert, I knew his music was extraordinary, and so the Carnegie wasn't so much a surprise as his changed appearance.

"How old are you? If you don't mind my asking."

"I'm in my middle earlies," he said, chuckling. I hadn't even seen him smile before, as though it were unnatural to him. I had to laugh when I realized his little mysteries were not that important, after all, and I sensed an ease between us.

"Why did you ask if Gloria cared about me?"

"Just a feeling. I had no place saying it. Forgive me." Gabriel was again his somber-faced self, the brooding artist.

"She's okay, she's young, even though she's got a kid," I said, wondering.

"Anyway, you have somebody," he said, the words tumbling from his mouth, resonant with a palpable loneliness. I asked him about Barbara, Gloria's friend, who had taken an interest in him at the party. She was cute and upbeat, I thought, even if overweight.

"Well, I like them plump," he said, frowning.

"More than Barbara?"

He nodded. I tried hard to contain my disbelief and keep a straight face. I was glad it was dark in the Bistro because I could feel my face flushing with embarrassment. I couldn't help feeling I was being made privy to a ridiculous sexual preference, if not a desperate one. What kind of man couldn't have all the super chubby women he wanted? I could understand how some men liked full-figured women, but rhino haunches? Gloria was svelte, and I had never thought about truly obese women and how some mysterious men found them a turn on.

"Well, yeah," he just said, holding out his arms in approximation of the girth he desired. I would have dearly liked to ask him why he had a thing about very big women. He was a bit flabby himself, but by no means a fatso. I told him I'd see what I could do. Gloria had lots of friends working at her office. I knew there had to be some sweet fat girl on the office staff just longing for a guy like Gabriel. As he returned to the little stage and took up his guitar, I wondered who he really was, until once again I was transported, gliding along on his notes like a river of diamonds.

Later that week, after I stopped in to pick up my unemployment check, I had lunch with Gloria just down the street from her office. She wouldn't often agree to meeting me during the week, preferring to keep our thing to the weekends. I especially liked the way she dressed for work, the collared blouses and floral polyester skirts that alternately clung and swirled with her sashay, and heels that raised her legs to the extraordinary. It was one of the reasons I liked seeing her during the week. Unfortunately, I could never interest her in nooners.

"Someone really fat? Be serious," Gloria said.

"Just think of it as doing some hopeless girl a favor."

"I'm telling you that guy is a kook."

But Gloria relented. There was such a girl in the office, one so shy that, despite her size, she seemed to magically appear at her post in the mornings and disappear at the end of the day. Gloria said she was sweet. I knew if Gloria ever started calling me *sweet,* I'd know it was all over.

The Christmas holidays were nearing when Gloria's company always had a bash at the boss's big house in Montecito, the posh section of town. She said she'd make sure the big office girl came and I could bring along Gabriel.

Maybe it was the coming holidays, I wasn't sure, but I felt I was running after Gloria, which I'd never felt before, and I think she was beginning to sense it. When she asked me why I hadn't tried to find a temporary job during the holiday season, it sounded like an accusation.

"What do you do with yourself all the time?"

"Trying to assess the continuous Now."

"Give me a break."

She couldn't stand anything that sounded intellectual. Maybe she was right to get on my case. But as long as I could get unemployment insurance and get by, I didn't want one of those jobs that were going nowhere, trainee this and trainee that. True, I wasn't getting far in my current situation, but at least I had time to think about things. I had put a makeshift skylight in one of the bedrooms of the cottage, and painted the walls flat white, my atelier. I did some good thinking there, wrote letters, made things.

Then I came down with a bad cold. I lay around for a week, and in the long hours spent reading, dozing or doing nothing, I became more aware of the rats, flurries of scratching and scuttling within the walls and in the crawl-space above. I fought the need to call Gloria every night, but generally lost. I agreed it was best that she didn't come by. There was nothing gained in her catching what I had. I lived off a big pot of chicken soup that I kept replenishing with chopped vegetables as it got low. For a diversion I set a rat trap. The trap seemed personal, more sporting, and I would be able to collect the dead. I mistakenly believed that if the rats ate poison they would lie down and die in the wall spaces and stink up the place. So I got up into the ceiling attic space and set a powerful trap with pieces of fried bacon.

When over the cold, I went to the unemployment office where, probably owing to the season, the clerks were not their usual surly selves. I didn't have to fill out any explanations, like contrition, and no one pressured me to go out on an interview for a job I didn't want. I'd put aside a little money for the season, enough to afford a little extra cheer. As for presents, I wasn't giving any. There wasn't any going around among the people I ran with, all of them poor like me. But I'd been working on a pendant for Gloria off and on for a few months—a slice of stag horn I had carved into an Indian woman's face and set into the head of an antique sterling fork which, with some help from a jewelry-making friend, I had pounded out into a buffalo head, using the big outside tines for the horns. Meanwhile I had Gabriel primed for the big evening in Montecito at the Starbuck estate. According to Gloria's description of her officemate's size, Gabriel would not be disappointed. As the party approached, anticipation of the blind date gave Gloria and me a common cause.

"I mean, Rhonda has a nice face, I'll give her that."

"What does she do?" I asked.

"She works in title search and archives."

"No, I mean what does she like to do?"

"I don't know, I didn't ask her. Cook, I suppose."

"What did you tell her about Gabriel?"

"What's there to tell?"

"Didn't she want to know who she's going out with?"

"Of course, I said he was a smart dresser and a great musician?"

"He's really a sensitive guy."

"He's polite, I guess, but he sure doesn't smile much."

"Maybe he doesn't have much to smile about."

Russ Desaulnier

I didn't know exactly how or why, but from the beginning his being a newcomer to town, there being something vulnerable about him, I felt the urge to help him. I did, in fact, urge all my friends to go see him at the Bistro. He made me think about those kids in elementary school who never get picked in the choose-up games, who always have the answers when called on by the teacher but who everyone tries to hammer when it comes time to play some rough house game, one of those kids who always had to stay in the house, practicing his music, while the rest of the kids were off playing around the neighborhood.

The Starbuck estate was a combination of Scarlett Ohara's Tara and a California hacienda, a facade of pillars facing a circular drive and, on the inside, a garden courtyard with a fountain in the middle. Facing the courtyard were huge rooms with tall French doors, and directly ahead was a hundred yards of sloping grass that looked more like a golf fairway than a backyard. Down at the end of the slope was a quasi-Greek gazebo with ivy-entwined columns, reminiscent of an Arcadian scene from a Maxfield Parrish poster.

Gloria met me and Gabriel at the Christmas tree, as planned. She was totally foxed out for the affair, black silky skirt split to the thigh, spaghetti strap top and eyes shadowed with blue. Gabriel wore a blazer and a cravat, looking almost handsome, distinguished anyway. Once he hit those strings, though, no one would dare question the Cary Grant impersonation.

And then there she was the mystery girl. I hung back and allowed Gloria to make the introductions. The girl, woman, as expected, was very big, but she had the face of a tired angel, a Rubenesque adult cherub. She was dressed in one of those tent-like things that opera stars sometimes wear, threaded with sparkling lamé, giving her an appearance not unlike the nearby Christmas tree. She did, indeed, have a chest of Wagnerian proportions, but when she spoke, it was the voice of a nervous girl with a hint of a Southern drawl. She seemed a little unsure of herself, but she was game. I shook her soft, moist hand. When Gabriel was introduced, he snapped to attention in a semi-Prussian manner, proffered his arm and said:

"Would Mademoiselle join me for a glass of punch?" Ronnie, as she asked to be called, shrugged with delight, took Gabriel's arm and glided away with him like a fluffy cumulus on a breeze. It occurred to me that absurdity is always relative.

Our mission appearing to be accomplished with the happy couple launched toward the proverbial sunset, Gloria and I were free to get into the Christmas spirit together. There we were in the baronial Starbuck living room glittering with Christmas hope, paintings of dour New England ancestors looking down on us. I produced the pendant from my pocket and wished Gloria a Merry Christmas.

"It's great. You know I love Indian stuff. I have the perfect fringed doe skin blouse to wear with it."

As she starting to inspect the piece, Mrs. Starbuck, the eminent hostess herself, intervened, ebullient and dripping with diamonds.

"I think Mr. Starbuck may have introduced us at the firm? Gloria wasn't it?" she said, her accent reminding me of Masterpiece Theater.

Gloria took a slight step back to admit her to our circle, the hand holding the pendant dropping to her side.

"Oh, Mrs. Starbuck, hello, such a nice party."

"And who is your friend?" When the light hit right, her diamonds were blinding.

"This is Herbie Johnson... Mrs. Starbuck." Gloria knows how I hate being called *Herbie*.

"A pleasure to meet you, Mrs. Starbuck," I said, trying to appear a little more sophisticated.

"And nice to meet you Mr. Johnson." At least she didn't call me *Herbie*.

Gloria carried on about how she liked Mrs. Starbuck's dress and then inquired if the Starbucks would be taking a winter cruise again. I wasn't really listening. Gloria, preoccupied with other things, had slipped my pendant into her little sequined evening bag. Across the room, Gabriel already had his guitar out, warming up with what sounded like some Albéniz, and Ronnie, next to him, was a beaming concert mistress. As he played, some distinguished men and women drifted in his direction. He didn't need my help any longer.

"Mr. Johnson?"

Mrs. Starbuck and Gloria had moved a couple steps away without my noticing. The great lady waited for him to join them, wherever it was they were going. Gloria's expression was impenetrable.

"I'll catch up," I said, excusing myself with a motion toward the punch bowl. I moved in the direction of the guitar instead, but now there was a wall of people surrounding Gabriel, so I slipped out a nearby French door that was ajar. The moonlit night was crisp but not cold, though I could see my breath. I flicked my half-smoked cigarette into the courtyard fountain and began walking down the grass slope toward the Greek gazebo, the notes of Gabriel's guitar fading as if tinkling shards of glass falling away into the well of the night. As I approached the gazebo ringed by Italian cypress, its marble columns gleaming in the moonlight, I dreamed of one of those barefoot Maxfield Parrish maidens playing a lyre and softly singing for me.

Marriage is our last, best chance to grow up.

—JOSEPH BARTH

# My Little White Picket Fence

There was something not right about her, like a brilliantly colored Amazonian frog, attractive but quite possibly toxic. I had met Melanie only once and was acquainted with her mainly through what my wife reported from the yoga class she took with her. Grace liked her because she was a Californian and easy to talk to and because she was all the right things—liberal, an environmental activist, New Age. A practicing member of some imported Buddhist sect, she ritually chanted but, gratefully, didn't preach. Younger than Grace and single, Melanie had an engaging effervescence, which had struck me in our initial meeting, but her intentness on my words I found patronizing. Having watched her at that night's ecological discussion and vegetarian potluck, I had noticed how she applied this patronizing manner to other people. I might not have given her much attention, but there was something familiar about her.

Having been in sales for twenty years, I was in the habit of evaluating how people pitched themselves. A sales pro and most mature, sincere people unconsciously walk that critical thin line between undersell and oversell. They project themselves as artlessly and unrehearsed as breathing. The inexperienced, the insecure and the insincere are often too quick or strong with the glad hand, too big with the smile, too intent upon your words, or the opposite, are opaquely reserved. Melanie broke all the rules of salesmanship when I met her. I wouldn't have cared except that my wife was taken with her. Why I should have been bothered by this fact was unclear to me, at first.

There was something more than her friendship to my wife that gnawed at the fringe of my awareness. Her appearance and mannerisms demanded attention. Her hair, for example, was straight, parted in the middle, long and silky. Her clothes tended to the ethnic, and she wore Birkenstock sandals. But she didn't come across like some spaced-out flower child. Grace wouldn't stay interested in such a person. Melanie espoused all the right causes, which I couldn't criticize, any more than I could her homemade breads which I had enjoyed on a few occasions when Grace had brought some home. But the profile she presented was too perfect, like her loaves of bread, too studied like her intent eyes, too predictable like her habit of sweeping her hair over a shoulder. Melanie's entrance from the wings of my life came when Grace had casually invited her to spend some time with us during the summer at our lake cottage. Fine. Grace would have a companion for those times when I would like to sit quietly and analyze the markets, jot down ideas for new purchase proposals, or just relax with a Ludlum thriller and a vodka and tonic. Our children never were without playmates at the lake, so they were usually occupied. Melanie and Grace could take walks and glory in the wonders of nature and find company in their condemnation of those who were polluting it. Fortunately for me, my investments group had begun several years ago to move away from heavy polluting industries, not so much because of conscience, but because such industries were in decline and losing out to foreign competition. I balanced myself with Grace's growing eco-awareness by agreeing several years ago to support simplification of our lives, especially in regard to our diet which has pretty much become vegetarian, and I have become more fit as a result.

One evening when I came home from work, Grace announced that Melanie had filled the only void in her life. She had found a man, a good-looking guy, a long hair and a jock who owned and ran a local record shop. She was wildly in love and she wanted to bring him along to our retreat at the lake, I assumed, for a romantic ordination of the relationship under the pines of nature's cathedral. I could tell Grace was uncertain when she made the announcement.

"She's wildly in love, is she? She just met him two days ago and now she's taking long showers with him? Love is grand," I said.

"Well, I didn't give her a *yes*."

"Nor did you give her a *no*. Look, Grace. I thought you would enjoy her company out at the cottage, but where would it leave you if she brings up her loverboy?"

"Well, I thought of that... after."

"Right. Maybe she invites people into her life she doesn't know, but I don't. We don't know this guy from Adam."

"This really puts me in a difficult situation."

"She put you in a difficult situation, not me."

"Melanie's just a free spirit. She's always got people staying at her apartment, friends from here and there."

"And she just presumes she can invite herself into other people's places, right?"

"We've been having such a good rapport; it'll just make things really weird If I have to tell her *no*."

"I hate that hippy hey-brother-can-I-crash-at-your-pad stuff. It's presumptuous and dated. Tell her I said *no*."

"Oh great, I'll look like a real wimp, like I have no mind of my own."

"Come on, Grace, you invited *her*, not some guy she just picked up off the street."

"She didn't just pick him up off the street."

"Well, wherever the hell she met him, does she know him? Okay, just because she's decided to sleep with a near stranger, doesn't mean I want him under my roof."

My voice had begun to rise. I was not angry with Grace, only with the fact that our peace had been invaded. Grace had been maneuvered. At any rate, the incident would not be erased with the turning off of the bed lamp. What had been at intimation of something amiss with this woman on the perimeter of my life was now a confirmed fact.

Although we decided that Grace would simply tell Melanie that it might be too crowded to invite an extra person to the cabin, we were both relieved when Melanie didn't pursue the topic at the following week's yoga session. Grace found out a few days later that Melanie had jumped the gun in assuming her infatuation was mutual. The new boyfriend had made it clear not long after the initial fireworks that he preferred a no-commitments friendship. So Melanie's summer plan was off. I thought it served her right.

"Well, what did I tell you?" I said, spearing some sliced tomatoes from the tray that Grace had laid out with the tofu burger dinner.

"Well, of course, she ran off mad-headed. But she was lonely. You can understand that?"

There was no challenge left in our discussion of the Melanie incident, and I was then able to feel some sympathy for Melanie. After all, loneliness had made fools of us all at one time or another. But I was still no less annoyed by the fact that she remained in Grace's life and a continuing possible source of intervention into mine. What was she going to engineer next? I told Grace to be circumspect in her dealings with her. I couldn't help thinking about that starry, blissed-out look on Melanie's face when she got with you one-on-one and talked about saving the spotted owls. I was surprised to learn she was taken seriously by a fair number of people, maintained a notable presence in several activist and New-Age groups, and was connected with a few local VIPs.

My next meeting with Melanie came when Grace and I went to a consciousness/fund raiser for protecting American forests, a cause which hoped to preserve the stately pines of the Pacific Northwest. I usually enjoyed going to these meetings, not only for their good causes, but because they made good social outings with substance. I often met professionals and businessmen I liked, as well as a few who chained themselves to Douglas firs in the path of lumbering crews, or who lay across lumber truck lanes or likened eating meat to murder. I had no objection to direct action. I had seen riot police and some blood in my day.

There, in part, was the rub: Melanie dressed and conducted herself as though she had just walked out of that era of mine, which one might not find so unusual in a college kid, an aged Berkeleyite or musician, but Melanie, at only thirty-five, seemed like a poseur and a mockery. All right, the causes were fine, but why the costumes, why the frequent use of Woodstock patois such as *mellow* and *far*

Russ Desaulnier

*out,* why the overly familiar manner, as if everyone she met was a long-lost relative?

We arrived late at the soiree which was being held in the spacious, vaulted living room of a beam and glass house in the southwest hills, the home of a prominent businessman. There was the usual mix of people, mostly mature couples like Grace and me and a few corduroyed grad-student types. On a large table was assembled various pamphlets and literature on a number of environmental causes, and another table was spread out with assorted refreshments—hummus dip, seaweed and Indian blue corn chips, vegetable sushi, bottles of Evian water and sparkling apple juice. People were talking in small groups, holding their cocktail glasses filled with the non-alcoholic beverages. Melanie was making her rounds with her patent flourishes, intense eyes, and tireless smile. Men were charmed by her, the women to a lesser degree. She was wearing a faded outfit of Balinese batik and, of course, her Birkenstock sandals. Her thick, near waist-length hair was partially taken up into a mound and held together with beaded Indian bands that glowed like the smile she trotted around the large room. Soon everyone prepared for the lecture portion of the evening, seating themselves in a block of folding chairs facing a screen for slides and a small table and chair provided for the guest speaker. I had become quite relaxed, as the day's work lifted from my mind and I sank as best one can into a folding chair. The speaker began by explaining statistics that projected the demise of our forests and the overall effects on the atmosphere, the increase in carbon dioxide, erosion, effects on crops, and the extinction of more forest species.

My attention wandered to the back of Melanie's head a few rows in front where small slivers of light were dancing off the iridescent beads in her Indian hair bands. And then like a small furtive beast of the forest night, memory crept up on me, rubbing itself seductively across my mind, purring its ancient song.

Nixon was broadening the scope of our involvement in Vietnam: we were angry, spoke rebellion, found a voice in the shouting of those about us. Everyone was doing it, just as everyone was smoking pot. Some of us participated with the SDS, going to the meetings which often featured some firebrand from the *LA Free Press* or *Berkeley Barb,* down on Anaheim Street in the old storefront near the slummy bars where the mini-skirted black hookers hung out. Painting placards, planning marches, discussing campus initiatives and endlessly listening to Bob Dylan or Crosby, Stills & Nash, we shared the elation of being young and having found a commonness. That was the most important thing, being together, and we often sealed our covenant with the passing of the tribal joint.

*... in Brazil last year about thirty million acres of forest fell to developers. More than half the world's trees are gone and yet man continues to slash and burn the earth's forest at a rate of two acres per second...*

The memory that had been slinking around my consciousness suddenly sank its teeth into me. The memory of Connie had flirted with me over the years but until now never so insistently or clearly. Framed by long, straight blond hair, her face floated through my mind, her pouty lower lip sensual and admonishing. "Define your terms," I could hear her saying. It was a stock retort from the lexicon of would-be intellectual-speak then in vogue. She particularly liked that one about terms. But she had other pet words like *validate, dichotomize* and *karma.* She had always said it was *karma* that she had come into my life.

She had insisted on being called Constance, never just Connie. "Let's be real," she would say. Her name was not to be changed, any more than a woman's God-given body hair should be shaved, or breasts encumbered with bras. Constance challenged everything, especially my naiveté.

I was a sophomore and she a senior. That she had bothered with me at all awed me. That she introduced me to many things I had never known made me love her with the special wonder that only a boy who loves a woman can know. I didn't carry her books for her around campus; that wasn't done, but I would have if she had asked. I did run occasional errands for her, tuned her VW bug, fixed a leaky faucet here, a shower head there. Going to her one-bedroom garage apartment on Obispo Street was like entering an art gallery, for her walls were covered with framed art prints. There were the obligatory Indian tapestries on the ceilings and the eradicable scent of joss stick. In her bedroom was a 1940s vanity with a giant round mirror reflecting her old ironwork bed which she had painted to appear like brass. And there were shelves and shelves of books, writers I had never heard of like Ouspensky, Herman Hesse, Wilhelm Reich, and Simone de Beauvoir. Constance ate a lot of brown rice and steamed vegetables and drank Chinese teas, which I thought tasted like steeped marijuana stems.

She was thin and tall and wore no makeup and you had to look close to see how beautiful she really was. She was the secretary to the Students for a Democratic Society chapter and that is where I met her, amidst the folding chairs, amidst the causes of another time.

*... cattle raising and multinational corporations continue to destroy forests in the name of development by converting vast tracts of forest to grazing land...*

THE BORDER                    117

I was pretty good-looking as a kid of twenty, lean and clean cut. Constance made me over and got me growing my hair longer with my first beard and mustache. With her I learned to feel good about face hair. I still hadn't declared my major either, until she convinced me to become an English major, saying it cut across every discipline, imparting a broader interpretation and knowledge of the world and life. I was still hanging out with her when I made the transition to my junior year and became an English major, signing up for everything from the Modern American Novel to an off-beat course on women writers which she convinced me to take. The instructor seemed like a man-hater, but I liked the stuff we read. I maintained my business minor, which kept peace with my father—and which I vaguely felt might become an ace in the hole a few years later.

*... almost all of the land converted to cattle ranches, num-bering in millions of acres, during the '70s has been aban-doned, leaving wasteland...*

Over the years Constance had sunk into the murky depths of memory along with the dozens of courses I took during college, save a few distilled attitudes and convictions. She herself was a *dichotomy* and an irony not then apparent to me, for she was at once real and illusory. When she occasionally allowed me into her bed, cultivating my boyish anxiousness into the deftness of a man familiar with women, artfully balancing boldness with shy femininity, she was real. Yet I couldn't hold her to the extent I felt held by my soaring illusion of love which I had to restrain like a Cyrano, for it was a time when free love and open relationships were code and anything resembling traditional romance, including marriage, implicated the straight world we were all sworn to oppose. Not that I gave marriage a thought. I was in no position to think of such a big step. But near the end of that spring term, despite promises to myself and to Constance, possessiveness had begun to take hold of me .

*... in the Northern Hemisphere we are decimating the forests with industrial pollution better known as acid rain...*

Constance graduated, but not finding much to interest her in the job market she went on to grad school. Understandably, she had less time for the SDS and me. She had taken some part-time work as a secretary at a Century 21 real estate office where the *straw men* in business suits, as she put it, went about dealing in *ticky tacky* houses. But she needed the money. I was working at a liquor store part-time and got the balance from my father, which I promised to pay back. But he just wanted good grades in repayment. So I doubled my efforts with my explications of Hemingway, Whitman and Eliot while reading Vonnegut and Brautigan on the side. But economists Ricardo and Keynes suffered, as my business course average fell to C.

I was anxious to discuss ideas with Constance because I wanted to show her how I had grown, expecting her admiration, or perhaps love. She had never used the word *love* with me. *Love* had too many definitions, she said, and was clouded by establishment conditioning. When it came to assigning labels, *love* usually failed as miserably as did words like *freedom* and *truth*. It was somehow tacitly understood that in matters of the heart, professions of love were of the old order, only bandied about by cornballs stuck in time. I had told her once when I got drunk that I loved her, and she silently put a finger across my lips.

*... The relationship between deforestation and the greenhouse effect* is *more interconnected than we had thought...*

I had gone over to her apartment for a candlelit spaghetti dinner. We had a spirited conversation through dinner, covering my term paper problem on the Beat Poets to the latest Vietnam news, the SDS, the campus furor over a less than student-friendly university president and finally her grad school problems. She was worried about finances, the pressures of keeping her apartment and paying the bills, while her seminars and thesis were demanding more time. She had stopped eating and was studying her wine glass.

"Have you met any interesting women in your classes?"

"Nope."

"It's none of my business, really."

"What's up?"

"You know I care a lot about you."

"You know how I feel."

"That's what I'm afraid of."

"What do you mean?"

She then launched into her astonishing story. Her voice got shaky and she stiffened, chin up, in a posture of challenge. Maybe it was conscience, or maybe she just wanted to test the limits of our open relationship. At any rate, she had to be upfront. She told me how she had become friendly with a real estate broker while working at the real estate office. He had received an offer on the occasion of a T.G.I.F. office cocktail party and made a business proposition, all very politely and logically, a measure of reality, as it were. He would keep her in rent and an unspecified amount of money monthly for an intimate arrangement involving no more than a few visits a month to her apartment, only a few since he was a happily married man.

"I have to finish up my Master's. Putting out a little doesn't matter."

"Selling yourself doesn't matter?"

"Are you going to put me through school?"

I should have called her what she was and just walked out, but instead I just sat, stunned and silent. Then she grew angry, telling me to stop looking at her with a sad expression.

"I can't believe how easy guys can be about a little sex, but once a woman takes that attitude, Christ, look out!"

Protest raged in me, but I didn't know where to start. After all, she was free to choose, but I had always secretly thought she would choose me, finally, if I waited, if I was persistent and loyal. My confused thoughts and feelings then began to congeal like the candle wax that dripped down the sides of the Chianti bottle on the dinner table. Finally, when I thought I might explode and lose what little dignity I had left, I got up, went for the door, turned and muttered my parting words, like something from a corny AM radio song, "I guess I was a fool for loving you."

I licked my wounds for several weeks after, but the power of recovery was great in those days and soon I had the unavoidable distraction of midterm exams. It was the confusion that lingered, how did you measure people, how did you measure the meaning of love? At the beginning of the following semester, I changed my major back to business but kept a minor in English for which I had already earned enough credits. My father seemed mystified but was delighted about my sudden change. And when I graduated the following year, the war had wound down and faded as an issue, as had Constance, who, I heard a few years later, had married a dentist and moved to Bakersfield. Karma... karma... ka...

"Are you with us?"

Grace was nudging me as applause arose for the guest speaker. Everyone was stirring from the folding chairs and once again gravitated to their respective little groups as the party broke up for the evening. I could see Melanie working the room.

"I hate that woman," I said, putting Grace's shawl over her shoulders.

"Who?"

"Melanie."

"I don't know why you should *hate* her."

It was true. There was no reason to hate Melanie. Even my tale, were I to tell it, would not make things any more clear to Grace. I couldn't clearly explain to myself what I was feeling. It was something more complex than simple hate threatening me like the resurfacing symptoms of an old malady that hadn't quite been given a lasting cure.

"She's not to be trusted."

"You make too much of her," Grace said, turning to face me.

"Maybe it's that I make too much of you and want nothing to ever come between us," I said, smiling so as not to appear too dramatic.

"Don't be silly."

"I mean it," I said.

Then we spotted Melanie making her way toward us with a polished middle-aged man in tow. She was upon us like an eager hostess of a Saturday TV kid's show.

"Wasn't that lecture just great, and this house, isn't it far out," she exclaimed.

It turned out the man with Melanie was the meeting's host, who hardly had any time to say anything as she reeled off his business profile and civic credits. I was embarrassed by this patronization and shook hands with the man in a way that I hoped to let him know I understood his sudden unease. Either he warmed to my gesture or to the fact that his arm was suddenly around Melanie's waist. He said he knew my company and counted it among his successful dealings in the past. Melanie bubbled on that Grace absolutely had to host a Gaia mixer sometime soon and that she, Melanie, would be glad to help.

Grace and I locked eyes for scarcely two or three heartbeats, but that moment contained the accumulated understandings of more than a decade of marriage.

"Melanie," Grace said in a dulcet tone, "I'm afraid that wouldn't be possible at our place. We're not centrally located and our house is far too small to accommodate such a wonderful get-together like tonight's, don't you think, dear?" Grace said, looking to me with mock disappointment.

I nodded in agreement. I could see the host was pleased by the implied praise of his home, but Melanie revealed a displeasure that dropped the corners of her mouth, as if pins had been pulled. But then she caught herself with a thin, tight smile.

"Well…" she said, struggling.

"Well…" Grace said, pressing.

"Well, see you at yoga."

"Yeah, see you at yoga."

While Melanie paused, looking for something else to say, I nodded a farewell smile to the host and put my arm around Grace's waist and began to move away. I knew then I should never have doubted my wife.

"Now *that* was far out," I said to her so that Melanie would overhear. Glancing back, I saw Melanie abruptly hook the uncomprehending host by the arm, fling her hair over a shoulder and sweep away like a sudden gust of autumn leaves.

Moments later, Grace and I were in the car heading back home down the manicured wood and stucco streets of our town. By now the kids would be asleep up in the small bedrooms of the second floor, and the babysitter would probably be watching television down in the den. I loved that house, our first, and the little white picket fence I had built myself. Most of all I loved the woman sitting next to me and she loved me, and those were inseparable facts needing no validation or definition.

# Bedtime Story

- - - - - - - - - - - - - - - - - -

"Tell me a story, Daddy," my six-year-old daughter asked. Jenny, perhaps because she is the only child of older parents, is at once babyish and precocious, dependent for having had too much attention, yet beyond her years because of the adult exchange that has been her constant example. I felt a twinge of guilt as her request caused me to reflect that I had all too often left bedtime stories to my wife. I usually got home late from the office, and by the time we had finished dinner and gotten Jenny ready for bed, I would be past having enough energy to give a good reading.

"Your daddy's tired, honey. Let him rest," my wife gently interjected. "I'll read you a story."

"I want you to tell me a bedtime story, pleeese, Daddy."

"Your dad's very tired, honey. He's worked all day."

"How about tomorrow night? I'm a little too tired tonight, honey," I added.

"You're always too tired," Jenny shot back.

Her tone and protruding lower lip tugged at my reserves, and so I got into her bed with her, and as she cuddled up to my side I began with the first and only story that came to mind, the story of the elves that helped the little old shoe-maker in the night. But Jenny wouldn't have it.

"Ah, Dad! I know that story!"

She didn't want me to read her any of her books because she was tired of them. The Sesame Street series, Dr. Seuss and several I-Can-Read books.

"Well, what would you like?"

I realized after asking that I sounded like an impatient, grumpy parent. Besides, how could she know what she wanted until she heard a story begin to unfold? Her expression begged my concentration. I felt a rush of guilt, a string of thoughts that counted off my delinquencies as a father. I recollected this moment or that when I had diverted Jenny in one way or another for the sake of my own preoccupations. These thoughts were followed by rationalizations that I was not, after all, a bad parent, that I provided well, often gave whole Sundays, gave moments when I was distracted by the hangover of the day's business. But did I give the effort required to create something for Jenny? Then it struck me, as her eyes gazed up at me, now bigger and more expectant, that I had perhaps become like so many parents who merely bought things for their children as substitutes for attention. I admired my wife who seemed to fall so easily into games with Jenny, who could play store with her, or doctor's office, or make up interviews to tape on her toy Sony recorder. I was almost always such a poor partner in Jenny's fantasies, helplessly looking for direction from her and ultimately deflating the pleasure she sought in sharing. Was I a failure as a father? I felt like an actor without his lines cast upon a stage before an audience of one whose power to inspire fright was no less than that of a full house. I felt myself darting in panic at the recesses of my mind. I had never been very good at remembering things I'd heard—anecdotes, jokes or the words to songs, never mind a worthy fable for the occasion.

Russ Desaulnier

"Come on, Daddy," Jenny entreated, now impatient.

"Okay, okay, let me think a bit."

I turned the dimmer switch, bringing the light down to a moonlight cast fit for gnomes, trolls and witches. Jenny's stuffed animals bunched up together on top of her chest of drawers were silhouetted in the low light, and I wished one of them would come alive as in a Disney animation and give me a sign. I was hesitant to grab at just any beginning that didn't promise a clear thread with which I could continue. Then, as if tuning in through the squeal and scramble of a short-wave radio reaching across great distance, I remembered *beavers*. I hadn't thought of *the great silver beavers of the north* in eons, a series of stories that my father had told me over forty years ago, on week nights when he came into my room after my mother had tucked me into bed or out on the back porch on lazy Sundays while he whittled a piece of wood. My mind reeled, trying to grasp at words and images that had been clouded and lost by the years, tales of a beaver named Chipper and his brethren, anthropomorphized, whose deeds were legendary to the Indian tribes of the north, according to my father. The tales had been passed along by the generations, known only to a very few white men of which my father (of course) had been one, having learned the legend of the beavers from a reclusive old Cree Indian who had fought in the Louis Riel Rebellion, one of the last of the Indian wars just after the turn of the century.

"Daddyeee?!"

"Yes, yes, yes. A long, long time ago, in the days of the great Indian tribes of the north, when the Chippewa Indians were a great nation, long before the coming of the white man, long before anyone can remember... Wait a minute. Before we get started here, did you brush your teeth yet?"

She sometimes would forget to brush and sometimes we would forget to remind her. At the moment I was glad of this, for I wanted to stall for a little time to get some focus on the elusive path to which I had committed myself. It was a path that had been blazed by my father whom I had buried almost seven years ago, and a big piece of my heart with him, now a subject that I had somewhat succeeded in tucking away, out of mind, like the old cigar box that had once held his cigars and now contained a few letters and odds and ends that I had acquired at the time of his death. I had hidden the cigar box deep in a big drawer of piled papers, old photo albums and the collected flotsam and jetsam of the years. I had thought that by that simple act I would initiate the process of burying my grief and the persistent ache of unresolved terms. I had felt cheated by life rather than by death, cheated by my father's not having reached out before it became too late.

Everyone had said he was a hard man, stolid, contained, difficult to know, despite his infectious smile, which I often imagine I see in my daughter's face. It was so long ago when things changed between me and my father, when the distance began, the emotional pushing and pulling that could never seem to be bridged, while my mother grieved helplessly at the sidelines. So that memory didn't invade too deeply into the territory of the present, I soothed myself with the summary that we had loved each other too much, like two rival brothers, who, being cut from the same serious-minded cloth, were unable to accept with good humor their essential differences. Certainly our lives and times were miles apart, mine the easier for his labors in machine shops which gave me an education and something better in life, as he had wanted. But by the time the Sixties arrived, the schism between us deepened. He never left me alone about my longish hair, sometimes just silently glaring at it.

"I'm ready, Daddy," Jenny announced, having returned from brushing her teeth, and she leaped back into the bed and drew the covers up around her chin.

"Let's see, where were we... ?"

"You were telling me about Chippy Indians, Daddy."

"That's *Chippewa,* honey. Chippewa Indians."

We settled again into the bed and I felt Jenny pull closer to me as I began to talk of the great forest of the north where the Chippewa lived and hunted. The little bed light now glowed as if it were our small campfire and the walls and furnishings of the room rose up like the shadows of the Minnesota woods. I remembered then how physical my father always had been, remembered the lingering smell of sweat and shaved steel which he brought to my bed with his tales about the great silver beavers. The society of the beavers was tribal and all things were decided by a conference among the elders. The chief among these was old Knobbler who was so named because he had lost a rear paw in a terrible battle with a lynx.

"What's a lynx, Daddy?"

"He's a kind of wildcat with lots of whiskers and he has big bushy eyebrows. And tonight's story is going to be about how old Knobbler's terrible fight with the lynx and his injury led to Chipper and his tribe of silver beavers entering into the legends of the Chippewa Indians."

I was surprised by my own announcement. I had no idea at that moment what story I was proposing, for I remembered no such story from my father, or any others. There were only the names: Chipper the great warrior beaver, wise old Knobbler and one other beaver hero called

Edgewise, who was the mightiest cutter of trees among all the beavers. I had only the recollection that my father's stories, which I couldn't count but for the approximate number of years he had told them, had always taken place in the wilds of the north in Minnesota or Manitoba. The stories were always about the primordial struggles among the beavers, muskrats, otters and other animals that lived and hunted along the waterways. Occasionally he wove into his stories the interventions of man, first the Indians and then the voracious white men who came seeking the beaver for his fur that fetched high prices from European clothiers and hatters.

"The story begins with the Indians who lived happily in the forests of the north, hunting, fishing and gathering what wild vegetables and fruits they could find. The great spirit of Manitou, who lived in all things, seemed to smile on his people of the north. And then one day a dark cloud descended upon the land."

I felt Jenny pull yet closer as my tone became ominous. A detail of some arcane history once learned somewhere, or perhaps just imagined, occurred to me, and I proceeded to tell a story about how quarrels arose among the western tribes and eastern tribes of the Chippewa nation and how they struggled to retain possession of the rich hunting grounds. I told her about terrible wars that took the lives of many Chippewa braves of both sides in this dispute. There was so much war and fear that there was little time for hunting, fishing and gathering, and the tribes, along with their other sufferings, were becoming hungry and weak. The great chief of the western tribes, Owl Moon Talker, who had never wanted the wars and who had tried many times to sue for peace, was full of sadness.

"What's a civil war, Daddy?"

"It's a war where people fight among themselves, friend against friend, brother against brother, even father against son." The old familiar aching over my father suddenly resurfaced as I tried to continue my tale. He had always been a warrior, (perhaps a little too angry for his own good) always at a low simmer with the world. As a young man of the Depression he had earned a few dollars slugging it out in club fights in tents and meeting halls in the small towns of the western prairies. In later years, when I was just a kid, he took up the fight on union picket lines for steelworkers' rights. I could only make feeble attempts to imagine his rugged world, but I could still recall his hands which were never quite clean of machine shop grime or clear of nasty nicks and gashes.

"Owl Moon Talker's son Deer Not There, a young brave of no more than sixteen, had gotten his name for his fleetness of foot and his ability to disappear at the bat of an eye like a deer into the bush. He was to spend ten days alone in the marsh country and keep vigil for a sign from the great spirit Manitou, a sign that would tell the people what should be done to end the terrible strife among the Indians.

So Deer Not There went to the marsh country where he built a lean-to in a dry spot in the marshes and made a small fire which he kept burning through the night. He slept for only short periods, always stirring himself to put more wood on the fire while he kept his vigil for a sign amidst the marshland's night choir of bullfrogs. During the day he collected blueberries and wild rice, and at night he would cook the rice in a fire-hardened gourd held just close enough to the fire to slowly bring the water to a boil. He would not hunt for game during his vigil, for he was forbidden to eat meat during the ten days of his sacred vigil.

Then it came to pass, on the second day of his vigil, while collecting berries, that Deer Not There came upon old Knobbler, who had not yet acquired his name. Knobbier was lying in the grass near a small creek that emptied into the big still marsh where Deer Not There was camped. Knobbier was faint and could barely move from loss of blood, for a hind paw had been severed in a fight with the lynx. The young brave took pity on the beaver and carried him to his lean-to, where he healed the beaver's wound with the herbal medicines his people carried in deerskin pouches when they trekked into the wilderness. As the beaver recovered, they told each other about their lives and their tribes. The beaver learned about things no beaver had ever imagined, things that were to make him wise and famous among all the beavers. At the end of the tenth day, Knobbier, who was to receive his name in the days after he returned to his people, bid farewell to Deer Not There and began his journey back to the silver beavers, swimming back up the creek from where the young Indian had found him."

"How could he swim without his leg, Daddy?" "Well, easy. A beaver uses his big round tail like a paddle." Her eyes were big with wonder. I felt wonder at having entered so deeply into my childhood forest of fantasy. Caught up in the act of telling what now surged in me, I wanted to push on like a kid who had just found his balance on a bicycle for the first time.

"When Deer Not There returned to his village, the other braves taunted him about his unbelievable story of having talked with a beaver. His father Chief Owl Moon Talker and the tribe's Medicine man believed him, but they could not guess how this strange experience might be a sign from the great spirit Manitou. The chief and the tribe had begun to feel hopeless, for the war with the western tribes raged on, and there was barely enough food to feed the warriors. With there being more war casualties every day, there were fewer warriors and braves to hunt for meat, and it had become too dangerous for the women and children to wander far from the village for gathering berries, nuts and wild vegetables. The tribe worried all the more because winter would soon come."

"What's a casualty, Daddy?"

"People who get killed. Indians killed in the war."

I continued by picking up the story back at the silver beaver great council lodge. Knobbier had called a meeting of the elders so that he might enlist them in a plan to help Deer Not There. He told the meeting of the terrible war and how the young Indian and his people were suffering great hardship. Chipper, always a defender of the oppressed and a devout follower of Knobbler, stepped forward and offered to be the first to help. Certainly the beavers couldn't fight against the enemies of Deer Not There, and so they had to find another way in which they could help Deer Not There and his people.

"Daddy, can I have a drink of water?"

I went to the kitchen for her water, a respite which I needed in order to ponder the direction of my story. My father had been wise in his way, generous and kind like old Knobbler. I began remembering how he would make his voice solemn and older when he would end his stories with Knobbler making a moral summation for all the beavers congregated in the hall of the great hut.

For all of his hardness, both real and reputed, my father had always done for others, even, it seemed at times, when it made little sense to do so. I recall him hefting refrigerators for friends changing houses, writing letters of recommendation for this person or that, sometimes lending money he never got back, spearheading neighborhood causes, writing letters of protest to the editorial page of the local paper. He had often slipped me extra money for my high school dates above my mother's objections, helped me with math homework and how to write a composition, for he always had ideas about things, especially politics. He always groused, for example, about the plight of the working class, about the "right-to-work" laws that he said threatened to oppress the American worker. He liked Harry Bridges and Harry Truman because they were no-nonsense fighters who understood the working class. I imagined my father as one of that principled breed of men in simpler, perhaps more glorious times who sacrificed for others; whereas, in these confusing times, I wondered about my potential for resolve and courage.

Then he changed. He seemed to give up caring about everything, save my mother, and began sighing a lot, though then only in his early sixties. His attention would wander, carried off by indifference to company, and he would give delayed, vacant responses of accord, reminding me a bit of a very tired Gary Cooper. I moved out of state, but I stayed in touch with the occasional call, only our conversations dwindled to little more than observations about the weather and other such banalities. He still was playing golf, but I could tell it didn't matter much to him because he never talked about his scores, about the thrills of having scrambled for pars on tough holes. Golf had become a filler like afternoon television, like walks in the mall. He'd often say, when there was a break in our meager conversations, that he was "just putting in time."

"Don't you think it's about lights out time, Mr. Story Teller," said my wife who came in just after I returned with the water. Jenny, despite her enthusiasm, was getting watery eyes from trying to stay awake.

"No, Mom, I want to know what Knobbler is going to do!"

"Knobbler?"

"Just an old story I knew as a kid."

"Aren't you getting tired?"

"Not at all. I feel quite good actually."

My wife shrugged and left us, and once again I entered the forest.

"Knobbler, understanding the plight of the Chippewas, knew that their greatest ally would be food, which would give them the strength to fight their enemies, who also were now suffering for lack of food.

Deer Not There's village was located at the side of a small creek, one of many that eventually joined up with rivers that flowed to the great lakes beyond. Although the tribe caught trout, catfish, sunfish and large succulent crayfish in the creek, it never yielded enough to feed the tribe. The creeks, waterways and marshes that plaited the area were the domain of the beaver nation of the north. The beavers had the power to shift the ebb and flow of the smaller waterways with great engineering skills, building great wood and mud dams overnight. Scouting missions were sent out by Knobbler with his lieutenants Edgewise and Chipper in command to report the conditions upstream from the Indian village. On a suggestion by the usually ingenious Edgewise, great cutter of trees, they would investigate the supply of fish for several miles upstream of the Indian village, and then, if their guess was right, they would proceed with a great plan which would require the help of many beavers, the grays from the south, and the big browns from the far north."

"I have to pee, Daddy."

Again a respite. But now I knew where I was going. Perhaps the path back through Chipper's forest had grown over with the years, but it was still there. My father, like Edgewise, the cutter of trees and engineer of dams, loved the challenge of a problem, anything requiring hard logic or mechanical divination, whether it was a sluggish carburetor in his Ford Fairlane or some gizmo in my mother's clunky Maytag washing machine. By some mysterious communion with such inanimate objects he was able to get them to cooperate. Despite my father's encouragements, blandishments and patient explanations—and finally to his disappointment— the world of machines and math was destined to remain a mystery to me.

"It came to pass one morning, when the sun was just beginning to break through the dark, that a great commotion echoed through the forest and the Indian village. The birds' usual sweet songs were now chaos of alarm, the chatter of chipmunks and squirrels became a chorus of panic, and there was a riot of splashing coming from the creek near the village, as if a whole tribe had taken to the water with canoes and were furiously paddling. Braves and warriors rushed from wigwams, bows and war clubs in hand, thinking that the village was being attacked by the enemy tribes, but what they beheld was a miracle. For what had been the lazy, easy flowing creek, when the last embers of the evening campfire had died and the tribe had retired, was now a great pond overflowing the gentle grassy banks. And it was churning with fish.

In amazement the Indians beheld a great dam of logs, sticks and brush that all but stopped the flow of the creek, forming a small shallow lake at their feet, while barrages of sharp whacking sounds, as if canoe paddles being slapped upon the water, echoed from upstream and the forest beyond. Even Chief Owl Moon Talker stood bewildered, but then a smile spread across his broad, wrinkled face. Deer Not There still couldn't make sense of the commotion. Then some young braves came running by him, beckoning him to come quick to the water that now foamed with the splashing dorsal fins and tails of panicked fish. A few of the braves were grasping fish in each hand and were returning to wigwams for baskets. And then as recognition began to set in among the villagers, the excitement increased. Women and children converged upon the creek banks to scoop up fish with their hands, baskets, paddles or anything they could find. The fish were so plentiful and so agitated that some jumped out onto the banks where they were scooped up by frantic children.

It didn't take long for the medicine man and chief Owl Moon Talker to know that Deer Not There's strange story of a talking beaver had, in fact, been a sign from the great Manitou. The beavers had not only thoroughly dammed the creek near the village, but had also, in great numbers, perhaps more than a thousand, beat the water with their tails for miles up the creek, at every eddy, every small back-water, where fish might be lingering, driving them, as in a cattle roundup, into a corral of water. The dam had been built in a wide arc rather than higher and narrower so that the dammed waters would remain shallow, making it easy to capture the panicked fish. At the right distance from the dam, Edgewise and Chipper felled a great pine across the creek which sunk with its thick needled branches into the water like a huge net preventing all but a few fish from swimming back up stream. The Indians rejoiced in this miraculous gift of food which would give them the strength to prevail over their enemies. That night the village had a great feast, roasting many trout, sunfish, bass, pickerel and catfish on freshly cut green sticks slanted over a huge fire in the center of the village. There was much dancing to drums, and the Medicine man made big medicine. The chief raised praise to the great spirit Manitou who had come to his son Deer Not There. The young Indian, for his kindness to the wounded Knobbler, was given the gift of food, and so his tribe was able to defeat their enemies in the west."

Jenny's eyes were drooping, but she struggled to keep them open. She snuggled closer, yawned.

"Aren't you tired, Daddy?"

"A little."

"I love you, Daddy."

"I love you, too."

"Daddy, what happened to the enemies?"

"The Medicine man, who was bitter in his hatred of the enemies, wanted to destroy them completely. By tradition the chief never opposed the advice of the Medicine man. But Deer Not There, seeing that his tribe was now stronger, saw no reason to make the enemy suffer anymore. His medicine, too, was great, and so he convinced the Medicine man and the chief to make a truce with the enemy tribes and allow them to retreat in peace. A truce was called, and all the warring chiefs met in a great pow wow. At Deer Not There's insistence the tribe would give half of its great bounty of fish to the starving, defeated enemy, if they would withdraw far to the west and never return. And so it came to pass that the defeated tribes left the lands of the Chippewa and moved away to the black hills and broad plains far to the west and took up new lives and new tribal names such as Cree, Mandan and Assiniboin.

It was decreed that Deer Not There, who one day would succeed his father as chief, would henceforth be considered a warrior and was allowed to wear the feather of the eagle. It was also decreed that the beavers forever would be holy and would be a brother to the Chippewa and would never again be hunted. This story has always been told among the Indians of the North, the story of the silver beavers, Old Knobbler, Edgewise and Chipper."

As I emerged from the trance of my story, I discovered that Jenny had fallen asleep. My wife looked in, smiling, as if to say, "job well done." I felt light from the telling, as though exhilarated by the imaginary crisp northern air of beaver country. Then smiling down on my sleeping daughter, I imagined my father's tender smile as he must have looked down on me. I imagined him lifting himself from my side, heavy with the weight of having stood on concrete machine shop floors all day, his mind numbed by the constant drone of the grinding, shaving, and drilling of steel. Then he would retire to bed with my mother and his Police Gazette magazine with its boxing news which he loved so much.

I then went directly to our den and the chest of drawers where I extracted my father's cigar box which I hadn't opened in several years. White Owl cigars had been the sponsor of the Friday night fights with sportscaster Mel Allen whose drawling accent always signaled my father's settling into the living room sofa with a cigar and a bottle of Pabst Blue Ribbon beer. I remembered sitting with Dad and my uncle Morrie the night Cuba's Kid Gavilan, despite his lightning speed and famed bolo punch, lost his bid for the middleweight title to Bobo Olson, and my Dad and uncle made jokes about the "keed" and how he had made a "beeg meestake."

The cigar box contained a few of my last letters to my father and some of his last letters to me, with their patent tone and phrasing that avoided issues. I had kept the letters with the intention of someday rereading them. There was an old photo of my father as a young man in satin boxer shorts in a fighting pose with six ounce gloves, another of him in Marine Corps uniform, a vote for Adlai Stevenson button, an AFL-CIO Union button with his imprinted name, a gold-plated golf tee, my old university cap-and-gown graduation picture, a leather-banded Timex watch, and finally a small wood and brass handled jackknife which I picked up and opened. The blade was made of good steel, was short but sturdy, like my father. The edge was not dull but could use a good sharpening. I thought I would buy a nice whetstone the next day and put a fine edge on the blade. The knife deserved some special care and, besides, maybe I would whittle or carve something sometime.

# Breaking Eighty

<hr>

The sweet morning air coming off the golf course begins to release my chest, coiled tight since Aunt Sally's call. She didn't want me to make the trip back East, as if that had occurred to me. Maybe I could say a prayer, she said. I struggled for things to say, asking about her boys, my cousins, about her arthritis, the weather. There had been so little communication over the years, mainly a few perfunctory words in yearly Christmas cards. I had always been such a nice boy, she said, and my uncle Morrie had always thought highly of me.

It was hard for me to imagine Morrie stretched out in a hospital bed, his face and body blanching and disappearing into death like an errant tee shot descending into the out-of-bounds of a dense wood. I kept seeing him on the tee when his lean, hard body used to wind up around his driver, unleashing his patent flat swing; kept seeing his big dark eyes from which he was forever brushing away a slick lock of Bryll-Creemed hair; saw that pinched-up mouth of his that seemed too small for his face, obstinate. He was one of those guys who could look pained even when he was happy.

Although I kept thinking of Morrie in a hospital bed with all those tubes and machines attached to him, I also kept thinking about myself, about the last time I had my cholesterol checked, whether or not I should take out more life insurance, execute a living will, spend more "quality time" with my grown son, take my wife out for a nice romantic dinner.

Shadows of my youth whisper to me through the morning mist of the fairways—my father, Uncle Frank, and the old slicer himself, Morrie. Golf was a way of life when I was growing up, dragging my bag around after those guys on our hometown municipal links. When we weren't out on the course, we'd be at the driving range or carpet putting for nickels in one or the other's living room. My mother and aunts Helen and Sally played out their parts happily, it seemed, hanging out together on those Saturdays or Sundays, sometimes both days, chatting, cooking and doing whatever it was they did when the men went out to play, with me, the "kid," tagging along.

Thinking about Morrie, my own life and the past began making me restless as a cat in a cage. My wife told me to distract myself.

"Go out and do something, you're making me nervous," she said.

I thought of my Scot Tourney clubs I had sold years ago when I came out to California. Of course, I could rent some clubs, if I were to play. But golfing might be just a little strange right now. *Fairway of dreams?* Too much passed out there on the fairways, another lifetime. Yet I couldn't deny there was a pull. I had shed my bag of clubs but not my memories. I remembered I had stored away an almost new pair of golf shoes I couldn't sell.

So here I am, crisp slacks and polo shirt for the occasion, reminded how easy it can be to pick up a round as a single, as there's always someone who doesn't muster for these early tee times. The starter has slotted me in with a threesome about twenty minutes after my leaving the clubhouse with a set of rented clubs, and a dozen new balls. On the tee we introduce around to each other, a couple of middle-aged guys like myself, and a third guy in his thirties, well-built and tanned. As the latecomer, I tee off last. I almost fall on my face in the process, despite having warmed up by hitting a couple buckets of balls on the practice range. They must think I'm a real duffer. My ball shaves the grass a hundred yards or so down the fairway and then dribbles out into the rough. I'm unfazed and breathe the sweet, grassy air.

The others have good tee shots, so when we get down the fairway, it's my turn to hit while they stand and watch. It looks like a good solid three iron to the green. It would have been as little as a five iron for me when I was eighteen. It then hits me that when Dad, Uncles Frank and Morrie and I were at the peak of those old feverish golf days, they were about the same age that I am now. The world has turned, but it stills take two shots to get on the green in regulation.

I whip out the five iron. The feel for the middle irons is lost the least because they have enough club loft to get the ball off the ground and into the air but still enough shaft length to allow a full, uncompromised swing. And a good swing, once grooved, stays with you like the memory of your first lay.

My threesome is now at the green and they are parking their electric carts near the fringe. They've probably been playing the course every weekend for years. Seeing them at the green, awaiting my approach, I am momentarily the "kid" again trailing in behind.

From where I lie, old Frank would have hit effortlessly. His ball would disappear up into the white haze of those early mornings and come out of nowhere like a meteor, thunk into the soft green and jump out of its impression with a powerful backspin. After such a shot he'd often make some quip like "straight as your pecker."

My five iron attempt lands about thirty yards from the green. A bunker, like a gaping mouth, separates me from the pin whose flag flies just above the bunker's crest. If I want to go for the pin, I have to just carry the bunker and stop the ball dead. Or I can roll up to the downside of the pin where I will have to come back across forty feet or so of fast green. This requires finesse, surgery like the kind Morrie often performed around the greens. He used to pucker his lips as though he was going to kiss the ball. He never had much of a long game, though. Just as Dad didn't have a middle game. Frank was off and on with his short game but generally had it *all* on most days.

I'm telling myself it doesn't matter what the hell happens, *just hit the goddamn ball.* I do, and it zings off the edge of the blade, instead of floating in the direction of the bunker. The ball thuds into the upper lip, miraculously flips up over the hump and dribbles onto the green. There is cheering from my threesome.

"You got lucky on that one," says Ernie, the sanguine fellow, who wears a cap with an Augusta, Georgia crest, the traditional Masters Open course.

I have rolled down the hump to within five feet of the pin. My putt is easy and flat, the kind Sam Snead became famous for missing in big tournaments. I should be able to do it with my eyes closed. So I do, sort of. A lucky par.

"Better thank Howard for that one," says the guy wearing lime green polyester pants that disappear under his beer belly.

"Howard?"

"You know, the great handicapper up there," he says, pointing to the sky.

My group can't possibly resent my par. It should be obvious I'm just a hacker. But they are all a little too smiley as I take the honors and tee up my ball for hole two. Like Uncle Frank used to do, I walk away from the ball and stand behind and sight up toward the green. It's a short, straight par four, but there's a big ditch about 180 yards out.

Remembering Frank's posture from when we used to go to Rook's driving range, I narrow my stance and think fluid. I lock my eyes on the ball and start the backswing.

When you hit a golf ball right, you know at impact. The feeling is so solid, it has the illusion of being soft. My ball takes off and climbs like a jet off a carrier.

"As straight as your dicks, eh boys," I say.

"Well, you're showing us the way," says Lime Pants.

Everyone clears the ditch and we all have an easy approach to the green. But I hit my second shot fat and come up short. Rattled, I get my nine iron halfway out of my bag for another attempt when I remember that both Dad and Morrie would have punched a middle iron and rolled up to the pin. So that is what I decide to do, first addressing the sky, *here goes nothing*. And nothing it is, my clubhead digging into the ground behind the ball, duffing it up to the fringe and leaving me thirty feet from the pin.

"Dick's not long enough," says Lime Green, the others chiming in with a chuckle. I chuckle, too, so as not to show my first disgust with the day's adventure. It serves me right for getting cocky. I'm only out here to get some air and get loose, after all. But in the squeak and chatter of birds from a stand of eucalyptus trees dividing the green from the next tee, I imagine I hear the sound of Uncle Frank sucking his teeth, as though he could never quite get rid of the debris of the golf course hot dogs that were his favorite food.

I can't see the cup and have to have Ernie hold the pin for my approach. This was where Dad excelled, as he did in billiards. *Hawkeye,* Frank used to call him. When he got on the green, he often made up for lost strokes with his special old-time wood-shafted putter. He used to say you just had to believe the ball was going in the cup, that downing a putt was ninety-percent image. Lock your head down and stroke through smoothly.

My ball starts off slowly but picks up the break in the green and accelerates toward the cup. The ball clinks against the bottom of the aluminum cup for another freak par.

We are heading over to the third tee. Ernie wants conversation. He compliments me on my par. He wants to know what I do and where I'm from, the usual. He's an insurance man with Allstate. I don't feel particularly social. But I tell him I haven't really played in ages, as though to provide an excuse for the disaster I feel will befall my game at any time. He responds that he hasn't been out in ages either, not since last week.

Feeling the spring in the well-maintained turf, the sweetness of the freshly cut fairway, the jangle of clubs, the fluke of being par after the first two holes, I whimsically imagine Morrie is with me, walking to the next tee. *Nice par, kid,* he is saying. Nearby Frank sucks his teeth, his usual uncommitting response. Dad beams, as though to say *that's my boy.* I think we all felt close to each other out there on the golf course, but that didn't alter the fact that every man comes to know some measure of his essential aloneness out on the course. Fluffed shots have a way of insinuating the shortcomings in one's life. *Hell, it's just a game,* Dad would say. But I could catch the stream of expletives from under his breath. After Morrie had a bad hole, his expression just deepened into a frozen wince. But Frank would just suck his teeth after a bad shot. A particularly emotional teenager, I often cussed like a sailor, sometimes threw clubs, even stomped off the course in a huff a few times. The men would shake their heads, and Dad would say something like *who the hell does he think he is, Arnold Palmer?*

The next seven holes go pretty much the same. I am in and out of trouble, saving pars with putts, topping shots that roll up on the green, hitting trees but bouncing into play. It is all incredibly lucky, even though I am hitting progressively better shots in between.

The ninth hole snack shack is backed up with patrons grabbing a bite and a sit-down before the long back nine. Behind the counter a large woman buzzsaws through the orders, grabbing hot dogs from the glass-encased hot dog rotisserie and slapping them into buns, while flipping sizzling burgers on the grill and tapping paper cups full of beer and Pepsi.

"What'll it be boys?" the big woman says, without even looking up.

I order a couple of hot dogs and line them with chopped onions and ketchup. For a moment I ponder how much these things will raise my cholesterol. A steady diet of this kind of stuff is what contributed to Frank's premature death. I suppose he never thought about food. He only needed fuel like a race car at a pit stop, the faster the better. When it wasn't hot dogs, it was chocolate bars that he kept in plentiful supply in his golf bag. Bad diet probably has a lot to do with why Morrie was in the hospital now. I offer my remaining hot dog to Ernie, who gladly accepts.

THE BORDER

"You look like you're hitting your pace," pipes the Tanned One to Lime Pants, who smiles at this recognition of his play over the last two holes.

"Yeah, yeah, you get lucky now and then," Lime Pants replies, trying to be modest.

The big woman behind the snack counter checks her order tickets clipped to a little wheel above her head.

"Hamburger well-done, whole wheat bun, black coffee." The Tanned One steps forward, pale winter skin flashing from inside the collar of his polo shirt. I figure he probably works on construction, though I don't ask.

"Hey, big hitter here is carding only three over for the front nine," Allstate says, drawing attention to me.

"He's on the money. Glad it's not mine," the Tanned One says.

"Hey, that's an idea. How about playing skins on the back nine?" says Lime Pants, who I can see is becoming expansive with the tall Budweiser he has knocked back.

"What the hell, why not? A buck a hole?" Allstate says, looking at me. I look to the Tanned One who hesitates and shrugs.

"Let's make it interesting, two bucks," I blurt. Lime Pants has nothing on me, I think. The way everyone is playing almost head to head, the back nine will probably be a wash anyway.

Lime Pants shoots back agreement like a challenge. Allstate looks to the Tanned One who again hesitates and then says: "You guys are tough, but what the hell, why not. I'm no one to be a party pooper."

The tenth through the twelfth are a wash, as expected, with no skins to anyone. The Tanned One pars them all, but one of us manages a par on each of the holes to tie him.

Ernie and Lime Pants fall off the pace in the following holes while the Tanned One and I, though turning in bogies on the fourteenth, push ahead like a couple of pros, putting away regulation pars and one bird each. I can't believe my incredible luck.

We're taking our time with our shots now, surveying every lie as though we were engineers, Lime Pants and Ernie deferring with that respect any seasoned golfer has for a good round when he sees one developing. They are oohing, aahing and clapping for our shots. I start worrying about choking around the fifteenth hole, but I begin sucking my teeth and it seems to help.

Sixteen is a long par four. The Tanned One hits a big drive and then drills a three iron straight for the pin. I go for the five wood with which I have now resumed a certain degree of my old intimacy and finesse, if not quite the old distance. I sweet swing it, down and through, sending it high and right but drawing into the green.

"How long did you say it's been since you played?" asks Ernie, who still needs a wedge to get on in three.

"So long I'd thought I'd forgotten."

I don't think any of the old gang had actually taught me to swing. I just picked it up like a gypsy kid does the violin. I was around golf all the time. Some families have grease monkeys, some have weekend carpenters, some football fanatics, but ours had the addiction of the "white pill," as Morrie used to call it. One of Morrie's prizes was a framed scorecard, witnessed and signed by us all, from when he had legitimately broken eighty, every weekend golfer's Everest, at Willowhurst, an upstate PGA rated course where we all once went for a weekend. Next to the card in its frame was a black and white snapshot of us all at the eighteenth hole, a triumphant Morrie in the middle, holding his card and giving the victory sign. I don't think he ever played a game like that one again.

The Tanned One pars sixteen, but I three-putt and take a bogie. I feel the old anger creeping into my chest, but I suck my teeth, look to the sky and repeat several times like a mantra, *it's only a game.* Lime Pants saves the day with a lucky wedge approach that hits the pin and drops a couple feet away, which he easily taps in to tie the Tanned One.

Seventeen is a short 140-yard par three. We all get on in one and two putt for pars all around. So the skins carry over, building up a pot of near $50 as we start into the homestretch toward the clubhouse. I am still holding, still looking at a 79 for the round. I am playing some magnificent golf, calling the shots, as they say.

We arrive at the eighteenth, a long par five where a big drive is needed, but going for the big ball usually means less control. Ernie and Lime Pants get off the tee nicely, staying clear of the water on the right down about 230 yards. The Tanned One seems very relaxed as he goes to the tee. He hasn't said much all day. Just ambles along. Then he hits, his body and legs corkscrewing through after impact. The ball starts right toward the water, rising like stages of a rocket, and just as I want to say "too bad," his ball draws left with top spin, descending in line with the pin some 275 yards out.

"Christ!" Lime Green gasps.

Allstate runs his tongue around his lips. The Tanned One picks up his tee and walks back to his bag ever so nonchalantly and says to Lime Pants: "As you said, we all get lucky sometimes." I wonder. Not only has his game improved since the ninth, but his swing is smoother.

Russ Desaulnier

I don't let his drive tempt me and I swing easy, knocking one down the left fairway, but leaving a good poke with a fairway wood and a wedge to the green. No one gets the water.

Again I reach for the security of the five wood. Dad, an old baseball player at heart, used to love the 3 iron with a three-quarter swing, punching low, neat sizzlers a consistent 180 yards. Morrie, on the other hand, could never hit long irons, usually slicing off to the right. But the 5 wood was his special fairway weapon. Frank, always the sweet swinger, made playing fairway woods look like a casual game of croquet.

I let the clubhead do the work, keeping my jaw slack so as not to power the shot. I just want to make sure I get on in three so I have a chance to go down in two for a par. The green is a big, mildly concave parabola tilted toward us with kidney-shaped sand traps at each side and one in back, easy to hit to, but hard to putt. We all get up within wedge distance and then wait for the Tanned One to hit his second. The green must be a good 225 yards away. The Tanned One stands looking at the green with his hands on his hips and his back to us.

He throws a wisp of grass in the air to test the breeze, goes to his bag and whips out a long iron, maybe a two or three, takes one practice swing and then steps up and hits his ball with barely any hesitation, as if he'd made the same shot a thousand times before.

Allstate just looks at me over his wire rim glasses, as if to say, "what's this?" Lime Pants, trying his best to be a good sport, says: "Nothing like saving the best for last."

I hate using the wedge. At this point in the game I don't trust my nerves enough to try the surgical control required for a short lob, so I go for my trusty five iron, and with a choked grip I punch up. The ball doesn't have quite enough steam and stops at the apron of the green.

Lime Pants sprays his shot into one of the kidney-shaped traps and Allstate, insurance man that he is, follows me with a low punch, only he comes up even shorter than I do.

The Tanned One is on the frog hair in two strokes and in a position to putt for a birdie. I watch Allstate try to negotiate his shot off the apron. It's tricky dichondra, the kind that feels like cushy carpeting. A ball tends to sit up on this kind of grass, and to avoid jamming the clubhead into this spongy stuff you have to pick the ball off clean and hope you judge your clubhead speed correctly. Allstate overhits and goes to the back of the green from where he'll have a tough downhill return to the pin.

Chip shots like the one I'm faced with were always my nemesis. When the pressure is on, it is easy to choke or peek too soon. As Morrie always used to say: *if you look up, you won't like what you see.* I remember how Morrie was so intent on following his own advice that he used to push his face to the right in an exaggerated manner so that his chin was almost touching his right shoulder, as if someone were pulling him by the ear. His head bent down and lips pulled right, looking like a spastic, he'd commence his swing.

After measuring off the distance to the pin, I mimic Morrie as I swing. The ball hits down from its flat arc and scoots right, passing the pin, but then runs out of steam, curling back behind the pin some ten feet away. A modest little cheer rises from Allstate and Lime Green who are surely thinking about the money they will shell out if the Tanned One isn't matched. The Tanned One has a long putt off the frog hair, maybe forty feet. He putts, but is short by about six feet. Our balls, which we replace with markers, are approximately opposite each other, north and south. Lime Pants is on now, but it cost him two extra strokes to get out of the trap. Allstate, in returning from the back of the green, has overshot the cup. If the Tanned One sinks his six-footer for a bird, we all sink with it.

It's around noon, the air still, with barely any movement in the nearby oaks. Both Allstate and Lime Pants have holed out, clearing the way for the final and deciding putts. Lime Pants stands poised with his cigarette smoke angling off in a white stream. Allstate winks at me in encouragement. The Tanned One taps his ball and it struggles up the grade to stop two inches short of the cup. He shows no emotion and just taps his ball in for a par. He presses me with a thin, perceptibly wicked smile before he turns and joins the others out of view at the edge of the green. I have to urinate, and my heart is working faster than I'd like, and my palms are feeling sweaty. My putt is with the grain of the grass, therefore faster, particularly since I'm going downhill. Using my putter for a plumb line, I measure a two-inch break to the left. It's a bitch. If I can sink this one, I'll par and all bets will be off, and I will break 80 for the first time in my life.

I am circling my ball, delaying and trying to relax rather than studying my putt. Allstate and Lime Pants shift about nervously. The Tanned One leans, unmoving, on his putter, cool.

The longest moment in any game is that time it takes for a critical putt to roll toward the cup. In any big tourney that's when the gallery sounds off the most tension in sighs and applause. As I set myself, weight slightly on my left foot, elbows out and clearing the body, I try to empty my mind of everything except the pendular motion of the putter head. And then contact, closing circuit with the cup, a thrill, a chilling sense that my life spreads out before me in a few strides of green. In a convulsion of stored tension, I hurl my putter off toward the trees banking the green, as my ball gathers speed, catches the break, then slows, hesitates at the lip, then falls. I slump into a kneel, looking for faces in the clouds. There is applause, except from the Tanned One, who shakes his head.

"By God, you carded a 79, old man," Allstate says. "Speak for yourself," I say. "Old man, nothing."

I am now thinking about the old man in the cardiac ward back East. Allstate and Lime Pants say they'll buy me a beer and they start for the clubhouse. The Tanned One just nods at me with that same thin smile, only it speaks of a good-natured resignation to the gods of golf. "Thanks for the game," he says and turns toward the first tee where a long line of afternoon golfers are waiting to get off.

I go to the payphone at the entrance to the clubhouse and call my wife for Sally and Morrie's number. I want to get a call through now, from here, while this feeling is with me. *Seventy-nine!* Maybe I can talk to him. Maybe if I tell him he was my inspiration on the course, it'll ignite a spark of life in him. I'll get his hospital number from Sally. Sure, heart attack patients often pull through—some oxygen, some jolts of adrenaline, or whatever it is they do. Haven't I seen it a hundred times on TV dramas?

My wife gives me the number and I tell her not to bother cooking tonight because I'll take her out for dinner. I ask her to track down our son at one of the numbers we have for him and invite him to join us. With a girlfriend if he likes. Wine, all the trimmings, on me. She is delighted, but asks me what I've been smoking. I tell her not to be funny and that I'll explain later.

Then I get through to Sally's where a male voice answers. "She's not here. Who's this?"

"It's cousin Joey. Who's this, Brenty?"

"Morrie Jr."

"No kidding, I didn't recognize your voice."

"He's gone, Joey. He didn't make it through the night. Mom is at the mortuary with Brent making arrangements... she was going..." he chokes.

I quietly say I'll call later and gently hang up the phone. Dazed, I walk to the pro shop to turn in my rented clubs. I show the surprised clerk the irreparably bent putter which had landed wrong when I threw it, and I mindlessly slap down a twenty. It's just a K-Mart cheapy, he says and gives me back five dollars. He is one of those big ruddy types, like a younger, beefier Nicklaus, who probably plays almost every day and shoots in the high seventies on his bad days. Figuring I might be in the market for a new set of clubs, he says they've got the new models in and I should look around. The smell of fresh leather and something like shoe polish fills the shop. Across one wall is an array of new sets of gleaming irons. Woods are in vertical boxes, their shiny black and mahogany-colored heads like skinny, long-necked birds.

How Morrie and the old boys lived for the weekends and the course clubhouse, the pleasure I could tell they took in their bantering familiarity with the staff, and their methodical survey of the latest golf wares, like kids in a toy store; their extravagance in treating themselves to packages of new Titleist balls, never thinking for a moment they'd lose them in a pond or in the woods before the day was over; their filling out their names on the score card as if signing a prayer; their trading complaints and hopes about golf swings and putting grips and establishing excuses before the inevitable hacking and duffing commenced. And this went on for years, past their retirements when the game seemed to be all they had left, although the relish I remember them having when I was a boy had long gone. The game became something to fill time like their poring over the morning paper at breakfast and their dallying with the daily crossword.

As I walk toward the exit to the restaurant and bar, I hesitate to admire a set of trim ebony-colored woods with brass inlays. The set includes a sleek 5 wood with a head the size of a pistol grip. I caress its glassy surface, remembering how this had been Morrie's favorite club. The clerk is studying me, expectant, with *sale* written across his smile.

"Naaah!" I say, shaking my head for emphasis, and I turn toward the bar where I'll have a drink to Morrie.

# I Like Rambo

This is getting to be too much, Ingersol thinks. He'd seen it all in Nam, but that was a war. He never wants to know anything like that again. But increasing incidents of violence reported in the paper could no longer be called isolated. They have begun to gather and form an impression that stalks him like an unseen but palpable beast.

"Shootings, muggings, rapes, Jeez!" he says, looking up from the *Courier* at his wife of twenty years who now seems fragile in her sleeveless night gown.

"You be careful going into town and keep your car doors locked."

He watches her putting slices of bread in the toaster, with the same balletic grace that marks most of her movements. The thought of that grace crippled or extinguished makes him toss the paper across the kitchen table.

"I always figured this stuff would never reach us. This has always been a quiet town."

"Well, we're not exactly having a crime wave, Harry."

Marilyn always tries to quiet him when he gets too worked up about something. But he is better now, calmer, after years of marriage, far from the kid who was in Nam, as distant as that country itself. Never again does he want his heart to beat like that... so fast and heavy, it seemed the Viet Cong patrol might hear him as he lay with McNeil in the brush, both frozen, each questioning the other with startled eyes, until the voices petered away down the trail, denying him and McNeil the chance to perform any heroics. Not long after, following the direction of the VC patrol, they witnessed their mortared corpses, delicate hairless bodies, almost feminine, torn and oozing. After the CO had designated a cleanup detail and left, Harley Bates, G company's most frequent volunteer for point-man, took a few ears for his collection.

It is a morning of shifting rain clouds, and intermittent shafts of light bounce off the pastels of their kitchen. The oak cabinets he and his wife chose together still glisten as they did the day he installed them. The calico curtains, with their lace edges appointed by his wife, are insignia of a gentle order that he'd not stopped to question these past years. His daughter, too, now in middle school, was on these workaday mornings a reassurance that the world is essentially good, that perhaps there is a force for good, even a God.

Lily, still in her nightie and engrossed in her latest hand computer game, barely greets him as she feels her way to the breakfast table.

"Are you winning?" he asks.

He gets no response and looks to his wife, who is pouring a glass of juice from a half-gallon carton of Minute Maid. She shrugs, also bewildered by the little plastic boxes with screens and buttons that their daughter carries around these days like an unrelenting itch.

"Third level," is the delayed reply.

"Is that good?"

"Awesome, I got fourth level!" Lily exclaims, reminding Ingersol how things a short twenty-five years ago were *far out*, how he and his comrades could exhale those words huddled around a joint of *Blue Expando,* as if the dying were somewhere else.

"Look, our daughter is awe-struck," he says.

"She'll also be late for school if she doesn't get her little butt in gear."

"I gotta get going too," Ingersol says, his mind shifting to the stack of unprocessed insurance policies and claims sitting on his desk where he keeps a photo of Marilyn and Lily to remind himself during the day of what is, after all, really important.

"Don't get hung up late at the office, Harry. We have an early dinner appointment, remember?"

Ingersol hasn't forgotten. He can't avoid the fact of his in-laws, his wife's sister and her husband. For her sake he abides them, the small talk, the fat laden dinners that make his arteries tingle in rebellion, their insistent references to God, as if oblique sermons to him, the faithless. But they are warm people, kind in their way, as his wife reminds him with her assertions that their daughter ought to have an extended family. What would Lily do if something happened to them?

"Didn't Norman come over and help you with the wiring of the garage?"

"I was willing to get an electrician."

"That's not the point. And what about how good he's been with Lily?"

"I know, you never let me forget. I can almost predict when a visit is on the horizon. I start hearing about Norman this and Alice that."

In between visits, Marilyn usually manages to bring him around to the next one. If he can just smile and nod through this visit and not drop himself into something, not let the visit drag out. Maybe tonight he'll excuse himself for having had a long day. His in-laws put a lot of store in an *honest day's work,* as though an eleventh command-ment, and so they can't very well fault him for begging off on that account.

The one-way traffic of Eleventh Street is heavy and slow, cars ahead a blur of liquid red tail-lights through his wind shield awash with rain, like the monsoon kind he'd learned to accept without shelter out on search and destroy patrols that year in the Bien Hoa sector. Even when a hamlet was nearby, they were ordered to do without. There was too much risk getting comfortable inside huts where they might be easy targets. It had gotten so you didn't know who the enemy was or where he was—could even be a teenage girl with an AK 47 hidden under a pile of grass, a grenade in a heap of mangoes. Your back was the front.

In penance, Ingersol now refuses to scratch an itch beneath his chin where mosquitoes once sucked unhin-dered while he and McNeil lay riveted. The twing twang of VC voices along that trail now merge into the slosh of cars four lanes wide, and his windshield wipers thump like incoming Hueys bringing replacements, which then, when the tide was turning, even Harley Bates was glad for, grin-ning through teeth rotted by too much Coca Cola.

Ingersol' s office is in the center of town, adjacent to the new multilevel parking lot and Main Street, which is under redevelopment. There have always been a few vagrants, especially in the summer, but never any problems. These people certainly never have guns; they are just looking for a peaceful handout, which he is not averse to giving if he happens to have some loose change. Although he is not superstitious, he feels that not giving a bit now and then

Russ Desaulnier

would be tempting fate, which saw him through Nam and has given him a good life since.

After coming back, Ingersol had gone into the Prudential Insurance training program and stayed with it, worked hard. That had been an effect of the war. After coming home from the war, security of any kind had seemed a good thing to have and hard work and a moderate amount of boredom were a small price to pay. Then finding Marilyn one day waiting tables at the Galaxy Cafe had caused him to linger after the lunch trade, ordering coffee refills he didn't need. In the young waitress's eyes, he saw the light of his father's anthem that a man had to build something for himself.

Will people start needing insurance against random homicide? A statistic Ingersol read at breakfast asserted that murder was the leading cause of on-the-job death among female office workers. How can that be? But then he doesn't provide the calculations that set the premium rates on the policies he writes. Some things made sense, like higher driver liability premiums for young males. How can you insure someone like a Harley Bates cruising roadside topless bars on Friday nights, wheeling an old eight cylinder, while drunk on rum and coke?

Now that he has finished reviewing the stack of claims and new policies on his desk, he is contemplating where he might take a leisurely lunch. He is interrupted by the office secretary calling through that there is an angry client in the lobby, demanding to see someone. A moment later the man is in his office.

"What is this?!" he blusters, slapping a paper onto Ingersol's desk.

The abruptness with which the man has swung into the office startles Ingersol.

"Relax and have a seat, Mr... ?"

"Bergstrom."

The man is not so big, but he has a chiseled face with deep-set small eyes and a compact body that suggests what he lacks in size he makes up for in ferocity.

"How can I help you, Mr. Bergstrom?"

"Call the damn mortgage company and do something."

"Excuse me, Mr. Bergstrom, I think I'm missing something."

"You don't miss a chance to screw people over."

"I beg your pardon."

Ingersol senses his throat tightening, his breath shortening. The man seated across from him looks coiled to spring like some forest predator.

"Because I'm late with my fire insurance, my mortgage holder slaps me with a foreclosure which is going to cost me fifteen hundred hard earned bucks to lift."

Ingersol punches the policy numbers from the foreclosure paper into his desk computer. It shows Bergstrom's name, the property address and policy profile, and that its current status is delinquent.

"Legally you are not covered should a fire occur, Mr. Bergstrom. I suspect that when your lien holder received notice of the premium delinquency they filed a foreclosure under the terms of the trust deed."

"Why didn't you people let me know about this?"

"We did, Mr. Bergstrom. We always send out reminders thirty days before a policy is coming up for renewal and the annual payment."

"I didn't get nothing."

"I can assure you it was sent out. In any case, Mr. Bergstrom, we can't take any responsibility. We allow a fifteen-

Russ Desaulnier

day grace period. But we have no control over lien hold-
ers once a policy falls delinquent." Ingersol, mustering a
business-like but benign demeanor, says he's truly sorry
and pushes the foreclosure paper across the table toward
the man. Ingersol resists telling the man he should have
read the terms of his trust deed and note. No use rubbing
it in. But the rules are the rules; negligence carries penalties.
The company sergeant had always harped about reading
for booby traps, which had accounted for nearly a dozen
of their casualties along the Bien Hoa trails.

There is nothing left to say. The man stands up, a vessel
of barely corked rage. In response, Ingersol shoots to his
feet, planting himself in readiness.

"Bullshit, bullshit," the man sneers, grasping at the
foreclosure paper. As he swings away, the arc of his hand
holding the crumpled document grazes and knocks over
Ingersol's desk portrait of Marilyn and Lily, but the man,
blinded and numbed by his anger, barrels on toward the
door, unaware of the picture and the insurance agent who
is left trembling like a man caught in a sudden winter rain.

Ingersol tries to concentrate on work that afternoon,
but the tightness in his stomach keeps distracting him. He
paces, he makes excuses to chat with the secretary, he finds
himself chatting over the phone with clients about irrel-
evancies, segueing into new topics when business is done,
as if a friendly voice could allay his sense of impending
siege beyond the office door.

At home and still distracted, Ingersol shaves and changes
his clothes with none of the agitation that usually accom-
panies these preparations for an evening with his in-laws.

"You all right?" Marilyn says, looking at him in the
dresser mirror.

"Fine, fine, yes, fine."

He shouldn't fault Norm and Alice just because they are simple people. They've never been anywhere, done much of anything, seen the world, as he has. They have, after all, raised good kids who stay out of trouble. Norm doesn't even smoke or drink, save a beer or two when watching a Sunday football game.

When Ingersol enters his in-laws' sprawling, shake-roofed house that night, the pungent smell of roast lamb arrests his appetite. It's not that he dislikes lamb, although he reserves his consumption of meat for special occasions. Events of the day have begun opening channels to deeply-stored impressions, the lamb now retrieving something he'd learned during the Tet offensive: the sickly smell of dead, ripe human flesh. Ingersol accepts the can of beer his brother-in-law offers and allows himself to be led into the living room. His wife and daughter disappear into the kitchen with Alice.

"Where the boys?" Ingersol says absently. He has never felt very comfortable initiating conversations with Norm, but he can always be safe talking shop, sports or Norm's sons. Ingersol hates talking shop outside the office and he barely knows anything about current sports news. Norm builds speculation houses and limited partnership developments and likes to talk investments and money.

"Nick's out on a date. You know how it is, you can't keep 'em home. Billy's down in the family room watching video ... say, how about that city referendum planned for the spring ... how you going to vote, Harry?" Norm winks and chuckles, as though Ingersol's response is a foregone conclusion.

"I don't know, yet, Norm."

"You're kidding."

"No, I'm not. So a property tax cut makes us a little money in the short term, but what's it going to do to this town in the long run?"

"Why, attract more business, more people, bring growth," He chuckles momentarily and then is suddenly straight faced.

"I don't know if I want more growth. Our schools are going to suffer."

"Hell, let 'em tighten their belts and get back to basics. That's what kids need, rather than all the nonsense."

"Then you don't mind cutting the football programs?"

"I didn't mean sports."

Ingersol shrugs. There's no use pursuing the discussion. He thinks of the fresh young faces of his brother-in-law's boys, faces like those of his old buddies, polished and grinning, heading for some R&R in Saigon. Some never got to see the next two decades. McNeil had his first piece in Saigon and was still talking about it when he stepped on a mine a week later. Cuevas, Morris, Jordan, Lindell, now just hard-to-find names etched on a big chunk of black granite in Washington. Harley became a statistic in his own way, getting ever more spooky toward the end of his tour before disappearing into the hinterlands of Kansas from where he had come. He probably peddled his decorations not long after for booze or drugs. He was smart enough to survive but not smart enough to flourish.

"Excuse me a bit, Norm, I'll go see what young Billy's up to if you don't mind."

Beer in hand, Ingersol pads across the heavily piled carpet of the living room, noting the furniture store-bought print of a Venetian scene, a cliche that nevertheless reminds him of how much there is to see in the world. As he comes down the carpeted stairs, he is met by the sound of heavy ordnance and men shouting. Once inside the darkened family room, he sees Billy glued to the TV, totally unaware he has entered the room. Sylvester Stallone, like a Super Bowl halfback, is dodging 50-millimeter machine gun fire from a low-flying helicopter. As the chopper passes, he snatches up a large caliber machine gun from a foxhole and returns fire, sending the aircraft spiraling to the ground where it explodes into a tremendous fireball.

"Hi Billy."

"Hi, Uncle Harry," Billy says barely breaking from his viewing. The smell of the cooked lamb seeps into Ingersol's brain. He waits in the dark for his nephew to give him some attention. Rambo kills. And kills. Ingersol flips on the main overhead light. Billy looks around, blinking and pausing Rambo's rampage with the remote control.

"What's wrong, Uncle Harry?"

"How's school, Billy?"

"It's okay."

"Isn't there something else to watch besides this stuff?"

"Rambo's great!"

"Rambo's crap!" Ingersol shoots back, his tone startling the twelve-year old boy.

"I like Rambo!" Norm's voice booms from behind Ingersol. Norm is standing at the top of the short flight of stairs, his bulk exaggerated by the angle, his face icy. Both Norm and Billy are motionless, waiting.

"Yes, well... right. Is dinner ready?"

"Yeah," Norm says, still cold. Alice says she wants everyone to see her cheese souffle before it falls."

At the table Norm is all business, first intoning a solemn grace, thanking the Lord for his bounty and for bringing loved ones together, then carving the leg of lamb so that thin flaps of pink roasted flesh fall away from the bone. Still repelled by the lamb, Ingersol takes a generous helping of the cheese souffle and a mound of peas to allay possible protests from Alice. After he takes a mouthful of the spongy cheese mixture, he comments how wonderful it is, evoking smiles first from Alice and then from his wife. He considers the possibility of walking into town in the morning to work off the calories, but then he wonders if that would be prudent, considering the early hour and his being in a suit with a briefcase.

There is little talk through dinner, except comments about the food. But Alice can't stand to see her dinner quickly disappear in silence.

"You know, the Harringates across the road are getting divorced. They're going to sell the house. We've been friends for more than twenty years. People leaving the block, kids growing up and leaving... " Alice sighed.

"What's happened to people's patience?" Marilyn says, cutting her lamb into dainty pieces.

"And loyalty!" Norman blurts. He recklessly chews meat bulging his cheek.

*Loyalty?* Ingersol knows the comment is meant for him and he wonders what gyrations of Norm's mind have reduced their bit of tension to a question of loyalty. He then wishes Norm's enthusiastic chomping would accidentally catch the inside of his mouth. For himself, he decides it best to keep his mouth shut.

Alice doesn't waste any time bringing out the apple pie a la mode, as if dessert will sweeten the atmosphere. Ingersol accepts a sliver, but without the ice cream. The kids wolf down their pie and then excuse themselves to go downstairs and play a computer game on the TV. The adults retire to the living room where Alice serves up coffee.

Ingersol will sit back and listen. Norman isn't making any leads either. So the women will have to carry the evening, Ingersol thinks. It's in their nature to do so without acknowledging the fact that a DMZ has been drawn between the two men, at least for this visit.

Norman has taken the easy chair nearest the living room TV, across the room from Ingersol, who contemplates his coffee. Norman flips on the TV and gets the news. He channel-surfs for a moment, stopping again at the news, which is giving an update on the tension building in Los Angeles over the trial of three black men who brutally beat up a truck driver during the LA riots.

"Niggers," Norman whispers, just loud enough to be heard.

Bridled by this bait, Ingersol rises and leaves the room for the toilet. In the hall, the years are framed in photos ranging from old black & whites to newly made Sears color specials. Every extension of Norm and Alice's family is represented. There is one of Ingersol and Marilyn on their wedding day outside the church, Norman and Alice, then much slimmer, among the wedding party. Things change, but most people do their best to ignore the fact. Even him.

It had, in fact, been a hard day at the office Ingersol tells his brother-in-law, recalling the wiry little man with the ferret face. An early night would be best. With their departure, good feelings and the habit of familial nostalgia is reconstituted, as though the impasse of minds was merely a small bump in the road. Norman, Alice and Billy stand together in the driveway waving as Ingersol backs out into the street.

On the way back, Marilyn says she needs milk and wants him to stop at a convenience store. Ingersol drives past a Seven Eleven on a part of 13th Street he doesn't like. At the next convenience store he tells Marilyn to stay in the car, setting the car doors on auto-lock before he gets out. It takes longer than he'd like to find the low fat. A few customers move about the store as though not sure what they've come for. At the magazine rack a middle-aged man thumbing through a *Playboy* glances at him. At the register a swarthy man, probably from a Middle-Eastern country, gives Ingersol change for a five; he stuffs it into his trouser pocket and heads quickly toward the door where the eye of a video camera films his exit.

"Hey, brother, can you spare a little change?"

A smell akin to Campbell's chicken noodle soup assails Ingersol. The man accosting him has ratty matted hair and heavily soiled clothing. His gleaming sapphire eyes in the grimy setting of his face look vaguely familiar. Ingersol drops a crumpled dollar bill, maybe two, into the man's hand and starts for the car, but he is stopped by a hand on his arm.

"Thanks, brother. Take care."

A smile across the unwashed face reveals teeth like Harley's used to be, crooked, yellowed and rotting.

Ingersol hurries to his car, the chicken soup still in his nostrils. His wife asks what the man has said. Just thanking him for the spare change, he tells her. But the man's eyes, crazed like the eyes of corralled mustangs Ingersol had once seen on a television show, linger through the shadows of the dimly lit suburban streets as they drive home. Ingersol tells his wife he will stay up for a while. Alice's coffee must have gotten to him, he says, and he has been stimulated by the evening air. Lily needs no encouragement to go to bed after a day of school and an evening out. His wife tells him not to stay up too late, kisses him and starts upstairs. He goes to the kitchen, double checks the back door and windows, makes a large mug of tea, takes it with him into the garage and sets it on the workbench. He takes the padlock off a high storage cabinet and slides out the tooled leather case that contains his father's old bird gun, a long double-barreled Holland & Holland 12-gauge shotgun: an heirloom and a gentleman's gun. For years he's said he was going to get rid of it when the next gun show and sale came to town. But then it would get forgotten like so many other things stuffed in the garage, until tonight. Shooting was a sport he had never been tempted to take up when younger, despite his father's enthusiasm. A little hiking, if anything, in the great outdoors was more to his taste. For one thing, he couldn't stand the still warm, slack-necked birds, the life and flight blown out of them. Guns, like power saws, have always given him a chill, have always made him feel uncertain about handling them. It is illogical, but to this day he feels more comfortable using a good handsaw, despite the extra work it requires. When his tour in Vietnam came to an end and he relinquished his M-16, he had hoped he'd never have to handle a gun again. After returning from a shoot, his father used to ritually clean, oil and polish the shotgun, contemplating it with admiration. Though neglected in recent years since his father's death, the barrels still shine and the fine waves of grain in the stock carved with a pair of flying mallards have become richer with time. The barrels fall smoothly away from the stock when released and snap back together easily and solidly, like the doors of an expensive European sports car. Ingersol wraps the barrels with some cloth for padding and secures them in the workbench vise. He ponders where to mark the cut, what length of the barrels would make a good compromise between the range and spread of the shot. As he reaches for the hacksaw, he remembers that the brass in Vietnam had dubbed sweeping firepower H & I, harassment and inter-diction, a comprehensive response that shredded jungle and ripped up paddies and water palms, everything and anything where an unseen enemy might be hidden. *Surefire.*

# Auto Biography

-------------------

W hen weekends roll around, there is no rest for those of us who have acquired the American dream, the house and all that goes with it. You can find us fixing, improving, replacing, or washing, as in the case of the family car in the driveway, the main accoutrement. I don't complain. I just do it, a habit and a duty, like my wife's clearing away the dishes from the dinner table, which I can see her doing through the kitchen window.

I gave up a long time ago trying to get one of our kids to do anything. They are not quite old enough to do certain chores with enough precision to satisfy minimum adult requirements, and no amount of money or promises of treats produce a better job. The flower bed will still have weeds, the car, supposedly washed, will still show wide swatches of unscrubbed grime. I would rather have the kids off playing with their neighborhood friends.

We'd take the car to the local wash, but like so many other things these days who can afford it on a regular basis? My wife Muriel likes our green Subaru spiffy and gleaming for Mondays, because that's when she goes on caravan with her real estate people, touring the latest homes to come on the market. Her newly found part-time career is a fair compromise with the necessity for us to bring in more money (another problem with the American dream is the cost of maintaining it once you get it). She can keep her own hours yet be there for the kids. She really doesn't put in a lot of hours and she gets an extended social life in the bargain, as there are many middle-aged married women occupying the ranks of our local real estate sales force. She closes the occasional deal, using the commissions for the extras we might not otherwise have. The arrangement also gives her an added sense of achievement and importance, so I am very glad to wash the car for her.

I guess I enjoy standing out here in my driveway at dusk, lazily but carefully sponging down the car, rinsing with the hose, surveying my little kingdom, sharing my elevated mood in exchanged greetings with passersby, locals walking their dogs and those just out for an evening stroll. When a man stands outside his house in a reflective state, as I am now, he can view his whole life before him, a summation, a culmination, and probably his final resting place. No wonder we're constantly tinkering, guys like me, making sure all the parts and surfaces of our edifices are neatly painted and polished. Ironically, there was a time when I would have abhorred the idea of washing down a station wagon in front of a suburban home.

I bought the Subaru wagon in the hope it would be around for some years. The *Consumer Digest* ratings all pointed to high practicality and reliability coupled with economy. Up here in the wet Northwest, I figured a four-wheel drive would be a prudent choice. Must be, considering how many of them I see around town. When the magazine talked about technical stuff like suspensions and ratios of this and that, I got lost, but I did understand that all the ratings were good, better anyway than those of the comparable American wagons. Could my old man see what's happening with so many people buying imported cars, he'd roll over in his grave. He was an old Ford worker and a proud UAW man. But he'd have to agree with my prudent choice.

Muriel smiles at me through the kitchen bay window. I recall the cursing and mishaps of trying to install the window several years ago, one of the first big home improvement jobs I attempted. The window is decorated with the proof of my wife's ability to nurture temperamental Boston ferns, which I had always found impossible when I was single and an apartment dweller. It seems so long ago that I was a single man, or maybe I just can no longer imagine any life without this lovely woman for whom I have never stopped feeling passionate love. This, I guess, is where I always wanted to be, here in front of a house like this, with a good car, for once, and a good wife.

Love and cars stretch across my life like a bumpy highway. There had been that grail-like love I pursued as a very young man and could, of course, never quite find. The question of love was as enigmatic as the powerful workings under the hoods of the many cars I owned (and which owned me) when I carried dates here and there. The Subaru's stereo and tape deck seem so sophisticated compared to the simple AM radio I and those pretty girls of my youth listened to while necking in the front seats of those old cars. The songs that then played on the AM stations are now called *golden oldies*.

When I was first driving my Dad's '56 Mercury on weekends with five bucks in my wallet and anticipating a hot night of necking with Judy Stromyer or Merita Lasalle, I'd wash and sometimes wax the car on Saturday afternoons. In those days there was a lot of chrome to polish, like so much armor on a medieval warhorse. That old blue and white Mercury had carried us from the East to California, the new world. Then, not long after, it was to carry me to every boy's dream world at the Paradise drive-in movie theater. It was all innocent enough, mainly a lot of heavy kissing and petting. After those movies, attended but not seen, the Merc's brilliant blue and opulent chrome made a presence at Stack's Drive-in Burgers. If you are old enough, you will recall that was the period when *cruising* and *parking,* then popular teenage pastimes, found their way into the American idiom. The cars that were then ritually paraded have since disappeared along with flattop and duck-tail haircuts. Cars then had a mystique they've never had again. Now it seems so many cars look alike. But think of '56 Corvettes, sport T Birds with the little rear windows like portholes, mid 60s Mustangs, chopped and nosed '49 Mercurys, Fords from the '30s converted to roadsters, candy-apple red '57 Chevy Belairs. These autos were as unique to our culture and times as were young Marlon Brando, James Dean and JFK.

Muriel is watching me with an approving smile and she is holding up a bottle of beer, offering. I nod. Yes, the mild rush of a beer would be good right now. The forest green of our Subaru begins to gleam from under the lather. Muriel has come out with the beer in one hand and a chamois in the other. "We don't want any nasty streaks, do we? Here, relax a bit."

I sit on the porch step and take a swig. At least I never drank when I drove. And I had only one accident in my life. On one of those Saturday night high school dates I was busy talking with Shirley Macintosh, a cheerleader, and I didn't see the light turn red. Although I caught the back end of a car as I ran the intersection, no one was hurt. It was a wonder because this was before we'd ever heard of seat belts. And because it was before the litigious times we now live in, the insurance companies settled everything without much ado.

After that, my privileges with the old Merc were severely curtailed, as you might well imagine. But being an only son and the apple of my father's eye, I was gradually able to beg myself back into grace, aided by the presentation of a 3.5 grade average. Not having the use of a car seriously limited one's romantic aspirations. There were a few guys at the high school who because of their cars were held in a certain awe by the rest of us. Billy Konsek had a metallic blue Ranchero Ford, a hybrid design of half coup, half pickup truck, with a custom Tijuana tuck-and-roll upholstery job and soft blue lights on the dash, while Phil Murton had the real classic, a chopped '49 maroon Merc, also with Naugahyde tuck-and-roll seats. In both cases, we easily imagined the libidinous adventures these two classmates had in these illustrious machines. Supporting a different kind of high school lifestyle, neither of those guys had time for football, or even study. Passing through my old high school town about fifteen years ago, I ran into Murton at a Gulf station, working as a mechanic. Konsek, it was rumored, was on his third marriage and was driving a delivery truck for Langendorf breads.

By 1960 I was in college and finally had my own car, a green 1950 Ford coup. My dad had bought the car for me when I got accepted into U.C.L.A. Not only did I have my own car, but becoming a university student had imbued me with a new sense of myself, of responsibility. It was at that time that I began the business of earnestly chasing women.

The popular venue of romance by then was no longer cars but dormitory rooms and cheap apartments. Yet when you live in Los Angeles, a lot of your life is necessarily spent in cars. That '50 Ford is memorable as the first and last car I could service to some degree, such as changing the plugs or cleaning the carburetor. It was so simple under the hood, like the times, that you could see the pavement below through the big spaces on either side of the engine block. In some ways the cars I drove then were as innocent as I was. It was in the time of that Ford that I began to lose my innocence, for I joined a typical beer-drinking fraternity and I fell in love with a freshman girl who was like no one I had ever known. She read. She introduced me to Sartre, Camus, Anaïs Nin, French wine and unencumbered sex. She was soft and pretty without demands, unsticky and forthright. I was pleased at her initial, open offer of intimacy early in our acquaintance, and when she had invited me into her tiny Santa Monica studio apartment, I think I felt very grown up. She had me drive her to various foreign movie houses in West LA, which is how I got to know that near mythical place. Dierdre amazed my still middle-class high school mind with films like *Hiroshima Mon Amour* and *Last Year at Marienbad*. In the year I was with her I began to feel like something of a sophisticate, leastwise not the bumpkin who had entered UCLA, and I began to let my hair grow longer. When we began to drift apart, as she had said we would, there was no fuss (as there was to be in most of my other romances). I can now see clearly that she was one of my first teachers, that all the other girls I had known to that point had been immature like myself.

Through the 60s my turnover in girls was about as regular as my turnover in cheap apartments and part-time jobs. I could never afford a good car, and so I wore out a succession of clunkers. There was a yellow '55 hardtop Dodge, a sort of old folks' car; then later, a huge four-door '60 Chevy with only gray primer for paint, which I had acquired cheaply at a police auction. Its main feature was that this entirely unimpressive clunker had a four-liter engine under the hood and could jack rabbit to highway speed in seconds because it had been a police pursuit car. But I was never much of a hot-rodder, and so the novelty of the Chevy's brute power soon passed.

The late 60s were marked by two cars. My own and my first wife's. Vicki was like her car: petite, pretty and speedy. The car was one of her first lines of expression, especially when she was angry, which was frequently during the single stormy year of our alliance. When we quarreled, she'd run off in her aerodynamic '65 Dodge Dart, peeling out from the driveway of our small apartment with a squeal, as if that were her last angry word. I learned to avoid arguing when she was at the wheel, since she would emphasize her words with harrowing accelerations and nervous jabs at the push buttons of the radio, an early form of channel surfing. You may ask what the arguments were about. I can't remember, but what do any young, unready-for-marriage people argue about? It might have been because she liked Frankie Valle and The Four Seasons and I didn't, or because I liked the new *Sergeant Pepper* album by the Beatles and she was indifferent. In general, I showed little enthusiasm for marriage, as I really hadn't wanted to get married to anyone in the first place. I seem to remember getting a little too expansive and romantic one Friday evening from too much cheap Gallo Red Mountain, which I had become accustomed to as an undergraduate. I may have unknowingly hinted at permanence which was taken literally. I don't really remember how it all came about. But before I knew it, I was receiving congratulatory calls from her family, and she had quietly bought an expensive bridal gown. My car at the time, a '61 Alfa Romeo Spider, was also petite, cute and speedy. Even more ironic was the Alpha's troublesome gear shift. I could never drive the car smoothly without a lot of grinding through the gears. One thing that can be said for that time was that I wasn't called up for Vietnam because I was married, was in grad school and was already beyond the gun-fodder age the draft board preferred.

By the spring of '68, Vicki and I had separated and filed for divorce, and I was now the owner of a master's degree and a '57 Plymouth Fury with its distinctive rear fenders like a pair of shark dorsal fins. Shifting its gears was a matter of pushing buttons on the dash much the same as one changes the speeds on a standard kitchen blender. Still too young to understand that my personal problems were portable, I looked to other vistas. Packing everything I owned into the Fury, appropriately named for that post-divorce period, I drove to San Francisco. The trip must have been too much for it, for not long after arriving in S.F. the Fury had none left and had a massive engine seizure of some sort, whereupon I left it where it had died, on a side street in the Mission district. I had to pay the city fifty dollars to tow it away and junk it.

I was working downtown in an employment consulting office, a headhunter outfit, where you screen applicants and fill positions for large companies who don't trust their own personnel departments. I didn't need a car in the city and learned to use the public transit system, a kind of divorce from the culture of Southern California in which I had grown up. But this was 1968 and everything was possible, which you felt when you walked down through the Haight, where I had found an inexpensive apartment. I was living a double life, shedding my business suit in the evenings for raggedy jeans and psychedelic shirts and partaking of the color that was the Haight during that "Summer of Love." The friends and influences of my neighborhood, rather than those of my downtown job, finally won out and I quit my job (prematurely, as I see it now), turned on and hit the road, the Interstate 80 to be exact.

I rode a lot of cars in the months that followed, with people I can't remember, for the rides were brief, sleepy or stoned, and nothing important was exchanged, nor did I learn much except that I was not cut out for the freedom of sleeping outdoors on cold nights, panhandling when broke and getting really funky for want of a shower. Albeit, there were a few memorable occasions, like rolling into Boston in the cab of a Peterbilt semi with a kind old trucker with whom we'd dropped acid. Another was coming down the Lake Erie front highway toward Ohio in the back of an open horse trailer where I and a pal froze in the November air. Yet another was a long ride en route to St. Louis in a late 50's pink Cadillac with four black musicians who didn't talk much but passed endless joints and grooved to their eight-track tape player blasting rhythm and blues at ear splitting volume.

With the '60s drawing to a close I was back in LA again and serious about living a more sane life. I got a job in a lumber yard and bought a '62 canary-yellow Le Mans Pontiac. It was the closest I ever got to owning a *low rider*, which, for those of you who don't know, is a car that has had its suspension lowered so that it rides barely a few inches from the road. It got me through the early 70s when I was teaching part-time at a local junior college and running a photography business out of a cheap, rambling apartment in a 1920s stucco 4-plex. Those were good days with a modest, but for once, steady income.

Then came (the?) Dawn, appearing one afternoon to have me do some portraits of her and her daughter. I was in my early thirties but I began acting like a teenager in love with love. Until Dawn, all my women (and cars) had been preliminaries. During my tenure with her, I held down a nine to five sales job, eventually moved in with her, played house, husband and father, and, as if to round out the illusion, she convinced me (I suppose I convinced myself) to buy a secondhand, white '65 Jaguar with a bird's eye cherry wood dash and black leather upholstery. It was a great buy at $1000, even viewing it for the first time under a coat of thick dust where it sat immobilized in a rundown wood garage in North Long Beach. The seller warned that it would mainly need a few hundred to get the brake system overhauled, a complete lube and major tune up. Finally, when we got her running and gussied up with a fresh wax job, she was quite a sight. The Jaguar's sophisticated aluminum engine was as mysterious to me as Dawn's inner workings and her little girl with whom I tentatively explored the role of surrogate father. This venture into domestic bliss lasted about as long as the Jaguar, which blew up a year later when a couple piston heads exploded as I tried to force the Jaguar to keep the pace in the fast lane up the Conejo grade on the 101 just north of the San Fernando Valley. I'd had my adventure into the world of high- maintenance cars and women. The Jaguar had cost me a bundle, while "the woman in the year of the Jaguar" had cost me my heart.

By the late '70s the price of gas had tripled and was approaching a dollar a gallon. One began seeing a lot more small cars on the road and the beginning of the Japanese import invasion. Always being an Anglophile, I opted for a cute baby-blue 1968 convertible Mark III Spitfire Triumph. It was a joy, save for its nagging problems with the master brake cylinder. But in California, one could drive such a car with the top down most of the year. I would often just jump in and out of it without opening the door. My spiffy little town-runabout. At last I had an accoutrement to my romantic romping that even Phil Murton and Billy Konsek would have approved. For four carefree years I scat about in that car from romance to romance, recovering my heart that had been so severely injured earlier in the decade.

By the time I was thirty-nine a shock of recognition or pre-forty jitters had begun to possess me. I didn't regret all the fun I was having. Most of the people I knew were also living it up as though things would never change. I mean, this was the *Hotel California* of song fame. I always had a little money or some part-time job or other, but I began to feel I should have a career, a home instead of endless apartments (which is yet another story), and instead of serial relationships, a wife.

I sold the Spitfire, by then thrashed, for a pittance, which I used as a down payment on a 1970 Ford Granada, a very middle-class car good for transporting clients in my new career as a California real estate agent. Real estate in the seventies was like the second gold rush. Inflation kept ratcheting up market values, yet people kept buying and speculating and almost anyone willing to take a six-week course for a license could go out there and stake his claim on the big sales commissions. I was successful for a time, until rising interest rates put the brakes on the market. I and my pals, dressed in our lawyerish three-piece suits, suddenly had the illusion that we were big time businessmen, and we spent a lot of money on weekend parties at the local bars. In keeping with my newly found persona, I drove my old Ford into the dealership on impulse one afternoon and drove out in a new '79 Mustang, the first *new* car I had ever owned.

I may not sound like a shy sort of man, but I am really, and so I was surprised to the point of being lightheaded when the young secretary of our office, almost half my age, easily became my mistress and (I admit it) a sort of trophy. She aspired to become a sales agent, but at twenty-one she had a lot to learn. I also had a lot to learn. What started casually with this young woman I began to take a little too seriously, and when she wasn't available quite as regularly as I came to want and in a way I wanted, the affair became a roller-coaster of emotions. I discovered I no longer had patience or energy for this sort of thing and decided it was time to forswear youngish women.

The Mustang, like my newly found love affair and career, began to run out of steam. Actually, the Mustang never had much power. The economical four-cylinder engine proved too weak to pull the car efficiently up hills and too small when you needed some real pickup. There I was nearing forty with a fading, barely-just-begun career, a wild love affair on the rocks and a car whose only good feature was, ironically, its peach color.

I think at this juncture I was somewhere in that limbo between feeling old and still being a boy, somewhere between hopelessness and hope. With business slacking off and the bank account I had built through my brief heyday dwindling, I was spending more time at the watering holes frequented by my old real estate cronies, waiting, I suppose, until I could make up my mind what to do next. It was in this time that I met Muriel. In retrospect, if I were to encapsulate our beginnings, they were not heady, not sweeping, not wild, not flights. But don't think my response was in some way subdued because the woman in question was unexciting. Quite the contrary, Muriel was beautiful and charming, even more so these days with gray highlights overtaking her hair. The largeness of her eyes in comparison to her small, delicate face has not changed, nor has her sudden outbursts of spontaneous girlish laughter. A careful listener and direct in her responses, she made me feel I could never be alone in her company. And I never have been since.

After a year of quiet and comfortable courting, we married and took a small apartment. I traded in the Mustang for a pair of little economical '78 Ford Fiestas that kept us on the road to our respective jobs. I'd essentially given up the now cooled real estate market, and while Muriel patiently worked in a medical office, I explored several other schemes to make a living, including a foray into the food service industry, all which failed. Finally, after a mass mailing, I got an interview for a modest paying high school teaching job up in the Northwest. I got hired and we moved, had children and have since tried to age gracefully. It has not always been easy, but then it hasn't been especially difficult. If there is such a thing as people being right for each other, then we have been so.

We now have only one car. That seems enough, as does our life together. I am near done chamoising the Subaru, and Muriel has come out on the porch and taken her place on the swing, which is her habit after dinner during these balmy summer evenings. She has some iced tea and I can see she has placed a fresh bottle of beer next to my side of the porch swing. She doesn't have to say anything. I will take my place beside her. I see the children in the kitchen peering into the fridge, looking for a drink or a snack to take with them for their favorite evening shows on the Nickelodeon channel. They perhaps watch too much television and I mildly protest, keeping in mind that I do see them occasionally reading. I find as I get into the heart of middle age that what I've had to learn all along is not to worry but to cultivate my sense of humor. The stories of my cars and my women are among those things which caused me the most grief in my life. I made some bad choices out of inexperience and impulse. But how else can the road be traveled? Don't most of us have to take a lot of blind alleys and dead-end roads before we find our way? I have to say, I am surprised, and thankful, that I've made it this far. With the exception of a bum knee that has curtailed my tennis, I'm pretty healthy, I have a long summer holiday from school with pay, the house is almost paid off and the Subaru, if I take good care of it, so they say, could last as long as I do. There is moisture in the evening air, and it has seized upon Muriel's hair, perming dime size curls along the hairline of her forehead, reminding me of women's hairstyles I've seen in books on ancient Rome. She swings gently, pushing with one foot, eyes closed, perhaps dreaming of a trip to Bora Bora or Tuscany, which we sometimes idly talk about but will probably never take. Now she opens her eyes, as if I had interrupted her dreaming, smiles and pats the seat next to her for me to come and rest.

Travel isn't always pretty. It isn't always comfortable. Sometimes it hurts, it even breaks your heart. But that's okay. The journey changes you; it should change you.
It leaves marks on your memory, on your consciousness, on your heart, and on your body. You take something with you.
Hopefully, you leave something good behind.

—ANTHONY BOURDAIN

# East is East

--------------------

A fter three months in Tokyo, Michael Rand still hadn't become accustomed to the crush of the crowd. The subway never seemed to have a slack time when he could get a seat. And always there were the faces, all wearing the same bored, impassive expression. There was more than the occasional commuter who would stare at him, but he had begun countering this by wearing dark glasses wherever he went. Somehow he felt camouflaged by the glasses. At any rate, fewer people looked his way.

But why should he be an oddity to be stared at? Wasn't he, after all, one among many fair-haired, light-complexioned *gaijins* inhabiting the city? Weren't Westerners seen at every turn of Japanese life-on billboards, on television, in movies, as mannequins in store windows? Why the gawking? These questions were absorbing Rand when his train jerked to a stop at lkejiri Ohashi station, the load of passengers within swaying like sea plants in a tidewater.

The sliding doors of thè car opened like dam gates, letting in more people than seemed possible for the car to hold. When the train made its next stop, Rand readjusted his stance within his cramped amount of space so that his shoulder was at a right angle to the businessman whose weight had dug into him when the train lurched. Next time, Rand vowed to himself, the businessman would do battle with a sharp elbow.

The squeeze of the crowd made it near impossible for Rand to continue reading his *Japan Times* newspaper. But the businessman, who was presently the object of Rand's agitation, continued to read a small illustrated magazine that looked like a comic book. The page Rand was able to glimpse over the businessman's shoulder revealed a series of drawings in which a naked young woman was trussed up with ropes in a very compromising position while an evil-looking man stood over her. Rand wondered how anyone could read such a magazine in public.

There were a few passengers reading pocket books, smaller and handier than the American variety, which lent themselves to the crowded conditions of the subway car. More than a few passengers just dozed, remarkably awakening for their train stops as though in perfectly timed Zen trances. It was a state of relaxation that was impossible for him, even when he was lulled by longer rides across Tokyo. There had been more than a few occasions, when Rand had managed to get a seat, that a sleeping passenger next to him had leaned unconsciously onto his shoulder. The sleepers, in most cases, sensing the imposition, shook themselves awake and sat upright again and resumed their dozing. In a few cases, Rand had to nudge them awake with his violated shoulder.

Inscrutable? He couldn't claim to understand the Japanese language, but the term *inscrutable* so often used by Americans to describe the Japanese was undeserved, was more a revelation of Western ignorance, a mystification based on popular cinematic images. Yet in the 60s, when so many of the traditional Western gods had died, hadn't Rand and his contemporaries looked to the East, listened to Ravi Shankar, read Alan Watts, ate brown rice diets and made attempts at Zen and yoga? Little had they known then that their contemporaries in Japan would cultivate the classic American materialism that Rand and his friends had gone to such lengths to disavow.

Rand surveyed the train car, composing theories upon the stony faces which were unmoved by the push and shove, the merciless extrusion of wincing, sweating flesh. Under such conditions could civility and calm prevail in America? Indeed, there was a civility here in Japan that seemed all the more admirable, considering the amount of stress and constriction of lifestyle which the average person had to endure. Already he had made a pleasant adjustment to the knowledge that he needn't worry about the usual potential hazards of returning home late at night along deserted subway platforms and down poorly lit streets.

The train pulled into Shibuya station, a major commercial center and crossroads in Tokyo and the location of the Rodgers English Center, his place of employment. It was ironic that he should have to come halfway around the world to find a job teaching English. English teachers in California had become as redundant as actors on Hollywood Boulevard.

He surfaced to the street, riding along in a black river of heads. At the first big intersection, a sea of people ebbed and flowed with the changing of the lights. Department stores alternately sucked in and spewed out waves of shoppers. Towering murals on the sides of the department stores idolized Alain Delon in his latest thriller and John Travolta in his newest musical. Another giant advertisement, for Izod polo shirts, featured Jack Nicklaus on a fairway, completing a golf swing. Written boldly across this scene was a logo in bold English: *For your happy and beautiful life.*

Rand crossed from Seibu department store to the big discount camera emporium and then under the trestle over which passed the Yamanote line. It would be good to come home that night to a hot meal. It was an especially cold, early winter in Tokyo, making the change from California for Toni and him all the more starkly abrupt. Undoubtedly, it all bound them more to each other, the isolation of their circumstance and now the cold. They would gratefully cuddle together near their kerosene heater each night. There was nothing like removing a marriage from its familiar surroundings to test its limits, for better or for worse. He hoped she would hold up. They had never been accustomed to more than a Californian one-bed-room apartment, but in Tokyo they were reduced to a dank, mildewy closet of an apartment that some fellow workers at the Rodgers Center thought a palace by Tokyo standards. Although the little apartment wasn't very comfortable, they had kicked the television habit and had rediscovered reading novels, and they often took long walks during which Toni took slides of the endless nooks and crannies of the city.

The Rodgers English Center was on the tenth floor of a new high rise building and consisted of a suite of rooms which would have made a comfortable apartment. Its least desirable quality, besides providing undeniable togetherness for the students who packed in every afternoon and evening, was its ability to make pronounced lateral swings during Tokyo's frequent earth tremors, which produced in Rand an ongoing mild anxiety.

The school was the creation of one Michiko Matsuda whom Rand had first met at a friend's dinner party in Los Angeles. The chance meeting had turned into an invitation to work at her English school in Tokyo. Toni was to be given some part-time work with children's classes, and Matsuda would provide an apartment in addition to his salary, which, if not high, promised to be regular. Because he and Toni had no children, no contracts and no particular prospects to hold them in California, they had decided to go for the lark of it. But it had bothered Rand that Matsuda had never seemed to give anything but a passing interest to his credentials or experience, save that he produce something for the LA Japanese Embassy in order to secure the appropriate visa.

The name of The Rodger's English Center she had acquired through a brief marriage to an American, along with a passable ability to speak English. After arriving in Japan, Rand rarely saw her, except for her phantom-like appearances, always with a long, thin More cigarette in hand. She would grab a few papers, make a phone call or two and be gone. In her constant stead was Jan, her administrative assistant, receptionist and overall vassal, as Rand saw her. Jan, a not unattractive but overly made-up woman in her late twenties, never gave her real Japanese name around the Center, but always went by her adopted American name as an emblem of her claim to American language and culture.

"Hello *Land-Sensei*," she now sang out through her usual Coca Cola smile as he came into the foyer. She, like most Japanese, had difficulty pronouncing the r sound, but in Jan's case the misuse was grating, somehow derisive. Had she not been left in charge of the Center's operation, he might have ignored her improbable existence, disco skirts, spiked heels and all. That she could presume any power of administration over him greatly disturbed his sense of proportion. After all, *he* knew what was best when it came to teaching English; *he* had the degrees and *he* was the native speaker. And *she* was going to presume?! This glorified receptionist whose quasi-pidgin English and garish sense of fashion prompted unsavory redneck humor? No way, he thought, kicking off his shoes in the foyer and pushing into a pair of slippers.

"*Land-Sensei,* would you please give dis test," she asked. Her manner with him had always been too saccharine.

Rand stood looking at her without expression. He, too, could assume an exterior of benign detachment.

"Dis Fujieda-san test book two," she continued tenuously. "Tape test he take... you remember?"

Rand remembered only too well having seen Fujieda, one of his prize pupils, being led away *(how easily they were led)* and administered the useless test, a tricky listening comprehension test of dubious value. Put to the test, Matsuda herself would not have passed.

"He must pass dis test, den he can go to book three," Jan said with a certain aplomb, as if Rand were going to debate that three followed two. Fujieda was a mature, educated man in his late thirties, an economist, a sportsman and a bit of a philosopher. He had communicated a great deal to Rand in their weekly sessions. Rand had finally succeeded in drawing him out and Fujieda began talking with an ease and enthusiasm, however imperfectly, that was beyond the scope of most students.

"He can handle book three," Rand said with finality.

"But he must pass test first," Jan replied shakily, unaccustomed to the confrontation in his tone. The test she was holding up in front of him was slightly vibrating at the edges.

The books were sold to the students at a profit and were the only tangible evidence that anyone was really studying anything, and they were also used to impose a loose

Russ Desaulnier

course for progress—of which there was rarely any, Fujieda excepted.

"Jan, Fujieda is quite capable of handling book three. But more important he needs to be in an advanced class. I mean he's here to learn how to converse, not pass tests."

When it came to the written and tape tests, Fujieda just didn't cut it. If anything, the tests set him back, made him think he could never improve. Rand wanted him admitted to his *aávanced free conversation* group.

"Excuse me, you must give test," she persisted. She would be faithful to the form, and the content be hanged. Acknowledgment of the test, the form, would cause him to have to retract his personal promotion of Fujieda to *Conversation Book 3* and the advanced conversation group. Again initiative would be wrested from him, again he would be diminished. It made no sense. Hadn't Matsuda encouraged his bringing *new ideas* to the Center, heralding his coming as the Center's investiture with a *real English teacher*? And hadn't he thrown himself into the challenge with enthusiasm and vigor? He deserved some credit, not this sabotage of his good faith.

"Give me the test," he said, trying to restrain his mounting annoyance. He would administer the test and change the answers if necessary to pass Fujieda. He jerked the test papers in an instant of reflex from Jan's hand, and then realized it was too late to retract the damage to Jan's composure. They momentarily stared at each other until they were distracted by opening doors and voices spilling into the hall.

It was the shifting of classes at the end of the hour, and leading the students out of the adjoining rooms were Owen and Garrison, two of Rand's teaching colleagues. The small hallway began to crowd, and as cigarettes were lit, the place took on the atmosphere of an apartment cocktail party. Jan's shrill voice rose above the gathering as she went about collecting monthly tuition fees, always concealed in plain envelopes, as if the sight of money would in some way sully the high purpose for which it flowed.

"Are you *genki* today?" Bernie Garrison inquired in his usual upbeat manner as he surveyed some student files. He liked sprinkling his English with the few Japanese words he knew.

"I'm not sure," Rand replied, still agitated.

"What's up, young man?"

"Just the usual shit and aggravation."

"Don't let it get to you, Man," Garrison chuckled sympathetically. He would have known perhaps as well as anyone the slings and arrows the *gaijin* was heir to in Tokyo, for he had been there for ten years. He was a retired U.S. Air Force Major, a glib Bill Cosby type who had been stationed in Japan after a tour of Vietnam and then had decided to stay on. All that anyone seemed to know about him was that he had some ex-wives and grown ex-children somewhere in the suburbs of Chicago, and he did a fair amount of drinking with his old service cronies at the New Sanno Hotel, Tokyo's stylish R&R center for American servicemen.

"You just lettin' things get under your skin, Rand. We all have. Still do, sometimes. You just around this place too much. Hell, I wouldn't be in nobody's army no more."

"Bernie, can I ask you something, well, personal business?"

"Shoot."

"Does Matsuda sponsor your visa?"

"Hell no! Got a friend takes care of that."

Visa sponsorship, it was rumored, could be a matter of Casablanca proportions in which the contracted foreigner was effectively held hostage by the visa sponsor. The Immigration Office was not sympathetic with the foreigner who fell out of the good graces of the sponsoring employer. It was a matter Rand had to investigate further.

"How's the Missus?" Garrison asked. Rand's mind was still on visas and he didn't register the question.

"Everything is a madhouse around here, and Matsuda in spite of herself seems to thrive on it. I've made suggestions for change which she asked for, but nothing gets done. I mean last week I wrote a curriculum brochure and this week she's forgotten she asked me to write one."

Garrison just shrugged and then, slipping into black dialect, which he had a habit of using for emphasis, he said:

"Matsuda just a head strong woman. She like to think she knows what she doin', but often she don't. Maybe she have good intentions, but things just kinda fall where they will. She always got her mind on other business. She don't care long as she feel like the big boss and nobody question her. Pretty much the same everywhere. Makes you wonder, don't it?"

It did make one wonder. How could so many Japanese companies be so successful if they were managed by such incompetent people? He could only imagine that the sheer intensity of the Japanese labor force pushed industry ahead despite its management, forgiving all the wasted motion and dead weight at the top. In the English teaching business in Japan, success was virtually guaranteed by an endless flow of young people hoping to practice a few phrases with a gaijin teacher. It was a seller's market, and any office with a stable of foreign teachers to advertise around town could count on steady business. Because of tradition or busy schedules, Rand wasn't sure which, Japanese students attended English classes only once a week. That anyone hoped to make any progress at that rate mystified him. A great many tenacious souls stayed with the weekly regimen for years. But that was good for the language schools.

"Listen Rand," Garrison said with the benevolence of the seasoned survivor, "you just relax, you hear. Don't worry about teaching. Just smile. Nothing going to change around here. This ain't exactly Harvard, you know."

Rand grunted acknowledgment. It wasn't a school by any definition he was familiar with. But it paid the bills. Yet he couldn't stop feeling the nagging insinuation that he had become a part of a pretense, and despite his qualifications, he was dispensable like the changing window displays of Seibu department store.

"And what conspiratorial undertakings have we here?" Owen injected with feigned hauteur, as he strutted up to where Rand was standing with Garrison.

"Not that any recent American undertakings have had anything but disastrous effects," he continued, reaching for Garrison's breast pocket, which Garrison proffered.

"Thanks for the cigarette, old chap." A fat paperback issue of *Nicholas Nickleby* was tucked under Owen's other arm.

Because of his Anglophilia that dated back to his undergraduate days, Rand was receptive to Owen, despite the Englishman's disconcerting appearance and his cocky manner.

"You wankers going to the party on Friday?" he inquired, lighting up his cigarette. His casual use of such epithets was his way of being friendly and it took some getting used to. Concerning the party, Garrison wasn't sure, but Rand indicated that he and Toni would probably go.

"Come on, are you coming or not? Don't be sodding wankers!" Owen looked at each of them. He always had an impertinent expression on his face, except when he was hung over. His pallid complexion, punked-out, auburn dyed hair and tight-fitted clothes gave him an almost Mephistophelian appearance. He was a Rock musician and singer aspiring to make his name in Tokyo while maintaining a cultural visa under which he was supposed to be studying the *shamisen.* Rand and Toni had heard him play and sing a few times at a small club and liked his stuff. He supported himself by working part-time at the Center, always entering and exiting with a stir. He was especially popular with the younger female students who hung around him like giggly Rock groupies.

"Owen, you look particularly pale these days. Spending too much time alone with yourself?" Rand quipped.

"Sod off, you," Owen reacted, grasping Rand's arm in mock aggression.

"He just spending too much time with his boyfriends in Roppongi," Garrison said, joining the assault. The insinuation of homosexuality was Garrison's ongoing response to Owen's flamboyant hair and clothes. The conservative Garrison, by contrast, was given to tweed sports jackets with leather elbow patches, and he never failed to wear a tie.

"Ass bandit," Garrison chortled.

"Come on, I'll get you in the gob. I'll show who's the puff," Owen reacted, taking a boxer's sparring stance toward Garrison who was at least a head taller and somewhat thicker than Owen's Mick Jagger-like frame. He could have easily flattened Owen in a real confrontation, but he affected a good natured, cowardly submission to Owen's mock bravado and then smothered the smaller man with a bear-like hug. They scuffled a bit and moved into the flow of students going toward the classrooms for the next period.

"Sod off, you big asshole," Owen's voice rose above the encircling students. He never refrained from loud vulgarities, as if he found a certain thrill in testing the limits of the students' comprehension. Matsuda had often admonished him, but would ultimately tolerate everything, even his hungover absences, since he kept a lot of young female students coming for more and more English lessons, lessons they could easily have given up for some other fad or fashion that might divert their spending money.

Jan had emerged from her crevice in the front office and was sorting out students for the next round of classes. Rand awaited the arrival of several new advanced students while perusing some exercises for the class. He generally eschewed standard drill forms for the more generative kinds of exercises in which the student was forced to reach into his own personal experience and stir up a little reflection and imagination, something which seemed to have been atrophied by an all too restrictive formal education. The textbooks provided by Matsuda, which she had asked him to evaluate, remained in place, sepulchers of language reminiscent of his boyhood Latin texts, better administered by accountants than language teachers.

Classes were about to begin when Joe Birelli lumbered through the door in a neat warm-up suit and Adidas jogging shoes. He had been a physical education teacher in New Jersey, and all the students with whom he was immensely popular called him Jersey Joe. Joe was a veteran at the Center and had established an enthusiastic following, which to Matsuda meant repeat business. Over the weeks of his tenure at the Center, Rand had come to realize that students came and went suddenly like the turnovers at a continuous double feature matinee. Even students with whom he felt he had a rapport would sometimes mysteriously disappear from classes without explanation. On some occasions Rand was asked, to his chagrin, why a student had disappeared, as if he had somehow been the cause. Maybe the student was broke, maybe a new hobby had come on the horizon. Maybe the student had become too busy with a new lover. God only knew why some students suddenly disappeared. And he was not God, as he had finally responded at the end of his patience with Matsuda in the first of such interrogations he had endured about a disappeared student. He had assured Matsuda that he was *busting his ass* and that it was likely he couldn't please everyone no matter how hard he tried. Jan, who had been at Matsuda's side, whined about not understanding his jargon which he quickly rephrased, but the more he explained his efforts, the more he met with an implacable silence from Matsuda and her yes person, Jan. The verdict was already in. He had failed in his responsibility.

"How you doing, Buddy?" Birelli greeted him with the restrained warmth of a John Wayne addressing the weary troops. He and Rand shared a mutual deference like that between two officers of equal rank but of different corps.

"Hey, Man, why don't you and the wife visit the *dojo* this weekend and shoot some pictures?" They had discussed this possibility before. Birelli had wanted some pointers on the new Nikon SLR he had bought, but he probably also wanted to show off his karate skills.

"This Sunday would be a good time to come. Some of the big guys will be there testing people for *dan* promotions. There'll probably be some contact." In this last statement Rand perceived a hint of relish. Although the monochromatic scheme of the karate gym might provide some interesting photographic experimentation, Rand's thoughts deferred to a Sunday walk with Toni around old town Tokyo, if it wasn't too cold, and then a nice *teishoku* lunch in some new restaurant.

"I'll see what Toni has planned," he said as if he didn't know. But then he felt slightly naked in his evasion. "How's your new Nikon treating you?" he said, changing the subject.

"Real cool, Man, cool," Birelli said, taking a student file from the cabinet. This was the Joe of mean streets.

Jan reemerged like a moray eel looking to feed on something, but Joe politely asked her to locate the audio tapes for *Book One,* since he couldn't find them. His request had the effect of a dismissal and she withdrew sullenly. Joe then moved toward Rand and sat down next to him.

"How do I shoot action in the *dojo?* I mean it ain't too bright in there," Joe asked.

"Use black and white. Monochrome will look better, too."

"Monochrome?"

"Black and white."

"If you need more speed, you push the ASA...

"Push the ASA?"

Joe really didn't know anything about film and handling a camera. And so Rand proceeded to explain to him the types of black and white film and available light shooting. Having acquired a momentum in his explanation and envisioning prints he would make of karate combatants, he launched a quick summary on darkroom technique which could enhance the original vision. He had watched Toni so many times in her old darkroom back in California that he had learned a repertoire of darkroom magic. In this case he suggested shooting for a grainy negative and then printing on very high contrast paper, his own particular vision of karate kicks and strikes.

"Hey, that was pretty interesting, Man."

"It was nothing."

"You're okay," Birelli pronounced as if having just validated Rand.

"Well, thanks." Rand cleared his throat and adjusted himself in his seat.

"I just do my thing, come and go, and just do my job, you know what I mean?" Birelli said. Rand wasn't sure of his meaning, but it seemed best to just nod agreement and listen.

"Yea, you probably *are* the best teacher we got around here," he said—as if confirming something from a prior discussion unknown to Rand.

"Ain't no real teachers here. So you gotta be the best," he muttered in *sotto voce* as he moved away toward the front office. "Try and make it Sunday."

"Rand wanted to stop him and tell him he wasn't the *best*. He didn't want to be the *best*. He was good on some days, but not *the best*. Suddenly he was embarrassed and a bit angry. Where did this brassy little rumor come from? Then running a mental thumb over the edges of recent days, he pulled out the last of his conferences with Matsuda and tried to remember...

"But Mr. Garrison and Mr. Birelli not lose any students," Matsuda had said, lighting up one of her extra-long More cigarettes, the first inhalation escaping through her nose like an exclamation point.

"So they have more hair than I do," he offered

"Some students complain he don't like them," chimed in Jan, who was at Matsuda's side with paper and pencil like a courtroom stenographer.

THE BORDER 201

"They think he don't like Japanese people," Jan concluded with a triumphant air.

"That's preposterous," Rand shot back. The women looked at each other in incomprehension.

"Meaning crazy," he added.

His momentary success at quelling his anger had allowed him to mentally focus on some of the faces of his students. Was it Koichi, the extra quiet one? Katsunori, the smirker? One of those sweet, timid housewives?

"Who said that about me, Jan? I want to know," he asked flatly, fixing her with a stare. Matsuda intervened.

"That would not be fair to the students."

"What about *fairness* to me?"

"Japanese students don't know how to talk to *sensei*."

"I thought we were talking fairness?"

"You must try to understand Japanese people," Matsuda continued.

"Can we stay with the issue here?" Rand was becoming exasperated.

"You maybe too severe with students," she said, unrelenting.

"Too severe? With whom? How? When?"

"You could tell more jokes. Be more friendly," she said. Jokes? What was this? The Comedy Store? What was he supposed to be? Emmett Kelly? Johnny Carson? Hadn't he always kept his classes lighthearted? It had been pointless to continue with Matsuda's hearing in hopes of an acquittal. Control had exhausted him.

"Look, I don't know what the hell is going on here, but I give my best to my classes. If that isn't good enough, we had better consider some other arrangement. I mean, I'm the most qualified teacher you've got and... "

*Voilà!* There it was. The fatal, errant words. *Most qualified.* Those words had been interpreted (or used), passed along as *best* like a hot, glowing ember of arrogance he hadn't intended. What intrigue, he thought, as he sat where Joe had left him.

"Hang in there, buddy." It was Joe beckoning from the doorway of a classroom. He smiled and then disappeared behind the door. Rand, realizing he was late for his next class, grabbed his file and headed to the classroom where he was met by an impatient Jan with two high school girls in tow.

"Would you please teach new student," Jan sang at him in her syrupy manner whenever clients were around. These were two new faces, no doubt off the street for a trial lesson before being signed up for a course and the big upfront tuition. If they didn't sign up, he might have to have another hearing with Matsuda. *God! Bring them in,* he thought, *I'll cajole them, I'll perform as if filling a tooth, tuning a car, coiffuring hair, anointing with oil, all in the allotted hour. Goodbye, you are taught now. Next please. Hello, my name is... and what is yours? Do I like Japan? Do I like raw fish? Do I know how to use chopsticks?!*

Jan and the new students stood waiting for his cue. He continued momentarily to peruse his class file as if to mark his control of the situation. But what did he control? Notions of freedom and choice of late seemed secondary to something much larger than himself.

Closing the filing cabinet abruptly, he looked up into Jan's waiting eyes. He then saw that she could never share his questioning of things at the Center any more than he could ever share her sense of belonging to the Center. She had arrived at her niche in her capital of the world. The Center and others like it, including more Matsudas and Jans, would go on long after his exit when he had become less than a memory, less than a tiny ripple on the great imperturbable pool of the *Japanese Way*.

"It's okay, no problem," he said very softly for her, for himself.

When Rand left the Center that night after classes, the air was crisp but not cold, strangely reminiscent of his high school days when the coolness of fall evenings would tingle on his forehead heated by long luxurious showers after the rigors of football practice. Shibuya was transformed. The plainness of the day's cityscape was now a pastiche of brilliant neon. Down the side street toward the subway, head-banded cooks solicited passers-by to try skewers of meat roasting on glowing braziers. There were others in bright colored *happi* coats soliciting entrance into dark, narrow doorways wreathed with suggestive photos of young women. Everywhere there were cries of *irasshaimase,* welcome.

Back in his neighborhood the narrow streets were empty, save for the occasional office worker making his way home in a cloud of fatigue and *sake*. A few of the small mom-and-pop grocery stores were still open for business. In a fruit shop that opened out onto the street, a wizened old man sat smoking a cigarette like a figure from an old woodblock print. A hunched-over old woman inspected his persimmons with the care of a jeweler. All was quiet as a museum. And then a light snow began to fall.

He should have been homesick for California, but he wasn't, even though he was always looking back. It was as if he had to come this far to see not just Japan, but himself. The changing seasons of Japan somehow cleared the vision, tempered the mind. The dimensions of life were reduced, the senses honed. There was his and Toni's two room apartment where they had only books, simple meals and each other. There was less, but more.

The silence of the street was then broken by a group of university students wearing 1950s style varsity jackets—one among many American retro fashions. A couple of the boys had their hair greased and combed into pompadours and duck-tails. Was there really anything new under the sun? The retreating laughter of the students left him whistling a few bars from *On Wisconsin* and his pace quickened with the memory of the sensation of emerging from a scrimmage line out into the open field to the roar of the crowd and the clear view of the end zone. As he strode toward his building, the wistful cry of the baked sweet potato vendor floated across the benign shadows of the night, *Ya-ki-mo, Ya-kl·mo.* He turned the key in the apartment door and swung the door open.

"I'm home, Honey," he called. At home as he would ever be.

# The Heart of Toyota

------------------

Keiko was soft and quiet and she kept their little apartment warm and very clean. She always had a hot American style breakfast of bacon and eggs or hot cereal waiting for him after he had shaved and dressed, and she always had a Japanese meal ready for him when he came home at night, each of the courses in its own separate decorative bowl or dish. He usually would take a relaxing soak in the *ofuro* which would already be drawn and waiting with a cover to hold in the heat. If he had tension in the neck and shoulders from the day's effort, she would knead it out with expert fingers and thumbs. Often these massages were a preamble to their making love, except when he felt extra tired. He worked long hours in his position as an English curriculum planner and teacher at Toyota Motor company, but the pay was good and his position secure. His life in Japan had a certain order which could be counted on, and he accepted it all gratefully. Like a great many other people in Japan, Rick and Keiko lived in a small, three-room high-rise apartment in a building known as a *mansion*. One of the rooms barely housed Keiko's piano where she gave private lessons to children during the week. She filled the balance of her time studying English and taking care of their home. He usually took their car to work but would leave it home if he was going

Russ Desaulnier

out after work with some of his colleagues. It was a custom for Japanese workers to fraternize after work hours, and he had come to like this custom since he felt special among his Japanese co-workers. They had always treated him with a certain deference, and it was good to drink and relax after the long day.

About once every couple of weeks he went to the Waon Cafe in Toyota City where he could always meet up with someone from the small group of local Americans, mainly English teachers, who frequented the place. The evenings spent with fellow expats seemed to keep in check occasional vague feelings of isolation, as if the Budweisers, billiards and male banter, like trips to McDonald's, filled some undeniable American craving.

Spring had come again and everyone, even his usually dour section manager, suddenly seemed brighter, as if everyone had unaccountably blossomed overnight along with the cherry trees that lined the avenues of the Toyota headquarters complex. He loved the change in the seasons because it was warm again and the early mornings and evenings became just right for resuming his ritual jogging. His runs were like meditations wherein he became absorbed in the cadence of his stride until he floated pure and mindless.

He got home early on this Friday night a little before 9 pm. He would be able to catch the Friday night bilingual movie. While he changed his clothes, Keiko began putting out their dinner arranged on lacquer trays. With a Kirin beer and the TV remote control, he made himself comfortable on the *tatami* floor in front of the small, low dining table. The movie would start in minutes. Then the phone rang. Keiko answered and anxiously motioned him to come to the phone while asking the caller in English to wait.

"Do you recognize my voice?" were the first words he heard as he put the receiver to his ear and said hello.

"Wait a minute," he said, though he recognized the voice immediately. He needed just a moment to collect a few thoughts. What was Serena doing here? How did she find him? Why? Suddenly he felt a collision of past and present, as images of California that he had laid to rest now flew at him like a cold wind off San Francisco Bay. He had lost track of time, as many expatriates seemed to do in Japan. But this sudden incursion of the past was now causing him to take stock. *Seven years.*

"What are you doing here?" he said. Keiko went about laying out the dinner trays. *Relax,* he thought, and he took a large draught from his bottle of Kirin.

"I got your number from your mother. It was no easy job finding her number to begin with. I heard from Van Brewer you'd gone off to Japan, good ole Van, he's still doing flea markets and making leather stuff, but not a stoner these days."

"Where did you run into Brewer?"

"I ran into him down on the Wharf with some young chick. He looked odd to me with all that same long hair and beard now kind of thinning and silvering. And leather. Some things don't change, do they? He's still living in the Haight. Anyway, you were mentioned, and so when we decided to take a trip to Japan, I thought it might be nice to at least say hello after all this time and... "

"You said *we?* "

"My boyfriend. I think you'd like him. Whaddya say? Could we get together with you and your wife?" Your mom mentioned that you had married a Japanese girl."

Having no time to weigh the uncertainties he felt or

Russ Desaulnier

for forming an excuse, Rick agreed. Something in him was wishing this phone call wasn't happening, and yet another part of him was curious about Serena. There was nothing to be afraid of, he told himself. But the sudden entrance of this time warp into his life presented subtleties of complication that he was unprepared to meet. This was this life and his California past was the past and somehow the two repelled each other. He had become unused to complication. In Japan, life had come to have a certain predictability. Even the ambiguities of everyday Japanese life and communication became predictable, and after a while they no longer mattered. You somehow stopped feeling the desire to fight things and you settled into the peaceful, inexorable flow. *Seven years.*

He was a long way from Berkeley where he had gone to school and even further from Marysville and his parents' little farm where he had grown up. Somewhere in the middle, in the belly of his past American life, was Serena, the first serious love of his postgraduate days when he had his first job in the city. They had both worked in offices down in the Montgomery Street business district, had loved the Renaissance Faire of San Rafael where they had met. There had been two wild years of drinking and love making and innumerable evenings at the smaller night spots in North Beach.

Then she had played around on him. He couldn't remember now how the suspicion had begun, but he had finally followed her over to Lake Street one evening to her lover's place and then cruised by early the next morning to find her car still parked nearby. Why else would she have stayed over if it wasn't sleeping with someone? He had never been able to bring himself to put it all out in the open.

He hadn't been able to do that, to tell her he had sneaked around corners, following her. The end was inevitable, and he wanted to at least salvage some pride, wanted to leave her guessing and guilty for her sin. So he cut himself adrift. He thought perhaps he could redeem something through being tough and bearing up. He thought if he didn't reveal his hurt and anger, if they were never witnessed, they would somehow cease to exist. All would be better swallowed and suffered until digested with time. It had seemed easier to walk away from it all.

Serena had seemed genuinely hurt by his rejection, his refusing to talk, his distancing from her, until she quit trying. Perhaps had she made a scene for him, a confession, something big, he might have relented. But she didn't, and it was just as well, because he couldn't erase from his mind her having made love with someone else. It was at that time he had quit cigarettes as an act of asceticism, took up jogging and learned about going into the pain of the run, through the wall and into an elevated, clearer consciousness. Up and down the hills above the Haight he pushed himself, as if the burning in his lungs would sear the open wound of his heart, which in denying he found energy for longer and longer runs. That was all around the beginning of Reagan's so-called trickle-down economic era that became a drought for many, including Rick, whose personnel firm just wasn't getting any business, and so he had been let go. He had continued jogging for months and lived on his unemployment insurance and pasta, but there had been no decent job offers. Finally, he got hired by answering an ad in the *Chronicle* promising jobs abroad.

He agreed to meet Serena and her boyfriend in Nagoya at their hotel in the Sakae district and then take them to a nearby restaurant. So he would take the train to downtown Nagoya and he would bring Keiko. Serena just assumed he would, had insisted. It would have been easier if he could have just gone by himself. But if he didn't agree to take Keiko, wouldn't it have seemed strange and required some impossible explanations? He didn't have to hide his life. He didn't have to do that for Serena. But why was she going to so much trouble to see him? What was there to talk about after all this time? Was she looking for some kind of comeuppance, vindication? A little gloating? Did she have a rich, good looking boyfriend in tow she wanted to show off? Surely, after seven years she couldn't be looking to get back in some way. But could it matter anyway? He had a good life. He was a happy man with a good job and a lovely wife. He had to relax.

*"Darega?"* Keiko broke his thought.

He told her in Japanese that some old friends were in town and that they would pick them up at the Princess Garden Hotel the following evening and go somewhere for dinner.

*"Honto?"* Really? There was a controlled hint of anxiety in her voice which she checked with the pouring of more beer into his glass from a fresh bottle of Kirin. It was in moments like this that a certain vulnerability shone through her that never failed to stir his desire. Admiring her small waist and narrow hips, he suggested that she wear her fitted black sheath with the mandarin collar when they went out.

*"Hai,"* she briskly responded.

They finished dinner quietly and soon after, when he could no longer keep his attention on the sit-com movie, he had Keiko rub his shoulders. Then they made love. He was more deliberate than usual, as if he hoped to find some response in both of them they had not yet known, until, exhausted, he drifted into sleep.

Waiting in the hotel lobby, he was searching for some images to connect himself with the woman he was about to meet again. It seemed that he had made such an effort for so long to forget everything associated with her. It had been a matter of survival. He had become good at detaching himself from not only unpleasant memories, but also from people and situations that called him to confrontation. He liked to think he was seeking the harmony in himself and in nature. That was another good thing about being in Japan: he didn't have to compete at every turn, with every word, day in, day out.

But now he had to remember something from those days with Serena. Specific scenes, days, moments, all blended into a soft focus, and despite his conscious resistance, he was drawn to memories of their lovemaking that had seemed to exist separately from them, as if a spirit with its own will that had swept them along.

He watched people coming and going to the information desk of the hotel. There was always something deliciously illicit, secret and furtive in the subdued style of plush hotel lobbies. He couldn't remember which hotel it had been, but he and Serena had once gone to a swank company champagne brunch and become daring with the champagne, trysting in a booth of a cavernous ladies' powder room, muffling laughter and pleasure. Serena had worked for the Dean Witter stock brokerage firm then. But what did she do now? Who was she now? He remembered that she had a degree in design, loved modem art, ethnic clothes, and little poetry books which she used to drag him to City Lights Bookstore to buy. There was one writer

Russ Desaulnier

she had especially liked who had a Spanish name that now escaped him.

Then he saw Serena coming out of the elevator with her boyfriend. Taller and older than Rick, he had sharp cheek bones, deep-set eyes and thick hair tied back in a small ponytail, and he wore an old corduroy sportscoat with crisp new designer jeans. Serena was dressed in a snug-fitting skirt, and she walked ahead, scanning the lobby. She seemed fuller in the hips than he remembered, but her hair was unchanged, taken up loosely as if it could all tumble down with the pulling of a few pins. Now she walked toward him, smiling, an eyebrow slightly arched and admonishing. Rick noted how her face was still unlined, except for the gentle circles beneath her eyes that had always added to her beauty in a tragic sort of way, and she still wasn't using makeup other than some lipstick the color of an evening sun. Her teeth, by contrast, were china white, unsullied by smoking, and her smile exposed that upper canine incisor that had come in a shade too high. Quieting himself, he took a deep breath and let it out slowly.

Introductions were made all around and there was a flurry of nervous small talk about their trip, about Japan, and then Rick led the way out into the street. Keiko took a position more or less slightly to the rear of his flank, keeping him between herself and the visitors. Serena's boyfriend, Barry, was gracious and tried to make small talk to Keiko who was trying to be warm and sociable despite her apparent nervousness. Serena hadn't stopped smiling and proceeded to fill in her side of the time gap.

"... and then after two years with the Broadway as a buyer, I did a short time back East with Bloomingdales before going with Norma Kamali. I've been to Hong Kong dozens of times but this is the first time to Japan. I've always wanted to see it, and so has Barry."

"I'm very interested in the raku techniques used by Japanese potters," Barry said.

"Barry throws pots for a hobby," Serena said, clarifying.

"Oh really?" Rick said, trying to appear interested.

There was a time when everyone in California was "throwing" pots and there had been a glut of ceramic ware with the same pretentious rustic crudeness. And then Rick had discovered that this ceramic style was essentially Japanese and highly prized, such renderings by well-known Japanese potters selling at prohibitive prices. To Rick such pieces looked like the accidents of kids at play rather than premeditated works of art.

"That's how we met. I took an adult education pottery class at city college that Barry was teaching," Serena said.

"Six months later we were living together. Matter of fact, this is like a special anniversary trip."

"Where you living now? Rick momentarily sensed himself inquiring by a reflex acquired from teaching too many ESL classes in which one often drilled students with banal questions.

"Five years, right Hon?" Barry said. "In the Heights."

"Posh. Yours?"

"Ours! We bought it two years ago," Serena said with undisguised pride.

But her smiling was warm and genuine. She seemed nothing less than delighted about seeing him again. She made an aside about how attractive she thought Keiko looked in her dress, guessing rightly that it was Italian made. She went on about how expensive women's clothes were in Japan, but how, despite the prices, most young women around town seemed too self-consciously overdressed; and how she liked kimono but not the constriction and how she would like to see some modern cuts with traditional patterns and colors. But she didn't pursue any questions about his and Keiko's marriage, about anything that could be personal.

"It's been a long time, as they say, hasn't it, Rick?" Serena said as she moved a pace ahead to Rick's side, leaving Barry with Keiko. It was about to begin, Rick thought.

"Where we are going is just up ahead under the International Hotel," he said, turning to Barry, who trailed behind politely chatting with Keiko. A moment later they descended some steep stairs to the Ginza restaurant.

The meal was elaborate, but not unlike the kind of fare that Keiko sometimes prepared for him. But the meal included some tender servings of Kobe beef that they rarely ate at home, and there was a serving of *toro sashimi,* raw slivers of flesh from the fat underside of the tuna. During the meal the talk revolved around what was a new experience for Serena and Barry, who had many questions for Keiko, who responded enthusiastically, mustering her most careful English to explain, missing only a few prepositions. Discussion about food spilled into other areas of Japanese culture including what Keiko recommended they should see when they went to Kyoto the next day. Everyone drank a fair amount of *sake* with the meal except Keiko. Barry, who had seemed a bit reserved before the meal, was now affable. His main business, he explained, was restoring old Victorian buildings from their gingerbread up to their spires. Also, according to Serena, he was one of the few people in the Bay area who could restore antique gilded picture frames. Barry was modest, referring to himself simply as a contractor. He wasn't without humor, either, joking about Serena's sense of drama, her flair for clothes being the proof. "She can change outfits three or four times before we get out the door," he said. Rick didn't have any such memory of her, but then he hadn't lived with her.

"He's critical because he never buys anything but jeans," Serena retorted.

"Serena is the only person I know who doesn't need a place to live. She only needs a big walk-in closet!"

Everyone laughed except Keiko, who didn't have any concept of a walk-in closet. Japanese bedrooms were often no bigger than a good-sized American walk-in.

He then remembered how Serena had often gotten looks when they had strolled down Montgomery Street arm in arm during lunch breaks. She had known how to dress for attention, with taste, unrevealing. Keiko was posed with her Japanese teacup held with both hands in front of her face, as if trying to hide.

"Barry has talent," Serena continued, not to be outdone, "but he has no sense of color. Everything has got to be earth colors. I sometimes think he's color blind. Take his pots... please."

"Okay, what's wrong with them?" Rick said, playing along with the good-natured fun which together with the *sake* was making him feel relaxed for the first time that evening.

"Nothing's wrong with them if you like the Stone Age," Serena said and then made a grunting noise as if to denote Neanderthal approval.

"My dear, there is a difference between brilliance and loudness," Barry came back, unruffled.

"What the hell was that supposed to mean?" She gave him a mock glare.

"We always know you are with us," Barry said, a little into his cups, and he leaned toward Serena affectionately trying to nuzzle her, but then he accidentally tipped a *sake* decanter, the clear liquid spilling over the edge of the table onto Serena's lap.

"Oh shit!" She flashed anger. "You lug!"

Keiko was quick to take up a hand towel and start mopping up the *sake*.

There was a friendly tension between Serena and Barry that drew Rick into their playful mood, and momentarily he forgot San Francisco. Then the flurry of action caused by the spill came to an end, and Rick wondered again if the evening wasn't being staged by Serena for some perverse reason.

"Hey Keiko, can you introduce me to a nice Japanese girl?" Barry said while grinning at Serena.

"You turkey!" Serena said, giving Barry a firm nudge with her elbow into his ribs to which he responded with fake pain.

"Why is it that men regress with a little alcohol," Serena said, lightly touching Keiko, who recoiled at the touch. It was apparent that neither Serena's comment nor her friendly gesture were understood, but Serena was the first to recover the awkward moment.

"Rick took you to San Francisco, didn't he?" she said slowly, carving out the words.

"One time," Keiko said, connected again, smiling. "We visit Rick's mother and we ride the cable car."

"And you had dinner at the Top of the Mark."

"Yes," Keiko replied, warming, unaware that she had confirmed a statement rather than answered a question, unaware of Serena's subtle, knowing look at Rick.

"Tarrentino's?" Serena continued on the trail, but she refrained from the social gesture of touching.

"Tarrentino's? Oh, yes. The crab was so delicious." Keiko looked at Rick as if to share the memories. Serena seemed to watch him with a curious, but mildly condescending smile, as though victoriously awaiting an expected reaction.

"And the 21 Club?" she said.

"No. No Club 21," Keiko answered, perplexed.

"The 21 Club, where's that?" Barry said, focusing in.

"Never mind, just a quaint little place from days of yore. I thought Rick might have taken her to," she said, bringing the nostalgic gambit to a close.

The 21 Club. The Hank, Wayne & Bob trio nightly on piano, bass and sax, a dark, smoke-filled hole in the wall in North Beach where it felt good to wallow, where it felt good to drink straight up and chain smoke. That's where, dressed to the teeth, they had often gone when they were down with work or with each other and they would purge themselves, the reality of their small troubles dissolving in the high camp of their action and the bluesy setting. In the end he had not gone back there, because the playing was over. He hadn't visited the 21 with Keiko because he no longer smoked, and he hated the suffocating smokiness of small bars. Nor was it a place that Keiko would have appreciated.

"Next time you guys come, I know the best deli in town, like the best grinder you ever ate," Barry said pouring more *sake*. Keiko looked to Rick, and he quickly explained in Japanese about delicatessens and grinder sandwiches.

"When are you coming back to the States, I mean permanently? You are coming back, aren't you?" Serena asked.

It was the stock question from every American visitor or short-term sojourner. They couldn't imagine how anyone could or would want to stay in Japan. For Rick the cultural shock that had once gnawed at him was no longer felt. He neither loved nor disliked his environment. He had acquired a kind of detachment from it all like that which he felt when he jogged past the five-kilometer mark where pain and pleasure neutralized each other. The thought of going back to the States now raised oppressive feelings of uncertainty.

"Someday, I suppose," was his vague, but honest answer. Then there was what seemed a long pause. He sensed that his lack of enthusiasm for returning to the United States had alienated his fellow Americans who, despite their sophistication, couldn't fathom, perhaps resented out of latent patriotism, one of their countrymen not longing to live in America, or worse, not dreaming of California.

Barry then broke the pause by suggesting they go for a nightcap at a club in the basement of their hotel. The night was still young, and so there were no objections. Besides there was something yet to be said, Rick thought, but he couldn't grasp the gist of it or form the words. He was hoping that the right moment and the right words would present themselves. He still had the dissonant feeling that he was being complicit in a bizarre pretense. Or was this evening a trial in which he found himself both defendant and judge? How could his present life in Japan possibly be served by unraveling a past that no longer mattered? He had listened to his insides carefully and there had been no residual of longing, of anger, of regret, nothing. If anything, the crossing of his lifelines made him feel strangely empty. He tried to move himself with fantasies of making love to Keiko, but the alcohol had taken him beyond desire.

The YA YA YA Club featured four Japanese moptop clones doing a respectable imitation of the Beatles. Barry ordered a bottle of Old Parr, and scotch and water was poured all around, with Keiko even agreeing to a mild drink. There was still room left on the small dance floor where a few drunken students swayed with eyes closed to "Yesterday."

Shortly after the drinks were served, Barry got everyone up on the dance floor for a slow dance and threw Rick and Serena together by commandeering Keiko onto the dance floor when the band began with "Hey Jude."

"I like Keiko," Serena said to him as soon as they began moving to the song. "She's young." Serena wasn't patronizing.

"I like Barry," he replied, although he had no feelings one way or the other.

"Well, you have a nice little town here, Nagoya, I mean."

"It's not bad."

"I wish we didn't have to leave in the morning."

They moved slowly across the floor, maintaining a space between their bodies. Barry was trying to simulate a slow kind of rock and roll dance, turning Keiko in circles and loops. Serena and Rick reviewed a few of their mutual points of reference, old friends and such, things that hadn't been touched upon during the dinner.

"Why did you come? Rick finally said, surprising himself. It was out. His head clearing with the sudden flow of adrenaline.

"Why? What do you mean?"

"Come on!"

"Come on nothing. Really! Hasn't it been fun tonight?"

"Yeah, well, sure."

"Oh Rick, lighten up. That was another life."

"Why the routine about all the old places?"

"No routine, it just sort of came out."

"Did you ever go back to the 21?"

"Not recently."

"I mean back then."

"When?"

"When... when we ..."

"When you did your disappearing act?"

"I was around."

"Right. If you were around, I didn't see you there."

"You looked for me at the 21?"

"No, I always went to seedy little bars by myself. Where did you get to anyway? Since we are dragging up history."

"I was around."

"Right. So you said. I never caught you at the 21, or anywhere else. Nor did you return my calls. I began feeling like those guys in western movies who never find anything except warm campfire ashes."

"I didn't know you were so concerned, Serena."

"What?" She laughed tenuously, her face alternately suggesting disbelief, then disgust, and finally a sorrow that seemed to deepen the circles beneath her eyes. She reached up and grazed his cheek with a light touch as if to extend sympathy, regret, or perhaps pity. Rick's heart began beating as if he had just started his morning run and he felt his voice sinking to his stomach. His practiced detachment was dissolving.

"I..." he began, but there were no words to follow.

Serena's attention trailed off as she looked across the dance floor to acknowledge Barry who was making some kind of anxious gesture to them while going back to the table with Keiko who appeared somehow awkward, unsure of herself and helpless.

"Excuse me, Rick, you were saying?"

"Nothing... nothing." He had caught himself, as if waking from a dream of falling. "Let's go sit down."

Back at the table Keiko reminded him that they had better be going if they were to catch the last train to Toyota City, since it was at least a ten-minute walk to the station. Barry said he and Serena would stay at the club a while longer and enjoy the music and a nightcap since they had only to go up the hotel elevator. He commented on how he thought Keiko's English was very good and that he had enjoyed meeting her, and then he shook Rick's hand. Rick and Serena could only say how nice it was to see each other again and gave each other a tenuous hug. As they let go of each other and stood apart, each with his and her respective mate, there seemed to be an interminable pause in which neither words nor gestures could be summoned. Then Serena extracted a small brightly wrapped package from her handbag and held it out to him, and as he took the little square package that felt like a book, she put a hand over his, holding him momentarily as if to communicate that he should take special care of it.

"A little something from America, a present. Open it later," she said, smiling, oracular, as if she'd just conferred the secret of Delphi.

He had pocketed the gift and they had rushed to the station to make the last train. The train was near full of late night revelers and redolent with alcohol, tobacco and sweat. Faces were flushed and saturnine with the effects of drink. Some travelers sat with their heads hung down in semi-sleep. Each stop was announced and at each stop more people got off until there were only a few people left as the train neared Toyota station and the end of the Meitetsu line.

"Serena is a beautiful woman," Keiko said, as though a cryptic encapsulation of the evening, and then she returned to her silence and the soporific hum of the train.

Russ Desaulnier

He then remembered the small package in his coat pocket, took it out and began unwrapping it. It was a little book of poetry by someone called Calvino, like the publications Serena always used to buy at City Lights Bookstore. Keiko gave it a disinterested glance. He was puzzled. Did Serena think he was in a distant outpost and her gift a cultural ration, a distillation of America for a deprived countryman? She couldn't know the Nagoya Maruzen bookstore was loaded with English paperbacks of every category. There wasn't anything you couldn't get in Japan these days, even good enchiladas. Besides he had never been a big fan of poetry; it was so complicated, the payoff unclear. But he would look the book over later when he wasn't tired.

The train would soon pull into Toyota station and then they would take a short cab ride home. Outside the train windows the countryside sped by, opaque and deep. Serena had said something during the evening that he thought he should remember, something about San Francisco, something important that he should have remembered, but he had forgotten what it was.

# The Spirit of the Royal Host

C *higau, chigau,"* wrong, wrong, I say, in my immigrant Japanese, pointing at the tiny portion of hash browns the waitress has brought and then at the generous serving pictured on the glossy menu. She takes my plate back to the kitchen, no doubt thinking I'm just another troublesome foreigner, for it would be a rare Japanese who'd complain. They endure.

I was frustrated and angered by such occurrences when I was new in Japan more than a decade ago. I've known expats to get worse rather than mellow with the years, some even getting out of control, escalating their frustrations into street scuffles. I don't get upset anymore with the comical things the Japanese do. Over the years, I've had to learn to accept that the Japanese perception of reality often defies truth. When I first came to my job at the university, I was assured my students were good at English. They were terrible. I was told the apartment the university was providing us was large. It was little more than a garret. I was further told the apartment was only ten minutes from the subway station. Maybe so for Carl Lewis.

It's been a few months since I came to the Royal Host cafe, because I was afraid I might start feeling nostalgic

Russ Desaulnier

and lonely. Although American style, the food never was great, but because the Royal Host is close to the university, my old buddies and I regularly lunched here for almost six years. There weren't many of us *gaijins* around in the mid-eighties, and I guess we were drawn together partly by that fact. These days, Nagoya's like Tokyo with Americans, Brits and Aussies on every street corner. Years ago when we lunched in these circular vinyl booths, it often crossed my mind that we were like those lonely GIs in the old black and white B war movies, huddled in a foxhole, complaining and talking about how much time they had left and what they were going to do when they got back to the States.

My plate has been returned, the hash browns still nothing like the picture, but an improvement. My eggs, ordered over easy, are overdone. I'm too hungry at this point to fuss. At least nowadays they have Heinz catsup on the tables, and I can give my eggs that good old American flavor. We Americans abroad do like to complain. It takes us a while, if ever, to get used to the fact that the world isn't American. And so the wannabe Royal Host coffee shop gave us a refreshing sense of home, one of the few places where you could hang out and get endless coffee refills.

We were all bad at Japanese. I still am. Perhaps in that we also found some bonding. We had discovered that fluency didn't seem to make much difference. Even if you manage to explain what you want, you often don't get what you want anyway. No substitutions, no flexibility in the menu. Rules and rigidity are everywhere. You'd think you'd find a beacon of light at the universities, but most are moribund with bureaucracy and old-boyism. At my school over the years I've suggested grouping students according to ability, creating an intensive curriculum, or just having some kind of rationalized program, any rationale, in the department. But there is no interest, no will. Ultimately, the study of English in Japan is an institutionalized fashion, and we foreign teachers are the window dressing. My buddies had their own war stories to tell, and together, from where we sat, we had a firsthand perspective and a collective store of irony that would have been hard to convey to the folks back home who were busy filling their garages with Toyotas and Hondas.

Thomas Burns III was the youngest of our threesome at thirty-five. Boyish, with large melancholy blue eyes, he was from an old Boston family whose fortunes had suffered in the 1929 crash and hadn't been restored with the succeeding generation. But the family had retained an abiding faith in education, managing to help young Tom through Dartmouth, where he paid them back by graduating cum laude in history. The family had also seen to his breeding, for it could never be said that Tom wasn't a well-mannered gentleman. This endeared him to my wife Tess, and Tom became a welcome, steady guest at our "large" Japanese apartment. When invited to dinner, he never failed to bring flowers and a good bottle of wine. And he could make the kids scream with delight at his playful and attentive antics. Apart from his women problems, Tom regularly exercised what seemed a didactic need to alert everyone to a world full of injustices and conspiracies, both past and present. But he was never dull company.

"They lost the war but they're still winning the peace," Tom was fond of saying about Japan and then would quote from the *Harvard Business Review* or *The Nation* on the number of Japanese lobbyists in Washington, how Japanese companies were taking over poor under-unionized states,

how they were hoarding government bonds as future political leverage, or how they were angling for a seat on the UN
security council without ever fully accounting for their war-
time atrocities. "Kurt Waldheim gets flak, why not them?"

Tom worked part-time at various schools, including
mine, and was still hunting a full-time position. Full-timers
receive bonuses two or three times a year, equal to about
six times their monthly base salary. In recent years, because
of a weakening dollar and a favorable exchange rate, some
of us full-timers have pushed into six figure incomes in
dollars. With this kind of money to be had, it's no surprise
there's been a flood of fortune-hunting newcomers, and no
surprise a lot of us old-timers have hung on, despite our
expat blues.

David Glassman, our other member, was a forty-four
year old confirmed bachelor. He was slight, bespeckled,
reserved, and not the kind of guy you'd expect was likely
to catch women's fancy. But in Nagoya at that time, when
any Westerner was a novelty, especially to a lot of curious,
young Japanese women, anything was possible. A Columbia
anthropology postgraduate from Westchester, New York,
David was a full-timer at Nagoya Technical College. Most
of us had been back to the States once or twice to visit
family, but not David, who'd only got as far as the West
Coast, apparently not concerned about seeing his aged
parents in the East.

"My mother never gives up. She's always asking me in
letters when am I going to find a nice girl and settle down
in my own country. My family doesn't know who I am, Man.
I don't even eat meat, least of all chopped liver."

With his Ben Franklin glasses, thinning hair worn in
a wispy tail, resembling that of a chipmunk, and his ever-

present beatific smile, he made me think of an aging elf. He wore an ever-changing assortment of ethnic clothing, accessories and jewelry—a Basque beret with a Greek tote bag one day, a north African bead necklace with a Peruvian vest the next. The trophies of a career traveler. He claimed to have been to forty-five countries and was staying in Japan just long enough to stake a few more years of roaming. If emotions stirred him, it was hard to tell, for his face rarely changed from that elfish look of secret glee, nor his speech from a quiet monotone. One had to wonder how he taught English, but he had done so all over the world.

"Come on, David, get excited for once, blow my mind," Tom said one afternoon when he was trying to wind David up about Israel's "illegal" bombing forays into Lebanon.

"Sorry not to fit your stereotype Zionist with an agenda," David countered, "but I don't really give a fuck about Israel. I'm going to Nepal." His elf eyes glittered.

"Who's talking stereotypes? Did you hear that, Hank? David used the F word," Tom said, satisfied.

Tess didn't care for David much. She said she couldn't respect anyone who came to her dinner table bearing a gift of cut-rate old fruit in a brown bag, nor could she trust anyone who barely acknowledged her kids.

Being as I was the family man and the oldest of the group, our association outside the Royal Host and the university lounge found its base with me. I prefer to be with Tess and the kids in the evenings if possible, so the guys would come to my place, particularly on the weekends. And Tess was glad for some American company. Since David and Tom have been gone, I've ventured out to meet some new expats, such as at a regular poker game across town on weekends when I needed some time out, even though

I don't much care for cards. But the spirit wasn't the same. There was too much cigarette smoke and talk about the NBA, NFL, NCAA, WBA, ad nauseam. I like company but not a male herd.

If Tom and David were around now, I'd gladly have them over for a dinner party, although Tess would probably insist I cook, which I can do. It would be her way of sending them a message. As she put it, she'd just burned out on them. She's had her own pressures, trying to raise two kids in this strange country, and she'd not had much of a life of her own in the bargain. Isolated, I would say, save for me and the kids, and the few people I brought home. For years there were only two other American women in the whole neighborhood, one who'd gone totally native, eschewing her own kind, and the other a forty-year old woman from the Midwest who'd mentally never left high school where she'd been a cheerleader. Tess has sacrificed a lot, and so I understand when she's sometimes got a bit of an edge. At times her candor can be pretty blunt. One evening, not long before Tom got married, when we'd all been drinking wine (I don't remember how it started), Tess told Tom and David, in her shoot-from-the-hip, kindly big-sister way, they needed to grow up and "get a life." Tom lacked "inner resources," and David was just "an aging, selfish bachelor."

In addition to getting married, Tom finally got himself a full-time job at a small college in Mie Prefecture. He wanted both things very badly. He was one of those men who can't bear living alone. David, on the other hand, was pretty much a loner. Anyway, neither David nor I got an invitation to Tom's wedding. He tried to tell us it was a very Japanese affair and it would have been awkward to have his *gaijin* friends at the ceremony. He promised a reception party at a later date, but it never materialized. I was disappointed when I received an embossed invitation to a second reception to be held in Boston that summer.

David and I continued lunching at the Royal Host without Tom, who had quit his part-time classes because my school was too far to drive from Mie Prefecture. The old saying about marriage parting friends was never more true. I'd met Tom's wife only once, and very briefly. She was twenty-nine and fairly attractive, had it not been for her sullenness. She was supposed to speak English well, but I would never have guessed by the little that came out of her. David was more acquainted, having met her and Tom downtown a few times when they were still just dating. He said they fought all the time. Her English could be like a volcano when ignited. One afternoon before a movie she exploded and stalked off, leaving David and Tom to watch the movie without her.

"Tom's pussy-whipped," David said. "She might be educated, but you know how little that means here. She's just another insecure Japanese chick, only she's got a mean streak. Tom was stupid to marry her. But then she isn't so smart either. The last time I was with them she asked me, straight-faced as the day is long, *Are you a hippy, David?*"

"Well, are you?" I said, trying not to laugh.

"Give me a break. She speaks English, but you still get a screwy Japanese mind. The shyness bullshit is just another excuse for hiding."

Maybe he was right because I never got to see Tom's fiancée again, even though I made numerous invitations to Tom to bring her along to our place. There was always an excuse why she couldn't join him when he came to our apartment. Tess and I just finally gave up on her. Then after the marriage, the obligatory Hawaiian honeymoon and his move to Mie, Tom became evasive and scarce. It was pretty obvious that he was sorting out a less than easy union. David and I couldn't figure out why Tom just hadn't taken up living with her. They were both adults, after all.

Not long after Tom's disappearance, David decided it was time to go to Nepal, promising he'd write when he got settled at an ashram. I got the impression David floated around the world ready to camp out with his sleeping bag wherever anyone would have him. I remember one spring vacation when he called a friend in Beijing to see if he could bunk in. During another school break, I got a postcard from Sulawesi, Indonesia on which he'd scrawled that he was staying in a remote village with a native family. I'd seen his collection of wannabe *National Geographic Magazine* photos in which he was proudly posed with exotic peoples from Llasa to the Louisiana bayous, all with stories to match.

I motion the waitress for more coffee. The service is always smiling and polite, as if the waitresses can't do enough. And all without tips. It's the same at the gas stations where two or three guys rush your car as you pull in, just the way it used to be in the States before self-serve, when guys used to wear uniforms and would clean your windshield without asking.

Tom believed both Kennedys had been removed by yet undiscovered deep and dark forces, and Japan had at its core something like Zionism. I wonder if he really believed the latter or just wanted to ruffle David's Jewish feathers. When Karel Van Wolfren's controversial book The *Enigma of Japanese Power* came out, Tom carried it around as though it were a bible from which he quoted like a born-again zealot. But Tom was convincing about Iraq's attack on Kuwait.

"We armed Saddam to counterbalance Iran, but then we realized he'd got a little too strong. So the State Department drops him a signal we're not interested in his border disputes with Kuwait. We know the result. The Pentagon got to try out their expensive high-tech weaponry and justify their obscene budgets, Bush got his Roman triumph, and Big Oil and the G-7 got to rearrange the balance of power in the Middle East and secure a continuing supply of cheap oil."

Tom was indeed well-read, but his sometimes tiresome insistence on making his points bordered on parading, as if he needed to impress people with what a smart guy he was. Most people have sketchy knowledge of history and politics patched together with a lot of opinions, and so, I think, he had found in our small pond he could swim like the proverbial big fish.

In earlier times, David liked to joke about Tom's girls, asking him at lunch if he had any new *trophy* to tell us about. But David himself never had a regular woman that I knew of. In addition to finding most Japanese women boring, he claimed to have suppressed his libido with meditation. We finally did get out of him once that he'd been dating a thirty-something Japanese woman and had taken her on a few hiking dates. He complained that she'd talked him into taking her to a French restaurant.

"I thought she was smart and liked traveling, but I find out she's only really interested in the best tour packages for shopping and scuba diving. A bummer evening, and expensive."

Tom, neither, was the experienced lady's man we'd been led to believe. A few months before he got married, Tom and I were having a bit of a head to head in my tiny apartment study.

"Should I marry her?" he asked.

I didn't know what to say, it being an improbable question and also I hardly knew anything about her or about them.

"Well, sure, I guess," I said, "if that's what you really want and you've thought it through." Was I supposed to say *no?* When I look back, I wish I had, but then I doubt it would have changed his course.

"She's not dippy like so many of the Japanese girls I've dated," he said.

Why didn't I just say then, *so that's a reason to get married?*

But do we ever have the right reply when we need it? Tom was caught up in his stormy needs and the nearest available port was going to do.

I'm on my third cup of coffee now. The place is starting to fill up, but no one is giving me the eye for lingering and taking up a booth. Matter of fact, I'm in the same booth where David and I had coffee just before he left for Nepal. He didn't have to pack much. All the while in Nagoya he'd lived in a dingy room at a Buddhist temple, where he shared a communal kitchen. I had to admire his simplicity. I agreed to buy his kerosene heater, the only thing of value in his room, which I figured Tess could use as an extra on really cold days. He asked me if I'd drive him to the airport and I agreed, although I never did like that long, tedious drive through a maze of side streets. Nowadays there's a direct express road that cuts the time in half. It crossed my mind that he could take a cab, but what the hell, I thought, he was one of my old buddies in the spirit of the Royal Host. When I told Tess I was taking him to the airport, she said, "That's a long drive at night. Can't he afford a cab?" All I could say was, "Well, he's a pal, after all." I really doubted I'd see him again, but maybe I wished I would; maybe I couldn't forget about all those lunches over the years like so many homesick pills. When we parted at the airport, he slipped me a little plastic Buddha on a key chain from the pocket of his Mexican poncho and solemnly said, "Stay mellow, Brother," as if he were a kind of Obi-one -Kinobi.

On the way back from the airport I resolved to get hold of Tom. I had resisted calling for weeks, after getting their perpetual answering machine on which his wife had recorded a message in Japanese. There was no English message. I had left a message once, but I think she must have got to it first and not passed it along, because Tom didn't return my call.

Finally one evening, after a couple drinks, I called and got through. She answered the phone in Japanese.

"May I speak to Tom, please? It's Hank," I said with the warmth of whiskey in my voice. No hello, no how-are-you, nothing. She was obviously holding the phone at arm's length, and I could hear her say, "It's one of your American friends," as cold and flat as Nebraska in winter. Tom got on the phone, sounding tired and subdued. He asked me about David, how were things at my school, the usual? I suggested our getting together for coffee or lunch that weekend, or sometime.

"Yea, sure, sure, sometime. I got a lot on my plate right now. But I'll get in touch." I could hear effort in his voice. Then I thought I'd lure out the old Tom I used to know.

"Hey, Man, how about that Bush fiasco in Tokyo with Miyazawa. What a bunch of fools the Japanese made of 'em, huh?"

"Yeah... they sure did," he replied, as if through the tunnel of daydream. I knew then that the spirit of the Royal Host was dead.

A couple, I'd say American, a little younger than Tess and I, are coming my way, led by the waitress. The expressions on their faces tell me they are happy with life. We make solid eye contact, a rarity among Westerners crossing paths these days. The waitress notes our smiling and veers them toward the empty booth next to mine.

"Where you from?" I say, as they sit down.

"Chicago," the man says.

"The Windy City."

"And you?" He smiles again.

"LA, eons ago. So what brings you to planet Japan?"

The play's the thing

—WILLIAM SHAKESPEARE

# The Breakfast Boys

- - - - - - - - - - - - - - - - - -

## A One Act Play

The scene is a typical diner like Denny's where three older men between 65 and 70 have just finished breakfast. They are seated in one of those semi-circle dining booths made for a group. They have hung their jackets over their seats. There is some continuous low background noise from other diners. At curtain rise, the waitress is collecting empty plates from the table where the boys appear glum.

**WAITRESS,** *{middle-aged, attractive)* More coffee? *(the boys nod)* I'll be back with more.

**LOUIE.** I still can't believe it.

**ALEX.** It's like he's sitting right there *(gesturing to empty seat)* and he's just gone to the head.

**JIM.** It's weird. He was the youngest.

**LOUIE.** The young and the best always go first.

**JIM.** Why didn't he ever say anything about his heart condition?

**ALEX.** He never talked about private stuff.

**LOUIE.** Do any of us talk about our hearts?

**ALEX.** I think Bobby was lonely.

**JIM.** That's probably why he never missed breakfast.

**ALEX.** There was no regular girlfriend in recent years that I knew of.

**LOUIS.** Guess what? I just met a hot babe last week!

**JIM &ALEX.** No?!!

**LOUIE.** Exactly, would I tell you guys if I had? Would Bobby have?

**ALEX.** Yeah, you would have because you'd want to brag if it was a babe!

**LOUIE.** The point is we don't talk much about our personal lives.

**JIM.** Hey, we're not a bunch of pussies.

**LOUIE.** Yeah, 1 know, real men talk about football.

**ALEX.** Or business?

**LOUIE.** Maybe we could have done something for Bobby, helped him in some way?

**ALEX.** I get out and walk in the mornings. I should have gotten him walking.

**LOUIE.** It gnaws at my gut when I think of Bobby just a pile of ash in an urn.

**ALEX.** It's actually a little nifty walnut box.

**LOUIE.** The container's not the point. Did you really care about Bobby, Alex?

**ALEX.** Screw you, Louie. I helped him out a lot of times you don't know about. I knew him before any of you did and I helped him.

**JIM.** Like how?

**ALEX.** When I was still working, I bailed him out several times with a few bucks and I also intervened a few times for him with his ex-wife.

**LOUIE.** Oh, really?! I remember the wife. Met her once. She made me think of an uptight little

Chihuahua.

**ALEX.** She wasn't bad. Bobby just treated her poorly and she finally did the right thing and dumped him.

**JIM.** We never knew any of this!? *(Jim and Louie look at each other in astonishment.)*

**LOUIE.** Like I said, we don't talk about our hearts.

**ALEX.** He felt bad about his personal mess. He asked me not to gossip about it.

**JIM.** God, you think you know people...

**LOUIE.** What do we really know about each other?

**JIM.** I know you hate USC.

**LOUIE.** What does it matter that I hate USC just because I went to UCLA almost 50 years ago? I felt stupid last season after painting my face blue and gold for a game. UCLA lost anyway.

**ALEX,** *(serious tone)* Bobby read.

**JIM.** We all read. So what?

**ALEX.** I don't mean Sports Illustrated, idiot. He read classics, Shakespeare, all kinds of stuff. He was deep.

**LOUIE.** Who knew?

**JIM.** Was he into drugs?

**ALEX.** No. But he was taking Lexapro or Zoloft, or something like that.

**LOUIE.** He didn't seem especially depressed or anything.

**JIM.** It doesn't always work like that.

**LOUIE.** Maybe we all need something.

**JIM.** Like being twenty years younger and a lot richer.

**LOUIE.** Seriously, we're all a bit nuts from being retired. Like this is our biggest event of the week, right?

**ALEX.** Speak for yourself.

**LOUIE.** That's all right for you to say. When you get

bored you just take a cruise on your fat retirement.

**ALEX.** Okay, Louie, I'm tired of this shit. Just to shut you up and get the record straight. The big money is my wife's, all right? All I got is my modest PERS check and Social Security. So, get off my case.

**JIM.** Will you two just cool it?!

**WAITRESS,** *(returning with a coffee pot)* You gents don't look very happy today. Can I get you something else, some fresh homemade apple pie perhaps?

**LOUIE,** *{sotto voce)* What I want ain't on the menu.

**ALEX,** *(intervening quickly in response to Louie's rudeness)* Why not? *(smiling pleasantly for the waitress as if an apology)* Apple pie all around. I'm buying. Make mine a la mode. *{Louie and Jim make affirmative gestures and the waitress exits)*

**LOUIE.** Well, thank you, Alex. Glad you can spare it.

**JIM.** Let it go, Louie.

**LOUIE.** Next week is my daughter's birthday and we haven't talked in two years. It's like I'm surrounded by death and loss.

**JIM.** So, give her a call.

**LOUIE.** It isn't that easy.

**ALEX.** Can't you just send her a card?

**LOUIE.** Last time I talked with her she said I abused her as a child.

**ALEX & JIM.** *(they react almost simultaneously, shocked)* No!? You didn't, *(and)* I don't believe it.

**LOUIE,** *(impatiently getting their meaning)* Oh, shit, nothing like that, of course not!! A few times I whacked her on the pants, but lightly. She was a pistol. Still is.

**ALEX.** So?

**JIM.** Weren't we all whacked about a little when we were kids?

**LOUIE.** That might be part of the problem.

**ALEX. I** cuffed my kids a few times; they don't seem any the worse for it.

**JIM.** Are we any the worse for it? My old man always whacked me when I got out of line.

**LOUIE.** She was always an angry kid. Maybe I made her that way.

**ALEX.** Everybody's trying to pass the buck these days. These entitled kids expect the world, and if they don't get it, it's everyone's fault but their own— you, me, the whole damn society.

**LOUIE,** *(sadly)* I miss her.

**JIM.** So, what are you going to do?

**LOUIE.** Not much I can do. Last time we talked she said if I started therapy, we could talk, maybe.

**ALEX.** Therapy for what? How's that going to patch things up?

**LOUIE,** *(a bit embarrassed here)* She says I might get my anger under control. Am I angry?

**ALEX.** You're opinionated as hell, but I don't know about angry. Are you?

**LOUIE.** I guess I get a little grumpy .

**JIM.** Don't we all.

**ALEX.** Look, Louie, just pick out a nice card and write a few words to your daughter about how you love her and miss her. *{There is a long pause in which everyone is pensive. Jim is visibly worried)*

**JIM.** I think Alice wants to leave me.

**LOUIE.** What? Nah! How long you been married, 30 years or so?

**ALEX.** What makes you think that? Has she said something?

**JIM.** No. She just seems distant. Like maybe I'm around too much since retiring. Maybe she sees too much of me.

**LOUIE.** Yeah, come to think of it you are kind of an ugly old fart, aren't you?

**ALEX.** Get out of the house, volunteer or something.

**LOUIE.** Retirement ain't all it's cracked up to be.

**ALEX.** You've got to deal with a whole new set of problems and challenges.

**JIM.** *{pensive with eyes toward the ceiling)* I feel I'm just putting in time, just maintaining and functioning. The past is always on my mind and I'm scared shitless of the future. It's like my life has passed by and there's nothing going forward.

**LOUIE.** You can say that again. I know exactly how you feel. *{The waitress arrives with three slices of apple pie and the breakfast check and then distributes the pie. Louie is solicitous and friendly)* You got kids?

**WAITRESS.** A boy in college, a girl just starting beauty school.

**LOUIE.** They sound like good kids.

**WAITRESS.** If your kids are happy and healthy, that's the best you can hope for. More coffee, fellas? *{they affirm non-verbally. Waitress exits)*

**ALEX.** Maybe we need bucket lists.

**LOUIE.** I would have thought you'd ticked off a lot of yours. Wasn't it two weeks in Hawaii last year?

**ALEX,** *(makes a disgusted face but then composes himself)* Jim, I mean, take on some personal challenge.

**LOUIE.** *(As though an aside but audible)* I do that

every day, just trying to take a healthy whizz.

**JIM.** Should I take up sky diving, or something?

**ALEX.** Nah, it doesn't have to be crazy or daring. Go to a gym, take a class, learn how to do something you've never done before.

**LOUIE.** That'll fill your bucket, yeah.

**JIM.** Louie, you ever thought of getting a cheap round trip flight to LA to see the UCLA-USC game? Don't you have a sister in LA you could stay with?

**LOUIE.** I've got other fish to fry. But since we're talking about solutions, Jim, you ever thought of just taking the wife out for a nice dinner and loosening up with a few drinks?

**ALEX.** Maybe even some dancing?

**JIM.** I can't dance.

**LOUIE.** Now there's a bucket list item, taking dance lessons with the wife. Do something together, whatever, besides watching television. Anyway, maybe things will be a bit clearer for all of us after the memorial on Saturday.

**ALEX.** That's right.

**JIM.** I don't think we need to take our wives, right?

**LOUIE.** They didn't know Bobby except for Alex's wife.

**ALEX.** She only knew about him, never liked him after I helped him with some money. She called him a loser.

**LOUIE.** So just the three of us are going, I guess.

**JIM.** This has got to be the worst thing about getting old, going to more memorials. (*The other two men shrug in discomfited agreement. They start moving out of the booth, getting their jackets.*)

THE BORDER                                    243

**LOUIE.** I reckon those of us left behind feel a bit closer to each other, *(he puts a hand on Jim's shoulder and then a hand on Alex who responds with a touch that bespeaks no hard feelings. They finish getting on their jackets and are getting out their wallets, Alex looking at the check left on the table earlier by the waitress.)*

**WAITRESS.** *(Arriving back at their table to bus the dishes and get the check)* That'll be it then, boys?

**ALEX.** That'll take care of mine, *(he returns the bill to the table with his share.)*

**JIM.** There! Keep the change, *(he puts some bills on top of Alex's share. The waitress has a stack of plates and is about to bus them away.)*

**LOUIE,** *(to the waitress)* You take good care of those kids of yours, okay? *(They exchange a smile, and she exits at stage left. Louie puts his share of money on the table and then he starts to exit right, trailing behind Alex and Jim who are almost offstage. He then stops and sighs, turns around and goes back to the table.)*

**LOUIE.** Ah, screw it, another ten bucks for the kids, *(he takes a bill from his wallet and puts it on the table and paperweights it with a cup, and then he exits)*

## END

It ain't the heat, it's the humility.

—YOGI BERRA

# One-Night Stand-Up

- - - - - - - - - - - - - - - - - - - -

W hen the fall rolls around, my mind often goes to football, although I gave up the game entirely after leaving high school. But it's hard to avoid being reminded of the game at this time of year. The television is full of the game, the newspaper, conversations overheard. A high school has its noisy practices on a field a few blocks away from my house. Adults all over town wear some sort of symbol of our university team whether it's the school color or a cap with a big O for Oregon. Across America similar behavior can be seen in other university hometowns. When I was in high school, I had the fever. I often think that this national obsession is a symptom of our history, a country made by war. How the ancient war-like Spartans would have loved our football. It is not an international team sport like soccer, hockey or basketball. It is singularly American. Well, I will let the social anthropologists take up that discussion.

I can never forget the summer and fall of my last year in high school in LA. I had already earned varsity letters in my sophomore and junior years, but in both those seasons I had sustained injuries that put me on the bench. In my sophomore year during a practice scrimmage I was tackled with a pile-driving shoulder pad to my thigh as I tried to turn the corner on an end run. The impact left my whole thigh solid black and blue for several weeks, requiring me to use a crutch to get around. The second injury came in my junior year when returning a punt in a scheduled league game. I wound up at the bottom of a pile of several tacklers which resulted in a twisted ankle, whereupon I spent the remainder of the game with my foot in a bucket of ice and I was hobbled for the balance of the season. Finally, in my senior year I was lucky enough to escape any disabling injuries, and so I was able to luxuriate in the highs of our Friday night games under lights. I think we Americans brought the expression *pumped up* to the vernacular. Along with my teammates, I was pumped up on those Friday nights. It was like a drug high I had become addicted to early in my short football career, however interrupted by the price of injuries. When you ran out on the field with your team under those intense floodlights in your clean, tight-fitted uniform and all that youthful testosterone busting at the seams, you felt something especially powerful, even invincible. The camaraderie felt with your teammates pushed your endorphins to yet greater heights. The coaches at this point were beloved demi-gods who held us mortal players in their hands.

But before all the color, music, cheerleaders and the restless hometown crowd, there were the weekly scrimmages and drills. And before even those were the summer practices before classes began in September. I don't think there was anyone among us who didn't think coach M was pushing the envelope. During the last two weeks of August before our first season game, we had three two-hour practices a day. As if that wasn't hard enough, a prolonged heat wave of 90 degree plus days added to our misery. Looking back now, I am surprised no one collapsed with heat stroke, or worse. Surely if any of us had entered army boot camp after graduation, we would have been prepared. I felt particularly sorry for some of our big linemen who had to carry so much more weight through those grueling days on the practice field.

For us seniors it was not just our last football season, for we were coming to the end of carefree young adult days. Some of us were going straight into the workaday world, some of us onto college. A few intrepid souls even got married upon graduation, or perhaps they were more grown up than the rest of us. My closest friend in that last season was Ted L. a 175 lb. all-league middle guard on offense and a ferocious linebacker on defense. He was such a close friend that I would occasionally stay over at his family's house and use a spare bedroom when I was on the outs with my parents. We also had great parties in his house when his parents and older sister were away. Home alone, as it were then. Lots of rock and roll, a few elicit beers and necking with girlfriends. My last, clear memory of partying in the rumpus room at the back of his house is framed with a big hit pop song of the time, *You Send Me* sung by Sam Cooke.

My fiftieth high school reunion was completely deflated of joy by the discovery that Ted had recently died in a car accident. There were no details, no kin to contact. But since then I have never stopped wondering if he didn't have one of his blacking out episodes. Once we were taking a leak during our football era when I looked over to say something to Ted at the next urinal, and he'd slumped down onto the porcelain bowl, recovering an instant later, telling me not to worry. It would pass, he assured me. But did it? Being a tiger as a middle guard, Ted perhaps took too many hits. With what we know now, perhaps those bruising football days had left him with brain damage that caught up to him with age, finally causing him to black out behind the wheel?

Rick C. was also not at the reunion, taken, I was told, by a massive heart attack. He was our smallish but wily quarterback with a great arm, and he represented some of my best and worst memories of my time on the field. He sensed when and where was the best time to call a certain play. He had a field general's sense of the other team's weaknesses and how best to take advantage. That season I dropped two of his perfectly thrown lateral passes delivered to my waiting hands at the sideline because I was too anxious to start sprinting the open field ahead before securing a good grip on the ball. Rick liked both our hardy tackles who often managed to open holes for the halfbacks on slant runs. Twice that season I redeemed myself with Rick, running two 30-yard touchdowns from those off-tackle slant plays that he called. I remember the exhilarated, floating feeling I had as I handed off the ball to the end zone referee while embracing the wild roar of our loyal crowd. What glory!

Jeff E. was there, best remembered for his homecoming game kick-off return of 90 yards. Our season would have fared better that season had he not suffered a broken arm in our fourth game of the season. I was faster than Jeff on a straight-away, but Jeff had a much better ability to run broken field and avoid tacklers. Laconic, he was reserved and serious, in addition to his football heroics, and he had great appeal for most of our underclassmen who had a hard time thinking of themselves as anything other than high school kids, and so they voted him in that fall semester to become student body president. Jeff wasn't especially approachable at the reunion. Or perhaps that was just me, always put off by strong, stolid types. We chatted briefly. He was working in a furniture manufacturing plant in Arizona. I acknowledged his memorable moment, dashing 90 yards on a kickoff return, but I got the name of the opposing high school wrong, which he quickly corrected with a clear hint of irritation. It was my guess that his life had never quite risen to the level that it had during that last football season of our senior year.

Randy M. looked almost the same after so many years, tallish, slim and hawk faced, but now he was sporting a stylish goatee and mustache. He'd made a career as a corporate attorney with CBS Entertainment. I could nose him out in the hundred-yard dash, always beating him by one or two tenths of a second. In football his field abilities weren't any better than mine. Where we both really shined was in the spring track meets. But he outdid me in the 220 dash where I had neither the leg length nor the stamina to keep the pace. We had been friends and teammates in the 440 x 4 relay event for the league title and double dated several times to dances. At the reunion, he joked about how he could never figure out how my comparatively short legs kept me ahead of him. Our reunion meeting was warm, but sadly we didn't connect beyond a brief interlude.

Judy S. was among the missing. Breast cancer. We'd had some marathon necking sessions that never went further. The length of those sessions, often in the front seat of a car at night, the romantic venue of the times, with the radio playing pop hits, bore proof to the youthful passion involved, and the restraint. Such were our times on the cusp of a decade and culture that were about to see an enormous change. I had always felt a bit uncomfortable with the fact that Judy was the daughter of a Methodist minister. We went steady for a few months, the customary exclusive dating arrangement of the era, until we both amicably moved on to new love interests, which I think was something of a relief for both of us—and probably for her pastor father. Much of the romance in those days was little more than an innocent ongoing game of spin-the-bottle.

Big Gary L. was holding court at his banquet table. He had been one of those great tackles on the team and became a steady, but minor presence in Hollywood movies into the 70s and 80s, making a career playing second tier characters, usually as the heavy, the bully, the imposing antagonist. I got to know him as a sophomore when a minor disagreement led to his choosing me off, from which I sensibly retreated. But in that last season on the gridiron, we became friends again, sealing the friendship when I made the most of the holes he'd plowed in defensive lines. I'd heard he'd lost his wife of thirty years and indeed he'd lost the rough edge I was expecting. Although he was a big man in our day, his size now would be comparable to that of the average halfback at the college level. People had become bigger in fifty years.

Paula B. looked almost unchanged with the same bobbed hair and no gray. She greeted me in passing with a sustained smile, looking back at me as she drifted away, as cute and distant as ever. I didn't recognize my old friend Elena A., truly a petite Mexican cutie in her day, who could dance a wonderfully choreographed routine to the 50s hit song *Tequila*. She was now round as a tortilla, and it was obvious I was trying too hard to read her name tag. Sensing my embarrassment, she told me in Spanish not to worry. Back in high school, we were just good friends and she lived a block away from me. I sometimes visited her house where she and her parents helped me learn a little Spanish in my beginner days and her mom fed me homemade Mexican delicacies.

Last, but not least, were Gina and Bill, married upon graduation. They both became lifelong high school teachers, he ascending to a district superintendent. They were always ahead of their years in my eyes, as though life had always presented to them a straight line and clear vision ahead. And here they were further down that line, not just grandparents but now great grandparents. They still sailed their forty-foot schooner to quaint seaports just south of the border. Gina, one of the organizers of the 50th reunion at the LA airport Hilton, had found me up in Oregon after seeing a couple of my stand-up routines on YouTube, and she asked me if I would present some comedy as part of the reunion festivities. Of course, the $50 reunion party fee would be waived. After all, she'd reminded me, I had been student body president, following Jeff E., in our last semester. She said it was incumbent on me to make the flight to LA and contribute to the entertainment. Most everyone would remember me, she assured, if their memory was still any good. Gina had been my student government secretary, as thorough an organizer now as she had been then. When she introduced me over the mic, the big rush to the sumptuous buffet had already occurred and most of my old classmates were settled at the big round banquet tables, eating, drinking and chatting. I took the mic off its stand and put the stand aside. I liked to move around a bit when I did my routines, not remain static behind the mic.

*Good evening ladies and gentlemen, friends and once-upon-a-time-classmates. You've entered another dimension, a dimension not only of sight and sound but of the mind, a journey into a wondrous land of imagination—your 50th high school class reunion of 1959. Indeed, tonight has all the makings of a Twilight Zone story and it just so happens that* it was also 50 years ago this month that Rod Serling's smash hit show began its first run on TV. How's that for a coincidence?! Now let's give it up for our hardworking reunion committee. Come on, stand up, you guys. Let's hear it everyone. (Applause)

Maybe we ought to have one of these gatherings every five years at this point...It really is wonderful to see you all here.... those I can recognize.

Being in LA again, wow, it's been a long time. What a sentimental journey. I'm all choked up and tearful. What can I say, coming from out of state, I'm not used to the Los Angeles smog.

I'd ask you all how you're doing, but I already know. You're trying to wrap your heads around fifty years! Just forget about it and pass the Scotch!

Some philosophers like to say life is just a dream. Okay, fine, but it's the wake-up call like tonight that really gets you.

An old friend comes up to me tonight and says, Man, you haven't changed at all. What? I say, I looked this bad fifty years ago? Get outta here!

Hey, when I turned sixty-five, I got rid of all the mirrors in the house and ever since I got back my self-esteem.

1959 was a great year for freedom: we graduated into the adult world and Searle company gave us the pill—that was some graduation present, huh ladies?

Now 2009 and we still have something to look forward to, huh, guys? Now we have **our** pills.

Speaking of romance, remember Johnny Mathis? I can still remember lines from his songs, but I can't remember what I had for lunch yesterday or sometimes what I went to the store for. By the way, why am I standing here with this mic? And who are you people?

THE BORDER                                   253

*You know, you're relieved when you retire, but it takes getting used to. I wasted a lot of afternoons watching reruns of Law and Order, until I finally figured out who the killer was.... BOREDOM!*

*Have you ever wondered why so many old codgers take to gardening? It's because that's the only way they've got left to get dirty.*

*Retirement should be a golden time, so long as you have engaging hobbies, an active social life and survive your first heart attack...and can remember you had one.*

*You know when you get to this stage of life you get to do some traveling...like five times a night to the bathroom.*

*Actually, I loved traveling. I used to love going off the beaten track in Mexico. But now it's where very few tourists go, and fewer come back. Hasta la vista, Baby.*

*After the wife and I had exhausted ourselves and our bank account with traveling, we took up dancing tango. I just wish women had to lead, then I'd get to blame my wife for something.*

*They say dancing is good for seniors. Puts life back into your vital organs, most of them anyway.*

*It's said tango is the vertical expression of a horizontal desire. Not really. It's a difficult dance, you're too busy thinking about your feet to think about booty.*

*At our age you start to look back and wonder about missed opportunities, like last week's Costco special on Econopacks of Metamucil and Aleve.*

*The other day I was reminiscing and having a few laughs with a couple of buddies about the crazy stuff we used to say and do, for example, how we called our women our old ladies. Who the hell is laughing now?*

*I think I spent a few years in San Francisco (??) All the*

Russ Desaulnier

*smoke left things a bit hazy! But kids these days will never forget, huh? They'll have their crazy moments indelibly written in tattoos.*

*We all want to age gracefully and slow the wrinkles, fix that cellulite cottage cheese around the torso and thighs. Get in shape, as it were. So, you go to your over-priced gym and pump iron, the whole sweaty enchilada, and what do you get? In shape cottage cheese.*

*As Betty Davis once said, getting old ain't for sissies. So better to make light of it and see the huge joke in it all. If you work at it enough, maybe you can die laughing.*

*A lot of us seniors these days don't know what we're more afraid of, kicking it early or not having enough money if we don't. My accountant tells me I've got only enough to last until I'm 75. So, screw it, I'm taking up cigars again and eating big steaks. Live long and prosper, old friends!*

I held up my hand with the Spock Vulcan salute and replaced the mic in its stand amidst spotty applause. I had forged ahead throughout my set, unbowed and animated despite half the tables remaining engrossed in their conversations. Gina, always sweet, gave me a hug as I left the stage, which was immediately being prepared for an Elvis Presley impersonator who had been hired to sing hits from our high school era. Gina asked me to join her and her husband Bill for a glass or two of champagne.

"Funny stuff," her husband Bill said, extending his hand as I sat at their table. "Don't feel bad, a lot of our old classmates never left the 50s. They're a bit drunk and distracted, and some of them still don't get irony."

"I'm not sure this was a good idea, doing this comedy thing." I said, trying to laugh it off. The champagne was much needed.

"Anyway, you can imagine what we've dealt with in education. I was finally relieved to retire," Gina, said pouring him a flute of champagne.

"Let me tell you, managing a school district with so many divergent views is like trying to run a gauntlet. In recent years getting a consensus on anything was tough. Choosing textbooks was a real headache. But I opposed their leaving out Darwin," Bill said, drawing an imaginary X.

"Kids don't listen because they have families who don't," Gina added

"So, I've gathered," I confirmed.

I sat and chatted with Gina and Bill about old times and our current lives through three more glasses of champagne, had a bite to eat and felt recovered, even a little happy. When I left them, I decided to slowly weave my way among the banquet tables, thinking I'd stop and chat wherever I saw a familiar face, or a welcoming smile. But I was unnoticed, no one holding eye contact or hailing me, as if fifty years had already slipped into eternity. There was nothing left to do but turn in, head for my room, maybe have a last drink from the tiny fridge, watch a little TV perhaps, call it a day, the reunion one-night stand was over.

# The Fearsome Blackfoot

In more innocent times, a certain frame cabin, the house of the Blackfoot tribe, wasn't visible from the main site of YMCA Camp Wanakita, for it was the last cabin in a string of others, also with Indian tribal names, on a meandering trail in the thick of the Ontario forest, a last outpost as it were for the older boys of twelve to thirteen. It was a good place to be because it was shaded and cooled by the thickness of the forest during the hot humid summers. The cabin was sided with heavy sheets of plywood which were slowly being gnawed away by porcupines. The roof was corrugated metal, and during two of the heavy downpours that summer we had to put down a few cans to catch the leaks. The interior of our sacred Blackfoot headquarters was just as rustic, furnished with six iron frame bunk beds and assorted orange crates fixed to the walls to serve as shelving for our personal items. As crude as it was, we brother warriors of the Blackfoot tribe thought it better than all the palaces in the world.

Barely a week had passed since the YMCA bus had brought us from the city of Hamilton, but we had already become as bound as brothers with secret signs and codes. We constructed a flagpole in front of the cabin from a fallen branch and we topped it with a square of cloth which we had all stamped with our right foot dipped in black paint.

Cuthbertson, Cuppy, had fashioned a sign with birch twigs some yards down the trail which read: Beware, Blackfoot Country. Blazing a trail through the thick brush, we found a small natural clearing near the cabin and put logs around the perimeter for seats and built a stone ringed fireplace in the center. It was to be our high council meeting place when medicine man Atkinson, Acky, sounded the ceremonial tom-tom. Having established ourselves as a great and fearsome tribe, we set our minds to what intrigues and adventures we would embark on. To do this we met after dark at the council circle. We dressed appropriately for the pow wow, using towels looped with a belt for loin cloths, wrapped ourselves in blankets, and wore a single feather in improvised headbands. Once everyone was sitting around the fire—that is, our collective flashlights bunched together in the center of the circle—we passed around the ceremonial black tempera paint and each smeared his face with an assortment of marks then passed the jar. Meanwhile Acky made strange motions and incantations over the fire. It didn't matter that we didn't understand his gibberish, because it made our ceremony more mysterious and potent in our imaginations already stirred by the embrace of the dark forest. In that circle we approached some ancient being within ourselves.

It was generally decided that we had to wage war. After all, that is what real Indian tribes did. But our war amounted to little more than mischief. We skulked away from our council circle with flashlights pointed downward and headed toward cabins down the trail. We would surround a cabin of 8 and 9 year-olds and start by making animal sounds in the dark, escalating the terror with small pebbles hurled at the cabin walls, and when we were satisfied we

Russ Desaulnier

had struck terror into the inhabitants of the cabin, we'd hoot and holler around the cabin, and then suddenly disappear back into the forest and make our way back to our council circle. These forays were usually followed by a quick dip into the lake down a short path from our cabin where paint and sweat were washed off.

One fateful night we took two younger campers captive, who happened to stumble upon us in route to one of our raids. Acky had us blindfold them and lead them back to our council circle. But by the time we got there, the boys couldn't stop wailing with terror so we took them back to their cabin, making them promise not to utter a word of what had happened, or the wrath of the Blackfoot would find them. After a week of these forays, we all got bored with the ritual. And besides, we got warnings from our counselor, Roscoe, who had gotten wind of our antics, and he warned us to cut out the funny stuff and join in the activities of the other campers. After that the tribe got restless and began to split up: Livsey, Pudge and Blair, three of our best, failed to show up at council meeting in the third week of camp. Little John, Acky and I agreed that all we needed was a new idea to bring the tribe together again. After another week passed, Acky made it known that there was to be a special council, and all were to come at the sound of the tom-tom. It was a moonlit night, and Little John and I were sitting cross-legged around our gathered bunch of flashlights while Acky played the call on the tom-tom. As I sat, my eyes followed the flashlight beams up into the black sky. I felt I had known this place my whole life and felt akin to the wild things that surely lurked just outside our circle.

"How!" Little John said in the deepest register of a voice that was just beginning to change.

"How!" said a group of voices in unison just as Pudge, Cuppy and Blair entered the circle of light. A few minutes later the rest arrived. Acky stopped the tom-tom beat and Little John spoke.

"Many moon pass, many Indian forget Blackfoot tribe. Medicine man Acky say this bad sign. Since last council fire great idea come from Great Spirit Manitou. But first we elect chief for all Blackfoot. All warriors in favor of me, raise hand."

I was so surprised by Little John's proposal I couldn't form the words to protest. Since the start of the tribe, having a chief was one subject we had managed to avoid. I think every one of us had thought about it. I had thought about becoming chief, but I never hinted at it. It was an idea that none of us could take a stand on.

"How come you gotta be chief, Fat Stuff?" Blair sneered.

"Cause I'm the biggest and chiefs gotta be big. That's how come."

"They ain't supposed to be big 'n dumb like you."

"You wanna make somethin' out of it, Baby Blair? Little John raised himself up and his pink face got red.

Little John lumbered slowly toward his smaller adversary with a menacing look as though he meant to kill. It was too late to stop them as they flew at each other, grappling and rolling in the dirt and pine needles. Everyone closed in around them, cheering and exhorting the straining bodies twisting on the ground. Then suddenly the fighters were on their feet and Blair had grasped a heavy chunk of wood.

"Come on, fatso, I'll bust your fat head," Blair cried, tears streaming down his cheeks. He was about to rush Little John when Acky and I simultaneously intervened, Acky wrestling Blair aside while I yanked the club from his hand.

"Shut up and listen!" I yelled as loud as I could. "Blair here got himself a bloody mouth and Little John almost got his head busted in. We can't fight like this. If we're going to have a chief, we're going to have to do it some other way. Isn't that right, Blair?"

"Yeah, guess so," he said, wiping away his tears.

"If Little John hadn't popped off,'" Acky said, "and given me a chance to say what I was gonna say there wouldn't have been all this trouble and we might've been getting to what the council meeting was for."

"Wait a minute..."

"Pipe down, John!" Pudge cut him off.

"Yeah, good idea." Livesy said, lining himself up next to Pudge.

"You've said enough for one council, John. Let Acky talk," Cuppy added, consoling with a hand on Little John's shoulder.

"First of all," Acky said, "Little John and Blair get to be special warriors and get to wear two feathers instead of one because they've done some real fighting. It'll be the tribe's way of giving them honor." There was a round of approval. Blair smiled faintly, wiping away some blood at the corner of his mouth.

Little John, his malice giving way to a sheepish smile, approached and put out his hand.

"I'm sorry, Blair. I'm sure glad you didn't clobber me."

"I really wasn't going to clobber you...I was just mad, that's all. You didn't hurt me. Just a little blood."

We all cheered and had a good laugh and swore there was nobody tougher than the Blackfoot in the whole camp.

"Tell them what we're gonna do," Acky said, pointing at me.

"We're gonna have a hunting party, a real hunting party. Acky and I were talking to old Bob the maintenance man and he told us there's a lynx or a bobcat around here somewhere. He showed us some tracks up behind Cabin 11. Acky and I thought it'd be great if we could hunt the cat down and kill him. He could be dangerous, so it would really be something if we could get him. Whoever kills him would get the tail in his head dress and be the chief. Anyways real tribes always go on hunting parties."

"What are we going to hunt with? Rocks?" Pudge said.

"Heck no!" Acky said. "You guys check out bows from the activities room at the lodge just like you're going to the archery range. Check out thirty pounders because old Bob said these cats got tough hides. You don't have to worry about arrows, because I lifted a carton from the storeroom, so we don't have to worry about having enough ammo."

We were abuzz with all the pros, cons and contingencies of this elevation of the Blackfoot to real hunters when taps sounded. As we headed back to the cabin with our flashlights, the words hunt, stalk and tail were heard the most. I was already thinking about where to look for the cat. I envisioned bringing him down with a perfect shot and I began thinking about a new headband I could make for the trophy tail.

When the coal oil lamps in our cabin were turned low and finally off with taps being played a final time from the central camp site, our excitement turned to whispers and those were slowly swallowed by the night and the chorus of Lake Koshlong's bullfrogs as we all drifted off to the happy hunting grounds of sleep.

As it turned out, there never was a bobcat and certainly no lynx as they are very rare and stay far from any humans.

Russ Desaulnier

What did become our prey, or should I say victim, was one of the porcupines that frequently came in the middle of the night to gnaw on the cabin siding for, as we were later told, the salt contained in the processed wood. Finally plans were made, the bows and arrows acquired and divided up. It was quite a feat that four of us managed to stay awake until two in the morning when the porcupine finally came around. We crept from the cabin, careful not to surprise the animal or awaken our sleeping mates. We surrounded the porcupine that spread its quills to make itself look twice as big, but only two arrows found their mark, which were not enough to stop the hapless creature from trying to waddle away. Panicked, we finally used heavy sticks, plentiful in the wooded vicinity of the cabin, to wildly club the big ball of spikes until it no longer moved. Then we all looked at each other in stunned, speechless amazement, and I think, sorrow and regret. We pulled the arrows from the carcass and dragged it on a beach towel further into the woods and buried it in a shallow grave we dug with the ends of the clubs. All of this came to pass with hardly any words between us. We were not proud Blackfoot that night, only completely exhausted and sad boys. The four of us never spoke of it again, never telling the others and certainly not Roscoe our counselor.

I have never spoken or written about this wanton act in sixty years until now.

# Forsaken

----------------------

C harlie Larsen loved his grown daughter Yvette with all the fervor a father can feel for an only child. There was no turning his affections to a sibling, no replacement. She had cut him out of her life so completely that all his pleas for reconciliation by card and email were left unanswered, as if she had disappeared into a vacuum. Old photos of her caused his heart to do flips and so he put all of them away in deep drawers. His failed efforts to file her away only convinced him that he couldn't let her go. His wife Donna claimed to have emotionally processed their daughter's apparent loss of love for them. He was sure the wound was still tender for her too. Donna was sensitive, but he knew how she could be tough when life called for it. That's how she grew up. All he could find to tell himself was the old saying, *you can lead a horse to water, but you can't make it drink.* Was he going to have to wait for Yvette to again find the love he knew she held in the depths of her heart? What he most remembered from the last time he saw her, when her tantrum and tears subsided, were her parting words: *I love you.*

It all began in Maui with Yvette's wedding to Laurie, her girlfriend of several years. It was hard to understand why they had to travel so far to get married. They could have had a cheaper and more inclusive wedding on the mainland. But Yvette and Laurie were doing what was currently in vogue and Yvette had noted she didn't have or want a wide circle of friends. When he and Donna got married at an Episcopal gray stone church thirty years ago, they had settled for a reception at a popular local Mexican restaurant with a dance floor, and they had invited over a hundred friends and acquaintances, although they had no contact with any of them now, save for a few who could be counted on one hand. In some ways his daughter Yvette was old for her years and too inclined to see the downside of possibilities. But then she had been hired to train in management by Chase Bank, not what Larsen might have hoped for her, but it was a solid beginning and she would no longer need his financial support.

The Maui hotel was typical, a huge concrete horseshoe-shaped warren around a curvy pool the size of a football field, surrounded by grassy grounds dotted by stands of tall slender palms. He and Donna had a room at the opposite end of the horseshoe building from the small wedding party's rooms that comprised Laurie's family and a few friends of the girls. There was no invitation to meet Laurie's family before the wedding, which should have sent up a red flag. They only met Laurie's mother by accident in passing in one of the lobbies, but there had been no offer to a sit-down to get acquainted. Later, Donna told him she didn't have a good feeling about the wedding, and so she purposely took a back seat and observed. He saw nothing except his daughter's joy.

The wedding took place on a beach cove, his daughter in a white tux and the bride in a typical white wedding gown of no memorable fashion. There were about a dozen in the wedding party plus a commercial crew of three who the girls had hired to organize and conduct the ceremony. Laurie's father, younger than Larsen, although white haired like himself, gave the bride away. It was almost impossible to make out what was spoken during the ceremony because of the wind and the lapping of waves on the beach, but perhaps it was just as well because the ukulele accompaniment by one of the wedding crew was less than amateurish. Larsen smiled inwardly when he considered what precious impulses inspired such romantic but impractical weddings. The last one he'd attended was that of an old college girlfriend who got married on a Malibu cliff. The groom had been somewhat of a romantic figure who owned a Chinese Junk on which they were going to honeymoon by sailing up and down the West Coast. That California marriage lasted all of four years. Perhaps lesbian marriages had better odds. He didn't know. He did know that this was his daughter's first real serious relationship and here she was committing her whole life based on what? The new wife, Laurie, a couple years older, was more experienced by all accounts. In any case, he just hoped for his daughter's lasting happiness.

The reception was a sit-down affair at a pricey island restaurant which he mostly remembered for his entertaining exchanges with two jolly overweight lesbians, office mates of Laurie, directly across the table from where he sat. What stood out for him was the absence of Laurie's father, sitting far out of reach of any exchanges.

Larsen had to get up and cross to a corner midway through dinner to toast with the father of the bride, who didn't rise but lifted his glass from his sitting position.

Shy? Retreating? How does a father of the bride claim the right to retreat at the wedding reception dinner for his daughter? He felt awkward offering a toast to someone who couldn't stand to toast his daughter's marriage! All the new father-in-law could offer was a weak smile and a thank you. All he knew of the new father-in-law is what Yvette had told him, that he was ex-Navy graduated from Annapolis and shy. Larsen had always had a distrust, and a little distaste, for people who came preceded by naming their prestigious alma mater as if a calling card meant to garner unearned respect or to intimidate. Should we consult their opinion on important matters, domestic and international? Well, perhaps so in the case of military academy grads; they might know which way the wind was blowing. The commander, as Larsen tacitly dubbed the father-in-law, might have been short on social grace but he was no dummy, working as a research engineer for Raytheon which contracted weaponry with the Pentagon. Possibly he'd known from the inside when conflict was on the horizon, alerted by ramped up production. Anyway, his etiquette was wanting. It was this presumed attitude toward the commander that got Larsen into trouble.

The next day after the wedding was hot, and everyone, including Larsen, kept close to the pool for dipping. Yvette had broken away from Laurie and the others to join him. When the father-in-law came up in their conversation, he commented, "I guess they don't teach good manners at the Naval Academy."

Little did he know that this bit of casual sarcasm was going to set off a shit storm. His comment on the father-in-law was to become like a yellow jacket sting, deep and lasting. He didn't give much thought to his bit of sarcasm nor did Yvette react at the time, and she invited him to join the contingent across the pool, including her new in-laws and family members.

The commander was flabby and pale in his bathing attire, younger but in no better shape than himself. But he was at least smiling and making eye contact, managing to partially rise from his deck chair to shake hands. The wife rose from her recliner to shake hands, greeting both him and Donna. Attempting a bit of humor, Larsen remarked what a beautiful day it was and questioned if there was such a thing as a bad day in paradise. The commander emphatically shot back, "Pearl Harbor!"

"That would be before your time," Larsen replied, trying to recover from his unlucky observation about weather.

"You're right about that but I did fly out of the Pearl Harbor naval base frequently on observation missions during the Vietnam war."

The direction of the meeting was set. From there on, Laurie's father launched into a stream of anecdotes about his flying for the Navy in the Pacific. There was no stopping him. Nor was there any reciprocal inquiry about Larsen's life, past or present. Funny how Yvette had led him to believe the father-in-law was shy. Larsen being cordial, added bits of supportive information about fighters and bombers he'd remembered from movies and his boyhood hobby of making balsam wood models of Spitfires, Me-109s, F-84s and MIGs.

"My family lived through the London blitz. So, I learned early about Heinkel bombers and Junkers," Larsen interjected, a true detail, and surely a showstopper.

But there was barely a pause and no raised eyebrows from the family, as if he had impolitely interrupted the commander who took a deep breath and carried on with his aeronautical career, taking the assembled group to every sector of the west Pacific. He was decidedly not shy in familiar territory. It had always seemed to Larsen that shyness is often a euphemism used by and for adults who suffer some other underlying deficiency. In any case, this commander was no admiral.

Back in the day when Yvette was still just dating Laurie, she revealed that Laurie was carrying nearly $100,000 in college debt. Was that a result of parental imposed self-reliance? Her sizeable debt suggested no largesse on the part of the commander. In contrast, Yvette got from him what she needed, when she needed it. She did her part, working part time, but she got his help. She even got his virtually new Corolla which he and Donna drove all the way from Oregon to San Diego to give her as a graduation present. She had no student debt. Other revelations included a family conflict about Laurie's troublesome younger brother, likened by Yvette to Bart Simpson, a rude ne'er do well wise ass, with whom the girls were having difficulties when they visited the family. But the commander refused to intervene. It seemed that Laurie's people were an insouciant, amicable bunch, who preferred not to confront issues. Was this the kind of family Yvette had always desired?

Early the next morning when Larsen was having coffee and rolls out on the wide patio that ringed the horseshoe, his daughter and new wife marched his way with determination in their stride and a lack of sleep written on their faces. They didn't waste any time with idle conversation and got right to their point, Laurie speaking first:

"I don't like you making nasty comments about my family." Shocked, he suddenly felt chilled by their grim faces. He had forgotten yesterday's remark.

"Excuse me?" Larsen replied, as if he'd not heard.

"Dad, when you and I sat at the pool yesterday, you said some pretty strong stuff." Then he remembered and he felt betrayed.

"That was a casual jest made in confidence, not for public consumption!"

"You tell mom everything, don't you?" His daughter misunderstood the parameters of intimacy.

"Not *everything!* Revealing some things just cause trouble and helps nothing!"

"Yeah, well, we were up most of the night as a result," Laurie shot back, the blue of her eyes suddenly electric.

"Oh, come on, you're making too much of this. I'm sorry, okay?"

"You can't attack my family like that," Laurie said, absorbing nothing of his apology. He made an exaggerated sigh.

"I wasn't *attacking* anyone. That's a little strong. Besides, *I'm* family now, yeah?!" Larsen felt himself tightening. His daughter seemed to be sneering at him the way a cat warns with narrowing eyes and ears shifting backward.

"Yvette, I'm not sure I know you anymore. I'm sorry for the indiscretion. Do we have to get so serious here?"

Neither Yvette nor Laurie were having it. Was this Yvette trying to prove that she belonged to someone else now, that any allegiance to him was finished? It was apparent he could no longer confide in her; anything said to his daughter went to the new wife. But Yvette was naïve and needy, he thought, not *everything* is shared among mature adults. Even after more than 30 years of marriage there was no point in sharing *everything* with Donna—not every quibbling remark or tone, the scent of snark in an email, an innocent flirtation. He had to remember Yvette's inexperience. A wedding is a big commitment and she perhaps felt compelled in her innocence to begin honoring her commitment with this excessive honesty. She could have just set aside his remark about the father-in-law. She must

Russ Desaulnier

have known it would upset Laurie. So why tell her? What was she trying to prove?

There are hot buttons in every family. For him it had been his parents' use in later years of the exhausted and surrendering assertion, *whatever.* When either of them was exasperated, their verbal hands-up-in-the-air was almost always the proverbial *whatever,* a term he hated and never used. For Yvette a hot button seemed to be anything that even obliquely could be construed as critical of her chosen love. This was the only explanation he could imagine.

On their only visit north, months before the marriage, Yvette and Laurie wanted a day at the beach. On the way to the coast they passed a clear-cut forest with a pathetic pretense to hide it from view behind a thin row of pines lining the shoulder of the highway. He had innocently pointed out the clear-cut, as he might to any visitor he was taking on a tour. Almost instantly, Yvette sank into a black mood all afternoon and refused to walk as a group when they got to the beach. Laurie didn't seem especially fazed, shrugging and raising her eyebrows in wonder. Yvette never accounted for that afternoon, claiming no memory of the incident. The only explanation he could construct is that Yvette had seen his comment as an attack on her lady love, an oblique damnation of Republican environmental policy. Yvette had given them advanced notice that Laurie's parents were Republican light, meaning they hadn't gone as extreme as Evangelicals. Of course, how could they be extremely conservative with a gay daughter? So, perhaps his pointing out a clear-cut was construed as an innuendo directed at Laurie and her family? He couldn't be sure. He was never able to get to the heart of that incident with Yvette. It wasn't the first time he and Donna were dumbfounded by Yvette's inexplicable outbursts. Her nature had turned combustible in her mid-teens, and they had walked on eggshells ever since.

Larsen recalled how as a young man he'd felt hurt by his parents' comments about girlfriends that were thinly veiled contempt. They didn't approve of most of his girlfriends, but that was not so unusual for parents of an only son. They never meant to hurt him. He hadn't meant any hurt when pointing out the forest clear cut. He was just innocently playing host and tour guide. When Laurie visited them, Donna for her part was warm and gracious and made every hospitable gesture possible. Both he and his wife were anxious to see their only child happy.

In the months leading up to her graduation with a degree plus honors in business from UC San Diego, they had their weekly phone call from Yvette, as they had throughout her undergraduate days. It seemed to him that all had gone well, but in retrospect all the phone conversations centered on Yvette's classes, *her* part time work, *her* friends, *her* world, but never was there a question about how he and Donna were doing. But this was accepted. After all, young adults are immersed in themselves and rarely have a thought for their parents' difficulties. Now older, Larsen often thought about his father, who had always been ready with encouragement and even a few dollars to help if he needed it over the years of his checkered teaching career. But he never gave much thought to his father's many years of groggy mornings and tenacious evenings, fighting LA traffic as he worked in precision machining sales in LA's huge aerospace industry. His father's love for him had been unshakable. In retrospect, he recognized that his model for loving Yvette was his father. How could Yvette desert him? How could she abandon his unflagging love, like his father's love for him? An only child in some sense remains one's baby in adulthood, a devotion that conflicts many a parent.

For several weeks after Maui, he did his best to sort out their parting in a few last desperate emails, but then as if surprise testimony for the prosecution, Yvette introduced accusations of *child abuse*. A bombshell. It appeared she'd been holding onto resentments for years and the destination wedding opened the flood gates.

"Don't you remember the spankings!"

"Very few times and always restrained and never on a bare ass. That should refresh your memory," he wrote back, exasperated by attempts to clearly remember all such events. He believed her imagination inflated such incidents more than his memory had failed him. Is that what her tantrum was about in the wake of his comments at the pool, her pounding on their hotel door and screaming to be let in? Was she planning all along to have an accounting, when her parents were no longer necessary, when it was time for her to make her final act of parting and fledging? Yet when she was let into their room, she was tearful, flushed and conflicted, as sorry as she was angry. It appeared she had no option but to abandon him and Donna. There could be no more relationship, no grandparenting should she and Laurie have children. Nothing. Then came more tears as she avowed her love before leaving the room. Had she been pressured, even forced to make such an awful choice?

Yes, he'd been exasperated a few times with Yvette when she was little, and he had given her a few whacks on the pants, but abuse?! Certainly not in any sense that the word conjures up in these times when every demographic has elevated the slightest trespasses to injury and even litigation. But how did the conflict get from a casual sarcasm to child abuse? Something was amiss. Did Laurie's family honor require his banishment and Yvette's estrangement? He couldn't believe that pain and anger ran so deep in his daughter that she would willingly take such a course. Had this come about as a price and reprisal imposed by Laurie? What had transpired during their sleepless night before their confrontation with him?

While growing up, Yvette was always given a wide latitude, perhaps too much, somewhat a result of his and Donna's readings in nouveau child rearing. But always like his father's love, his love for Yvette always prevailed. There was nothing he wouldn't do for her, then or now.

It has now been eight years and no word from her, despite his pleas which he could not bring himself to make in emails anymore. It all felt like a betrayal, or a loss of love. Larsen had never been able to forget when he betrayed his father by foolishly suing him over a petty real estate deal. Why couldn't they have talked it through? The folly of youth, and the ingratitude! The quibble never got to court because his disgusted father settled. There wasn't a lot of money involved, but the principle of it all! It had been a betrayal of trust and love for which he never stopped feeling shame forty years later and was still unable to forgive himself.

Yvette had turned on him as if all his love counted for nothing. What about all the good times? He had always played with her, as had his father with him, handmade her Halloween costumes, taught her chess, read to her, helped with homework assignments, taught her how to ride a bicycle, how to pitch a softball, how to paddle a canoe, rocked her to sleep when she was sick, took her out for countless lunches at restaurants she liked and kept on paying her way far beyond restaurant tabs. Yet she waited for her marriage to raise isolated childhood incidents, as if she'd been holding them back like poison arrows for a calculated showdown. His poolside sarcasm about the new father-in-law surely caused a ruckus, but Yvette's emails in the wake of the Maui incident were full of unexpected shocking, unfair recriminations.

Larsen believed her years with them deserved reasonably good marks, on par at least with his own childhood experience from where he drew his example for fathering her. Perhaps we need to age past fifty to feel our mortality and understand our earliest experiences and the parents who helped form us. He hoped he would live long enough, when aging might bring Yvette that epiphany, and she would email, make a phone call, or better, show up at his doorstep. Meanwhile, her complete break seemed like an exercise in proud, unbending resolution, a desperate proof of love for an angered spouse. In any case, her Maui reaction was wildly disproportionate.

But why shouldn't he try just one last time? His last email was over a year ago. He'd decided after that unanswered attempt he wouldn't write anymore until Yvette made some gesture in his direction. But then hope got the better of him. Sometimes she came to him in dreams in which he saw her so vividly he could feel tears and intense joy in his dream state. Despite himself, he turned on his computer and went to his mailbox, tapped the new message button, brought up her email address at the top of a blank page and he began writing:

Dear Yvette,

*Tell any neutral adult about your estrangement from us and he or she will not understand why you can't at least communicate with us and attempt some reconciliation. Trying to avoid your issues with me and mom will not make them go away. They will only fester, and if it should become too late to reconcile, you'll only carry regret the rest of your life. We still haven't been able to get to the bottom of your tantrum in Hawaii, nor your angry demonstration months earlier when you and Laurie visited with us and we drove out to the coast. I'm not sure you can explain your rage even to yourself. In any case, you were not an abused child. Ninety nine percent of the time you were loved, and indulged. Now, as an adult, don't you think it might be more balanced of you to account for the difficulties we had when you were growing up? During your early teens, mom was dealing with depression and chronic insomnia while my job kept me away for much of the time.*

*It has now been eight years that we've neither seen you nor had any response to our attempts to contact you. Is that adult? Over time, holding onto anger only leads to bitterness. You will do yourself a favor by confronting your feelings, either to us or to a professional family counselor—in which case we would be glad to join you. Living a thousand miles from you, we are hardly going to interfere in your life. We simply would like to clear the air with you and establish some connection and reconciliation. It's clear to me you were pressured to take this hard stance toward us. You showed no offense that afternoon when I first made my indiscreet remark. So, what happened during that sleepless night with Laurie when you became so upset? I'm betting Laurie encouraged your break with us, and more likely, demanded it.*

*There is no virtue in your estrangement, nor does it have any benefits or prove anything. If Laurie is carrying an attitude about us, she needs to learn to forgive, as do you. If she is the animus behind your unjust separation from us, then her sin and yours are much greater than my little sarcasm about Laurie's father. I was indiscreet but you were naive and fool-ish to repeat my sarcasm to Laurie. I think you got yourself into something deeper than you had expected. And so, I think you felt compelled to build a larger case against me to cover your mistake. Abuse? Really! See your estrangement for what it is: pride, pettiness and naivete. For her part, is Laurie being fair and reasonable? But it's not too late for us to reconcile.*

*Mom and I have always loved you since the day you were born. And that love for you has not changed. Please forgive me and mom for any hurt we may have caused you. Always wishing you and Laurie health and happiness,*

*Dad*

Larsen was about to tap the SEND key, but then he stalled like a car out of gas...

# Just a Few Passes

---------------------

I t wasn't bad, just uncomfortable, McClaren thought. The dimensions of his life were narrowing, no doubt like his arteries. Family, except for his octogenarian mother, his wife and daughter, had been narrowed by the ascension of the neo-conservative regime of George W. Bush, which spoke for almost everyone on both sides of the family. He and his wife Muriel were the odd couple on the Coast, he the retired liberal teacher and Muriel the wayward sister because she had decided long ago to settle out West rather than stay in Des Moines, grow fat, and be a good church-going Christian. The schism was mutual with little communication except for the most perfunctory exchanges. When Christmas rolled around, he and his wife, anticipating receiving the usual stream of Christian cards, sent Pagan cards celebrating the winter solstice.

Friends also seemed in short supply, or perhaps this was just more social fallout of the era. The McClarens' Danish teak dining set gathered dust more often than it provided seating for dinner parties, which he and Muriel had always loved. They had tried for a while but there were so few reciprocations their enthusiasm dwindled, and their entertaining was reduced to occasional sharing with their lonely, fast-food fed divorced friends.

When he had retired four years ago, McClaren had believed retirement would be a jolly time of at least bimonthly elegant meals with contemporaries and after-dinner cigars on the porch, minds and fellowship soaring in contempt of the not so far off inevitable. The expansive walls and vaulted ceilings of their home's impressive architecture now often felt claustrophobic. Their wide collection of art that graced the walls seemed a moot feature when there were so few visitors to admire it. His attempts to escape list-less days lay evidenced in bookmarked novels and piles of opened, half-read magazines. He hadn't touched the Native American flute in the den, which his wife had bought him as a retirement gift three years ago. It lay unused in a desk drawer, waiting for his efforts to learn the easy pentatonic scale so that his life would not pass without having learned to play a musical instrument.

He had been hopeful of correspondence, and there had been e-mail exchanges about Bush with a few politi-cally like-minded correspondents, but these had become a tiresome choir of ranting. The days dissolved one into another without any broad strokes to define the weeks and months. He and Muriel went to weekend dances, or saw the occasional critically acclaimed movie or play, but a feeling of routine still dogged him. He wrote a few short reviews of movies and e-mailed them, but there was little response. With a few old friends he had tried to broach the subject of aging, but this was met with easy encouragements best reserved for Hallmark greeting cards.

He enjoyed dancing the Argentine tango with Muriel, and their local dance community had held promise for a while, but despite the smiles and greetings at the dance hall, there remained an aloofness that seemed to infect almost everyone. McClaren could only assume that the women so infected were those he rarely or never danced with. The men were less a mystery, he concluded. They couldn't set aside an abiding and intimidating sense of competition. Athletic and rhythmic since a boy in middle school, he had become a respectable *tanguero* without too much effort and had found with Muriel, a true lover of dancing, the mysteries of precisely timed turns while keeping their shoulders in parallel frame. Maybe some unattached regulars resented them for dancing so well with an ease that only comes with long-term marriage. He could never quite get past the discomfort of people he knew acting like strangers, passing him by at the dance hall without making eye contact. There were many good moments of dancing, but the dance social scene was narrow, like the house, like the extended family, like the horizons.

But *narrowed* was perhaps not the best word to describe his life. Maybe it was just *static*. There was no measurable forward movement except the advance, however slowly, of the thinning of his hair and the spread of spider veins in his legs. In the brightly lit bathroom mirror, he noted the early signs of cellulite on the surface of his solar plexus. But he was still well proportioned and mostly lean, remarkably well preserved by comparison to his contemporaries he saw in the showers at his fitness club.

He and Muriel decided some travel was in order to broaden the view, and there was no better choice than Mexico that held the jewel among his memories, that brief moment when as a young man he had dreamed audaciously of becoming a professional bullfighter. Perhaps he could taste the flavor of his youthful illusions again. On the practical side, he and Muriel would be able to fill their drug prescriptions cheaply and he could get his dental implants crowned at a fraction of the cost at home. They decided on San Miguel Allende in the central Mexican highlands for its tourist-friendly reputation and colonial charm and because Muriel wanted a place where English had some currency. They would find a cheap apartment, settle in for two months, maybe find some tango dancing and hopefully see some bullfighting.

From the moment they took the short ride from the international airport in Leon to their hotel for a one-night stay before heading on to San Miguel by bus, McClaren was seized by familiar smells that summoned up his youth. Perhaps it was the open-air meat and tortilla stalls everywhere that imbued the air with the unmistakable smell of Mexico. Like the smells, Spanish phrases and vocabulary came back to him in unexpected flashes. This pleased Muriel who was relying on his Spanish to ease their way. In turn he was reminded of her vulnerability, although it was her easy-going nature that had made their passage of twenty-five years together possible.

*She* was the rock. She was even forgiving about their first night in San Miguel spent in a converted colonial nunnery which he had booked from Oregon on the advice of a Lonely Planet travel book. Imposing and picturesque from the outside, it was a warren of cold, bare rooms that made one think about how the nuns had to endure for Christ. The drafty building was beset by one of the coldest Januarys on record; and so, the McClarens clung together through a night of fitful sleep in their unheated room where a simple wooden cross hung above the bed.

San Miguel was the picture of what most Americans would expect of romantic old Mexico. The centuries old cobblestoned streets were alley narrow, and rich earth-colored colonial stucco buildings rose three and four stories on either side. It was in one of these buildings within a few blocks of the main town square, El Jardin, where they found refuge from the nunnery. After several days they became accustomed to the traffic and the afternoon pollution that collected in the narrow canyon-like streets, and they learned to walk carefully on the narrow, raised sidewalks. McClaren spent a lot of time just wandering around snapping photos with his new Canon digital camera. After inquiring in a dozen offices, he found an English-speaking dentist abreast of the latest advances who could finish the crowns on his implants for a third of what it would cost back home. When they weren't together, Muriel occupied herself with combing the artisan marketplace that sold an endless array of silver jewelry, bead work and tourist kitsch. She had to take a few small things back for their daughter and some family members. Although it was next to impossible to have real conversations with the family, Muriel was always thoughtful and felt compelled to make a few gestures toward them.

*Cuanto cuesta?* He coached his wife, who acquired a reasonable facsimile of a few handy phrases. But ultimately it was money that talked in San Miguel, and they discovered many of the vendors knew enough English for simple commerce. Conchita Garcia, a doctor and their new landlady, who ran her practice out of a ground floor office, spoke a fair amount of English. The McClarens weren't especially impressed with their apartment on the shady side of the courtyard, but it was the tourist high season after all, and anything seemed like a find after the nunnery, especially since they rented their spacious new place for a bargain at

$450 a month including linens and maid service. He deferred to the good doctor Conchita in Spanish, and their chance meetings in the courtyard settled into a mutually happy mix of Spanish and English. He was glad to accept her offer of medical services, should he need any, and so he agreed to a $30 consultation for the purpose of getting a Lorazepam prescription to calm his nerves and sleeplessness that had been exacerbated with travel. Although San Miguel was high on the Mexican economic scale, medicine was still a bargain, which he enthusiastically praised along with the town's colonial quaintness to e-mail correspondents back home who all had reason to complain about the skyrocketing cost of health insurance and drugs in the era of George W. Bush.

The McClarens shared meals in countless tiny restaurants and toured the many art gallery receptions where there was always a free glass of wine, if not so much good art. Most people they met were either traveling North American newlyweds or longtime residents, many years older than the McClarens, in particular the old widows. Wrinkled like prunes and dripping in bulky Mexican jewelry, they held plastic wine glasses and invariably began by inquiring where the McClarens hailed from. It was similar ancient women, only dignified, sober and very British, that he and Muriel encountered one lunchtime, sitting next to them at the Pegasus, a favorite little restaurant frequented by *gringos*. One of the women had worked in British intelligence and been a translator at the Nuremberg Trials. Both women were markedly educated with their proper London accents and they weren't shy about admitting to a loathing for the current resident of the White House.

The McClarens found a cyber-café, cum-tourist office just around the corner from their building on Calle Hernandez, which became their office away from home. The coffee was roasted on site and filled the shop with a powerful aroma that drifted out the front door onto the street. The shop was owned by a Mexican woman whose English was impeccable and she ran the adjoining tourist office. The coffee shop was run for her by a short, jolly mestizo named Paco. He generously tipped Paco for making him special *cafe con leche* and for generously conversing in Spanish with him, often about bullfighting.

He had carried with him to Mexico a handbook size album of photos from his bullfighting days, a modest little collection that captured the few times he had been in the ring. He'd anticipated the photos might be of help to open conversations on occasion and gain him a small measure of engagement. The photos had made the desired impression on Paco and on the good Dr. Conchita, who complimented him by saying he had *la sagaz de la raza*. Mexico ran in his blood. Indeed, he liked to feel he had a special emotional connection to Mexico, or perhaps this was merely nostalgia for his youth. In any case, Dr. Conchita filled all the prescriptions they requested.

Muriel had been doing her own exploration and shopping. She had found a little tango group that met weekly, although the McClarens turned out to be the only ones who knew what they were doing aside from the local teacher. Muriel had also negotiated a purchase of two dozen finely beaded bracelets handmade by the Huichol Indians, which she was sure she could sell back home for forty dollars each. She had signed up for weekly Spanish lessons with one of the girls at the tourism cum coffee shop, where his coffee man Paco had taken to making McClaren's morning *cafe con leche* as soon as he saw him coming in the door. He was buoyed by his newly found small neighborhood where his use of Spanish became more fluent each day. Several of the older wintering Canadians in their apartment building had overheard him chatting in Spanish with landlady Conchita and approached him to help them out with a little Spanish translation. He was only glad to oblige.

From the courtyard dominated by a broken Moorish fountain, one exited onto Calle Mesones through two huge doors of ancient wood with large brass hinges, constructed as if to keep out the many revolutions that had racked San Miguel and other towns since the days of the Spanish. Always seated just outside on the threshold of the great doors from morning until early afternoon was an old leathery faced woman who sold avocados, limes and papayas. McClaren would reserve buying these items from the old woman rather than at the big market so that he could give her the business and have a little chat. On one of his regular stops at the gates to chat and buy some avocados from the old lady, a striking young woman, perhaps in her middle 30s, passed them by. Maybe it was her unusual short hairstyle, a departure from the long hairstyles usually worn by most young Mexican women. Her eyes, vaguely sinople, suggesting Aztec ancestry, made him stare, and he felt himself flush and then averted his eyes, but not before he noticed she had smiled as if amused by the awe she inspired in a foreign man so much older than herself. He feigned attention to the old woman's avocados, but looked up to watch the young woman from behind, as she walked on up the street, her narrow hips accented by a smooth knee-length skirt.

He banished any further thoughts of this vision which had unexpectedly spiked his heartbeat. But then she passed him in the same place intermittently over the following weeks, as if Calle Mesones was her regular route to her home or job. After crossing her path a dozen or so times, he realized he was disappointed when she didn't appear for a day or two. He rebuked himself for being a foolish old man. In his twenty-five years with Muriel he'd been careful to avoid situations which could lead to overstepping the boundaries of marriage, even though there may have been a flirtatious teaching colleague here, a precocious, overly friendly graduate student there. The passing raven beauty of San Miguel's Calle Mesones, who now disturbed that protected place in his heart, recalled his dalliance with dark beauties when he was young and magnificent in the blue silk and gold brocade of his bullfighter's suit. Contrary to those days, Mexican women were now freer. American influence in Mexico had extended beyond NAFTA. Many young Mexican women wore the low-slung jeans, baring their navels like their American counterparts who paraded in the shopping malls. Times had changed, but this was a mature, tastefully dressed woman who kept crossing his path. Perhaps if he were to see such a woman back home it would have made no difference. But everything in Mexico had been playing with his senses since they'd arrived.

At the coffee shop he got online, while awaiting the arrival of his *cafe con leche* from Paco. After his initial flurry of email announcements of their arrival in San Miguel, the email had been limited. The well-wishing responses trailed off into forwards of tiresome gags and circulated commentaries excoriating Bush's most recent depredations. Now the correspondence was down to two of his bachelor friends his own age and his college-overwhelmed daughter.

Russ Desaulnier

*Oye, torero, tu cafe con leche!* Paco intervened, setting the coffee and a sweet Mexican bread on the computer desk.

Paco wondered if McClaren had seen an advertisement in the newspaper sports section announcing a bullfight festival coming to San Miguel. He'd been watching the Sunday televised fights from Mexico City and was planning to go into nearby Leon for a bullfight or two, but something in San Miguel would be splendid. He'd missed the small advertisement announcing the coming event. This festive affair in San Miguel's ring was to celebrate the occasion of the provincial elections with six young bulls from Garfias to be fought by practicing amateurs, one of them an American, Steve DeHaas of Houston.

DeHaas was a name he'd not thought of in decades. Their paths had crossed only once, and briefly, at a free-for-all caping of young bulls in Nogales forty years ago. But McClaren remembered his name, for he had been one among the few, perhaps about a dozen in all, of aspiring American boys in that era of the early 60s. Four of them had gone professional with some success. Although De Haas remained amateur, he stayed active and was still getting in the ring as an amateur *practico*. This McClaren would have to see.

The nights were growing warmer and there was more activity in the street as the festival approached. Sometimes the McClarens couldn't get to sleep because of carousers below in the street. Every night until eleven an elderly Mexican begged at the corner, playing old 1940s American hits on an off-key accordion. And there was more traffic than usual, vacationing Mexicans in from Mexico City, clogging the town with SUVs. Even the McClarens' favorite barbecue chicken restaurant at the top of Calle Mesones across from the colonial cathedral was packed every night with tables pushed together for extended families, including grand-mothers and toddlers.

On the morning of the festivities, the McClarens swung open the heavy shutters of their apartment windows so that they could watch the parade. Each four or five contingents of marchers had a brass band. There was a dozen or so student groups dressed in their clean, pressed student uni-forms, occasionally a baton twirler, and several 70s vintage convertible cars with beauty queens in embroidered blouses and dresses seated up on the backs of the rear seats. Fol-lowing them were macho platoons reminiscent of Pancho Villa with traditional Mexican sombreros, bullet studded bandoleers and sabers and rifles slung at the sides of their horses. After them came the regular military with machine guns and armored vehicles. A dissonant brass band follow-ing behind the army contingents oddly lacked the polish one would expect in such a martial display.

The parade ended just after noon and the McClarens decided to have lunch at the Pegasus again. The popular restaurant was a few blocks up by the main square, which was filled with festivity. Taco and ice cream vendors were doing a brisk business, children played while watching families occupied the park benches, and a small band in the central gazebo played romantic Mexican ballads like *Besame Mucho* and *Ojos Verdes*. As the McClarens turned the corner in the direction of the Pegasus, they were brought up short by a group trying to squeeze by them on the narrow sidewalk. Drawing in toward the wall, the McClarens let them pass. The last to pass was *the mysteri-ous Mexican beauty.* She wore a brightly embroidered skirt and a low-cut blouse exposing her narrow shoulders. Every time he saw her, she was dressed distinctively, neither rich nor in the peasant manner of the maids at the apartment complex, but simple enough to express her good taste. Her perfume, an unnameable floral scent that caught his nose and filtered into his blood, was familiar, and as he tried to remember who else had worn the scent, the San Miguel mystery woman smiled at him in passing and said *gracias*.

"This way, Jimmy." Muriel said, dragging him along.

When they sat down at the Pegasus and ordered coffees, the image of the mystery woman wouldn't leave his mind. Rather than any excitement, he felt a low-grade sorrow for himself. He was already in his sixties, long married and going nowhere. This was an unwelcome thought occasioned by this woman crossing his path perhaps too many times. But then the world was always full of young, beautiful women, and old men had to come to terms with that. How very much he loved Muriel; yet part of him, perhaps a newly reawakened part, struggled. Perhaps his being in Mexico sharpened his sense of mortality, and it emerged with the weight of self-sorrow. Or was this simply his moment in life, as other men experience, when he had to recognize the end of possibilities and acknowledge that boredom was as inevitable as losing teeth. Was this his season to be a foolish old man? He resolved to focus his mind elsewhere and not allow himself to be swept along in something that had no possibility of going anywhere.

"Earth to Jimmy," Muriel was saying. She had always said this to him over the years when his eyes glazed over in thought.

"Are you starting to feel at home here?" he solicited.

'The apartment could be on the sunny side, but we can go up on the roof and sunbathe in the deck chairs. It's an adventure. How about you?"

"I'll feel better when I get my teeth done."

It was an evasive answer because there was no way to talk about his thoughts, nor did he understand the full import of their time in Mexico. He had expected to be moved but not disturbed by awakened memories.

"How are the *gordas?*" he asked. She'd ordered the meat and vegetable stuffed cornmeal pancakes.

"They're good but no more of these for a week."

McClaren knew this meant she wanted to exercise and diet to halt gaining weight. They both had tried to stay with the Atkins Diet of protein and vegetables and a minimum of carbohydrates. Muriel had become sensitive about gaining weight and took to wearing styles of clothing that disguised her figure. But her physical changes were not so significant, although she was not that same svelte girl she had been. She was by American standards still quite trim, and she always dressed stylishly. And her silver hair, now longer than ever, turned the heads of men his age and also the heads of a few younger men wherever they went. He was careful not to call attention to her weight gains because she was sensitive on the topic and because he refused to admit to himself that her physical changes held any importance. He still loved her deeply, but it was true that he didn't always feel the same excitement, or should he? He wasn't a young stud anymore. With the years, wasn't marriage supposed to become something higher and deeper than desire? Yet the frequent presence of a beautiful vision, his San Miguel mystery woman, could momentarily challenge his deepest held constructions of reality.

The McClarens were told they didn't have to purchase tickets in advance for the San Miguel bullfight and could buy cheap tickets at the bullring because a sellout wasn't anticipated. Many of the Canadians and Americans in town found the bullfight tradition revolting and there was less interest among Mexicans than there had been in the past. Movies, computer games and soccer had intervened. And for many, bullfighting was just a relic of the culture. Although when the Spanish ace, Enrique Ponce, recently appeared in the big Plaza Mexico, which McClaren watched on TV, the ring was full to the rim with 50,000 fans. The San Miguel festival featured unknowns other than Mariano Ramos, a bullfighter of some fame thirty years ago. In these informal festivals with young bulls, it was traditional for participants to dress in the *traje corto,* the tight, high-waisted pants and short cut jacket. Perhaps DeHass had been invited for novelty and in hopes of drawing on the many North American tourists in town.

The San Miguel ring was Moorish in style with ornate arches at its upper circumference which enclosed and covered the upper rows. Small by bullring standards, it had a capacity of 3000 people. Although he counted only about 700 people, all the receipts would go to charity. The unknown amateur bullfighters, DeHass included, most likely paid to be on the program, as was custom, which would defray the high cost of the bulls.

The ex-pro Ramos drew the biggest animal of the day, maybe 400 kilos, while the rest of the bulls were more comfortable at 300 kilos or less. The old pro pleased the crowd with some pretty passes but had to make too many thrusts with the sword before taking down his adversary. The Garfias bulls had a lot of play in them, and for young bulls were more than adequately armed. Several of the younger men did well, garnering a few trophy ears and turns of the ring to applause. The crowd seemed to be knowledgeable, showing appreciation where it was merited, and accordingly, the judge of the plaza was not overly generous in his granting of awards to the bullfighters. The last bull was for DeHaas. He was taller than his Mexican cohorts, lean and distinguished with his full head of salt and pepper hair. He cut a fine figure in his tight-fitting Andalusian suit and flat brimmed Cordobes hat. McClaren, who usually didn't drink, had two Modelo beers to quench a parched mouth and to calm himself. By the time the clarion sounded for DeHass' bull to enter the ring, he was talking incessantly to Muriel, explaining everything like a sports newscaster.

DeHass's bull, a chunky saber-horned specimen, about 300 kilos and three fifths the size of the monsters the pros fought, sprinted into the ring, assaulted the protective barrier a few times, and then trotted off into the middle of the ring.

DeHaas squeezed his way from behind the narrow space of the barrier, stepped into the ring and called the bull, which spun around and charged. DeHass unfurled the gold and magenta cape, drawing the horns knifing past his chest, and then another and another to 700 simultaneous *oles* as McClaren clicked away with his new Canon. DeHaas moved about the ring and the bull with an air of knowledge and confidence, his moves purposeful and without hesitation. In the last act before the kill, he drew the bull in tight circles around his body to enthusiastic shouts from the stands. When the bull was played out and at a standstill, DeHaas raised and sighted down the curved blade of the sword. There was no lunge and thrust, but rather a slow joining of man and animal, as if the bull, ignoring its pain, willingly impaled itself to the hilt in its effort to gore the man. DeHaas was awarded two ears and slowly walked the circumference of the ring to cheers, thrown bouquets of flowers and a few hats. By now McClaren had lit a cigar, his first in four years since he retired, as if celebrating the most important event since that happy milestone.

The San Miguel bullring was an integral part of the village with multi-colored stucco homes rising above the upper rim of the shallow ring. In a few lucky instances the people living there would have been able to watch the show from their balconies. Entering and leaving the ring, one went through a ramped passage leading to large swinging gates and a typical San Miguel cobblestoned street. Next to the gates was a small convenience store selling fresh foods as well as beer and sodas. They bought a couple apple sodas and waited near the gates for DeHaas to exit.

It didn't take long for the seven hundred or so people to file out through the gates and out to a long line of backed up taxis. The participants were the last to come out, carry-ing capes and leather sword cases. Chatting and laughing with a couple Mexican photographers who'd been shooting earlier from behind the inner ring barriers, DeHass came down the ramp and McClaren stood in his path.

"Steve, nice fight... James McClaren. Early sixties?"

Still appearing pumped up, DeHaas didn't register the name at first. But the man was gracious, even a bit embar-rassed that he was supposed to know someone, a fellow American, and couldn't remember. DeHaas excused himself from the Mexican photographers and after a few more hints, recalled McClaren's name. It was always wonderfully odd how the longer the gap in time, the greater the surprise and interest when two old acquaintances meet, particularly if the time and events joining them had been powerful enough, such as war or a youthful craziness like bullfighting. McClaren had similar meetings with contemporaries he'd met from his San Francisco days and the *summer of love* in '68, and with fellow college alumnae who invariably waxed brotherly, sharing stories about notorious professors and parties. Perhaps it was the joy of discovering that our memories, unique reminders of our essential loneliness, are indeed shared by others; we may be inconsequential, but we are not entirely alone.

Neither man had much memory of the other except their names. What they held in common was being members of a small exclusive club of Americans associated decades ago with a unique art form of foreign derring-do. McClaren had been curious to see DeHaas but was now a little envious that someone as old as he could still be enjoying a glory usually reserved for youth. The afternoon of watching bullfights had stirred his wondering if he could again, with some training, go in the ring. The thought hovered at the far edge of possibility, as had his suppressed spike of emotion for the mysterious pretty woman of San Miguel.

They were men forty years beyond their nexus in the 1960s, but he couldn't identify with his numerical age, nor apparently did DeHaas, who seemed genuinely thrilled at their unlikely meeting and invited the McClarens to join him for dinner that evening at his hotel. They declined sharing his cab from the bullring to the center of town, since the walk back to their apartment from the bullring was short and downhill and probably faster than by car during the festival jammed streets.

At their apartment, he fed the day's photos into his laptop for editing, using Photoshop, which helped him make pro quality black and whites but there was no way for him to get connected online. Technology still had limits in

Mexico. Muriel was feeling tired from the afternoon and the walking and so she lay down. He decided to leave her undisturbed and walked over to the cyber-café for a coffee and to send off an email or two about the afternoon. The writer Henry James was right about Americans traveling so that they'd have something to talk about.

*Como fueron los toros, matador?* How were the bulls? It was Paco. He'd had to work in the shop that afternoon and asked about the American bullfighter. McClaren told him the American fought with grace and honor and said he'd bring in some photos later.

Paco, a grin on his face, asked if he was going to give the bulls a try again, and he laughed and said he was too old. But even as he said this there was the thought in the back of his mind that perhaps he could handle a small animal. But no, he couldn't afford a possible accident. Things happen. DeHaas was a different case; he'd stayed at it off and on over the years in little festivals.

He was on the cafe's computer writing a friend back home, telling him about the afternoon in the splendid little bullring when Paco brought his *cafe con leche* and a small *pandulce* for dipping. His change from a fifty-peso bill was in a separate dish. McClaren hadn't paid much attention to money since he had arrived, the prices of everything being so inexpensive compared to back home. But now he couldn't help noticing there were too few coins in the dish. Some of the coins, inset with brass centers, looked alike and if one didn't look closely, which he never did, the coins could easily be misidentified. His change was 20 pesos short, about two dollars US; probably just a mistake. The shortage was so inconsequential, it would seem petty to take issue with Paco. But he didn't leave a tip this time when he left, wondering about all the previous times he scooped up change without counting.

The McClarens joined DeHass at the Villa Jacaranda Hotel where he was waiting at a table when they showed up in the dining room. He had already ordered a bottle of red wine and offered them both a glass. He was warm and solicitous. They marveled at the years, how they could be sitting there four decades later.

"I seem to recall hearing you went off to Spain and had problems and then gave it up," DeHass said.

"That's pretty much the story," McClaren replied, giving him some of the details about his inability to get into the Spanish bullfighter's union and how he finally ran out of money and hope. Then they rolled through the years of their respective chronologies. DeHaas had logged a long career of international sales and service in farm equipment that took him throughout Latin America, allowing him to dabble with the bulls. He'd never entertained becoming a professional, but he'd maintained a steady commitment to fighting young bulls in festivals.

"Every time you do it you just hope your animal comes out brave."

Muriel wasn't entirely comprehending and so McClaren explained that a brave bull charges true and with great commitment. Tenuous bulls, afraid and wary, are unpredictable and sometimes can pull up short and hook in the middle of a pass.

"I don't think I could do it again," McClaren announced.

"I hope not," his wife chimed in.

"Health insurance doesn't cover much, never mind bullfighting injuries. What do you do?" he asked DeHass.

"Nothing. I just don't allow myself to think about it."

DeHaas told them how he bought into festivals and everyone except the featured famous old timers had to buy his own bull for usually about $700 US. DeHaas had fought as many as half a dozen times a year and traveled to Spain and various locations in Mexico. He said his last marriage broke up partly on account of his hobby.

Everyone ordered barbecued chicken, real yard bird chicken, probably one of the best dishes in San Miguel and throughout Mexico for the money, even cheap in the white table clothed, upscale Villa Jacaranda Hotel. *For the kicks* would be the first guess why anyone would still be fighting bulls at DeHass's age, but McClaren asked anyway.

"The only thing more beautiful than the love of a woman is bullfighting and there's only one thing more difficult— that's *not* bullfighting."

"I know women who feel that way about shopping," Muriel said.

"I had a college writing teacher who once said that about writing," McClaren added.

"There's nothing difficult about drinking a good glass of red," DeHaas said, raising his glass to them, and he commented on how some Mexican Cabernets could now hold their own among the best. But there was nothing pretentious about the man, not often the case with people who chose to talk about wine. Dressed down for the evening, he simply wore a muted plaid shirt, plain sport coat and new jeans. He could make strangers feel he'd known them for years.

"I see you're wearing those beaded bracelets made by the locals," he said, addressing Muriel.

"I bought a bunch of them," Muriel replied, proudly raising her wrists. "Only sixty pesos each."

"You should have paid less," DeHass said.

"Sixty seemed fair to me," Muriel replied.

"You should have bargained," DeHaas countered.

"The price was already a giveaway."

"They expect to be bargained down."

He could read his wife's disapproval, one of those moments that made him proud of her.

"Well, I thought of the extra as a donation to a lovely but poor people."

DeHaas acknowledged her comment with a smile, raising his glass to her. The prices of all the artisan wares were already priced tragically low. It would have been unseemly for comparatively rich North Americans to bargain for the difference of a dollar, which might feed a hungry child for a day.

Talk about bullfighting and the past had wound down by 10 pm. DeHass had to be in Leon early for his flight to LA. He expressed hope he'd see them again, perhaps at one the festivals he'd be in along the border for which he'd make sure they got front row seats, and he would keep in touch by email. DeHass's last words were for McClaren to think about joining one of the festivals, even if it were for just for a few *capetazos,* just a few passes with the cape.

Just a few passes. The idea hung with McClaren in the days that followed.

By the end of February, the weather had warmed so that he and Muriel spent afternoons sunning themselves on the chaise lounges on the roof of the building. They took an occasional glass of wine with the snowbird Canadians on the second floor, ate a lot of chicken dinners on Calle Mesones, watched English language movies on TV, and sometimes danced at a little club they'd found a few blocks away on Hidalgo, but there was very little tango. They read a number of novels borrowed from the San Miguel Biblioteca which had a large store of English language paperbacks, no doubt inherited from the constant turnover of tourists. The library, like most buildings, was a huge stucco block which hid a magnificent Spanish courtyard on the inside, featuring a working fountain and canopied garden tables where one could sip coffee or a cold drink from the concession, read and people watch.

The bullfighting bug in McClaren's blood had retreated with the passing of the weeks since DeHaas came to town and he had become accustomed to seeing dark beauties. There had been several Mexican beauties in his youth: Mariloli, Blanca, Esperanza, and then Isabel who had been special. The San Miguel beauty whom he'd not seen for a while recalled his memories of Isabel and the unbounded passion he once felt. Both women possessed an appearance of sympathetic intelligence that pretty features alone cannot convey, or perhaps these characteristics were now merely suggested by the mystery woman whom he discovered in the library patio, glasses on the bridge of her nose, intently reading a paperback. McClaren sat nearby, taking in some sun and reading a newspaper. In such a small town it was inevitable he would run into the same people sooner or later, especially the vacationing North Americans who stood out with their huge cameras and gauche attire. The library patio was a new venue for his sighting of the San Miguel mystery woman who sat with her skirted legs crossed, elbows akimbo on the table, one hand holding up a paperback, and her ringless left hand, bent at the wrist like a slender fishing bird, and probed her drink with a straw. The movement seemed like a response to what she was reading, a stirring of the drink with excitement, thought McClaren, discreetly looking her way over the top of the bullfight section of his *Esto* newspaper. When she sipped her drink, she would reflexively push back her hair, even though short, before taking a sip. She took a blasé look around the courtyard and McClaren was quick to look away into his *Esto* newspaper. He had never doubted he loved Muriel. He could not imagine his life without her, could not entertain ever hurting her with some foolish indiscretion, breaking the longest continuous line of commitment he'd made to anything in his life, even longer than his career in teaching. The mystery woman represented the impossible and so why should he hang around and dream? One grows older but the women are forever young, as King David lamented. There had been a famous bullfighter who had bemoaned something similar, that the bulls always came into the ring at four years old while he grew older and more mortal. McClaren had to leave.

He forced himself to avert his eyes, folded his paper and stood up as if to assure himself of solid ground beneath so that he could stride away before he dwelled any further on this woman. He walked slowly toward the exit from the courtyard, and as if in a parting gesture, he took a last glance her way. In the time it had taken him to walk to the exit, a shiny black-haired and chiseled-face young man had taken a seat next to her, and her slender hand that had stirred the drink now lay across the table in the hand of the young man.

McClaren read in the *Esto* newspaper that Leon, an hour bus ride away, would have a string of corridas to celebrate the city's founding, the first featuring the Spanish sensation Enrique Ponce. So later that afternoon, he told Muriel they should take a few days in Leon, where they had first landed from LA. Muriel didn't need any convincing. They would go into Leon for the weekend and see some of the city, the *Feria* and a corrida with big name matadors.

Much of Leon was still what it had been a hundred years ago. The McClarens stayed at the Leon Hotel right off the main square. Old and musty, it was a better deal than the modern glass and steel hotels on the highway leading out of the center of town to the international airport. The hotel still had an elevator with a collapsible brass screen and an elevator boy who took you for the ride with a brass handled control that looked like it belonged on a ship. The lobby and restaurant were no less old, charming and darkly lit. It made a contrasting backdrop when several of the suited-up bullfighters appeared in the lobby on Sunday afternoon, ready to be transported to the big downtown bullring, La Luz. They were like a bouquet of brilliant flowers amidst the old drab seediness of the lobby. For McClaren the scene was reminiscent of the lobby of the Bahia Hotel of Ensenada forty years ago when he had appeared dressed for a bullfight, the subject of curious and admiring eyes.

He had bought two forty-dollar front row seats on the sunny side of the La Luz bullring. It was a perfectly clear blue-sky day, the February sun sitting just above the rim of the ring when the clarion sounded for the entry of the bullfighters. Three drunken Mexican cowboys sat behind them and jeered through every bullfight except for those of Enrique Ponce, who awed the most demanding fans down to the least knowledgeable like Muriel. What Ponce did in the ring was simultaneously sublime and primordial, whereas the Mexican El Zotoluco indulged in a kind of exaggerated bravado in front of his bulls and his passes were more forced than graceful. Ponce was balletic and effortless, drawing his bulls by his body as though waving aside waist high grass on a meditative stroll in the country. Muriel needed no explanations and sat in awe like everyone else in the crowd as they joined in the *oles*. Rafael Ortega was athletic, more than aesthetic, tremendous and breathtaking like a high jumper or vaulter clearing new heights. All the men fought well and killed cleanly, the kind of afternoon of the bulls which the aficionado hoped for when the beauty and glory transcended the blood.

Emotionally drained by the fights, the pressing exiting crowd and the slow cab ride back to the hotel in heavy traffic, they stopped in the lobby restaurant for a fortifying cup of English tea with milk and sugar before returning to their room. It had been a satisfying day. Muriel commented how she was happy to see him more exuberant than he had been since retiring. Indeed, the narrowing spirit he had felt had diffused. Sleep was becoming a little more regular and less wakeful with twilight reruns of lost decades, as if refrains of mortality's song. Sometimes he had not been able to fall back asleep after waking at four in the morning, and so he would make tea and wait for the delivery boy to sling the morning paper which announced its arrival with a dull thud against the front door.

The hotel dining room was starting to fill with patrons after their third cup of tea when they were ready to go up to their room for a hot shower. About to pay at the cash register, he found his wallet was empty except for his pictures of Muriel and their daughter. The credit cards and cash were gone. The blood drained from his head and he had to sit down. Several moments of heavy silence elapsed before Muriel scolded him for not being mindful of his wallet. She'd told him not to keep his wallet in his back pocket. He had put it in a front pocket but then reflexively returned it to the back pocket. But hadn't he touched the wallet in his pants pocket continuously upon entering and leaving the bullring? But there were moments when he may have been distracted long enough for the wallet to be removed, cleaned of its valuables and returned without his knowing. Maybe when he had stood up shouting *oles* at the action in the ring, maybe in a moment when they squeezed through the entering or exiting crowd. Fortunately, Muriel had kept a list of everything and half their money in her purse. The next hour was spent with long distance telephone calls canceling their Mastercard and Visa. They didn't speak most of that evening as Muriel fumed and McClaren was in a kind of shock, but not so much at losing two hundred in cash or canceling the cards. Fortunately, his wife still had an ATM card which they had left with their passports at the hotel desk security. It was the humiliation that slammed him. Beyond feeling robbed, he felt betrayed.

They were not quite finished with Mexico, despite this blow to their enthusiasm. After returning to San Miguel, they waited long enough for McClaren to have his newly made crowns screwed onto the implants and then they packed up and made for Lake Chapala near Guadalajara, one of Mexico's other famous enclaves of North American ex-patriots, a kind of 'Mexico-lite' where one could go all day without having to use a single word of Spanish. In Chapala, they stayed with a distant Canadian relative, unaffected by the family divisions, who had vacant cottages on the property that overlooked the fifty-mile long lake. With warm easy days, and a swimming pool at their disposal, McClaren and his much-relieved wife settled into two weeks of real vacation, as opposed to adventure, until their return date and their flight home from nearby Guadalajara.

When they got back home, McClaren had somewhat forgotten about the brewing political storms occasioned by the ugly situation in Iraq and the coming runoff between Bush and Kerry. He had crossed swords a few times in Chapala with a few well-off retirees but all in all had let the swimming pool and the local hot springs soak away these concerns. Bush had come to office when he had retired, a bit of irony never lost on him. Stress levels were supposed to diminish when one retired, but instead every morning he had read the paper and was saddened and angered—another treaty broken, another environmental law weakened, another labor protection removed ad nauseam. He chafed at all the stupidity around him. Shortly after returning from Mexico, he was reminded that escape was merely a mirage. While eating some chewy meat, one of his cut-rate crowns done in San Miguel became loose. He would have to have it redone, and until his dental appointment he would be made to chew crow.

Was he becoming an aging curmudgeon with nothing else to distinguish his remaining years? Again, sleeping through nights had become difficult and reading the morning paper an exercise in controlling anger. And so, when he received an email from DeHaas, to whom he'd graciously sent several perfectly captured and Photoshop-edited passes of the bullfight in San Miguel, it took McClaren days to respond to the letter.

*Dear Jim,*

*It was indeed enjoyable to meet you and your lovely wife Muriel in San Miguel. And thank you for the great photos. You still have an eye for bullfighting. The photos you took were snapped at the right moment of the passes.*

*We are having a festival in Tijuana in a few months which is open to old practicos and you would be welcome if you wanted to buy one of the two year old bulls, usually under 300 kilos, or just participate with a few cape passes, as my guest at no charge. Some other old timers, guys who came up in our conversation in San Miguel, will be participating—Bill Randall, Bruce Harvey, and David Ross to name a few. Let me know. I'm off to Juarez next week for an international taurine clubs fight. Again, it was good seeing you after all these years. Stay in touch.*

*Steve*

For days McClaren tossed around the festival offer, some days thinking he could take up the challenge. He had even pulled out his old cape from an attic trunk and made a few imaginary passes in the privacy of the garage, envisioning the horns following the edge of the lure. Yes, perhaps he could get in and make just a few passes. He'd not forgotten how to swing the cape. But could he keep his feet still? His old fighting garb, the *traje corto,* was a bit moth eaten but usable and could be let out to accommodate the inches his waist had increased over the years. He was on the edge of this dream for some days, but as the fog of imagined glory gradually lifted, the truth became apparent, as did his thinning hair in the light of day. Innocence might be revisited but cannot be recouped.

The passion he'd once felt for bullfighting had been so large there had been little room in his heart for fear. The heart may remember such fullness but it could never be the same. Reluctantly, he wrote back to DeHass:

*Dear Steve,*

*Glad you like the photos I sent. Meeting you in S.M. and seeing you fight after all these years was a trip down memory lane I hadn 't expected when my wife and I went to Mexico. Since the old days, my life has taken me a lot of places. I suppose if I had kept my cape in the ring off and on over the years as you have, I'd be down there for the old-timers practico festival in Tijuana.*

*If I could get up the nerve, it would be wonderful to carry it off again. But there's no health coverage for this sort of thing. Getting seriously injured is a concern I can't get by. I have a family and a lot of responsibilities to consider. But thanks for the kind offer and I wish you every luck in the Tijuana festival and future actions.*

*Meanwhile I have concluded, while I putter around my house, dance on weekends with Muriel and walk the dog daily, that I had better get active again and do what I can to help the Democratic party defeat Bush. I've had enough of big business welfare and imperial war.*

*Regards, Jim*

McLaren hadn't thought about loosely dropping political comments. Until one really understood and knew one's company, it was best to hold one's peace, especially in the polarizing era of George W. Bush. DeHaas was a consummate gentleman, solicitous and soft spoken. When they had met in San Miguel, they hadn't ventured outside the ring into politics. It hadn't occurred to McClaren that DeHaas, having spent so many years in South America where he would have observed some of the world's direst poverty and political oppression, would be anything less than an informed internationalist and tolerant progressive.

But his return email read:

*Dear Jim,*

*Well, sorry you don't think you can join us for the festival in Tijuana.*

*In regard to the changes in the country you wish to make, we don't need to make the same mistake we made in Vietnam with a lack of commitment and determination. Considering Kerry's views of Vietnam, we are best advised to stick with Bush. As to our domestic scene, we have lived too long in an entitlement state where people have been coddled and have come to think the world owes them something. And then there are those of us who accept the price of our own actions. I think the difference is summed up by your concern for health insurance, when I am only worried about whether I draw a brave bull.*

*Regards, Steve*

For McClaren the return letter from DeHaas was the tip of an iceberg. He felt tired simply contemplating where to start. At their age, where could they begin a discussion to resolve their differences? Hadn't their articles of belief worn traces into their pride? To recant any of it now would be tantamount to admitting they had lived forty years under false notions. Fighting bulls over the years as a hobby must have galvanized DeHass's rural Texas breeding. The arena was such a perfect metaphor of struggle and survival, it was no surprise it had become a part of his Wild West view of life. And DeHaas was not alone. Survivor games dominated the popular media, and the supreme cowboy in the White House was exhorting Americans to exercise personal responsibility. *Be tough and look out for yourself, Bud.* Upon deleting DeHass's message from the inbox and the possibility of a reply, he felt relieved and his adrenaline that had been rushing to pick up the gauntlet settled and receded.

It was already two weeks since the McClarens had returned from Mexico. The central valley of Oregon was bursting with spring and the days were getting longer. They were spending more time in the yard, planting flowers and manicuring away the straggle and weeds left by winter. He liked midday best when the sun was at its warmest and brightest and bore directly on his cap and shoulders, when there were no shadows and the day had no sense of movement. The absence of regular dancing while they had been in Mexico had whetted their appetite, and so, they were anxious to get back to dancing at the club. On their first night back, they eagerly took to the dance floor for a series of upbeat *milongas,* tangos with a Cuban twist requiring speed, timing and concentration. McClaren strode into the music with a confident gentle arm around Muriel, and when they found the syncopating heart of the music, without losing a step, as though on unified autopilot, they laughed, and the lines in his wife's face vanished.